MADISON

THE LT. KATE GAZZARA MURDER FILES
BOOK 19

BLAIR HOWARD

Copyright © April 2024 Madison: Case 19
Blair Howard
All rights reserved.

Printed 2024 Cleveland, TN
Print ISBN-13: 979-8-9891031-9-5
Library of Congress Control Number: 2024907884
Email: BlairHoward@BlairHowardBooks.com
www.blairhowardbooks.com

Disclaimer: Madison is a work of fiction, the product of the author's imagination. The persons and events depicted in this novel were also created by the author's imagination; no resemblance to actual persons or events is intended.

For Jo

1

_____

Tuesday, June 14, 2022, 7:35 a.m.

"I DON'T KNOW WHY IT ALWAYS HAS TO RAIN," SHELLY SEWARD muttered under her breath as she fumbled with the umbrella, worn from more than a decade of use. Maybe she wouldn't have been in such a foul mood if she'd taken the time to buy a new one. But that morning, well, it was what it was.

Rain pattered on the sidewalk as she trudged onward, the dreary overcast skies making Eighth Street a little less attractive. She used to love it here, but that was before Elliott broke up with her. Now, she wished she'd never moved to Chattanooga. With a sigh and a pang of heartache, she dug into the pocket of her lightweight rain jacket as she headed toward the insurance office where she worked.

Shelly took out her phone, unsurprised to see that Elliott hadn't texted her back. He never did—well, once, when he unloaded his guilt for leaving her for his secretary. Once he'd gotten it off his chest, he was as good as gone.

Funny how that works, she thought. After all, she worked as a secretary, too, at a small insurance firm just off Eighth Street. It wasn't nearly as extravagant as Elliott's high-rise tech job, but it counted for something—and she was loved by the people she worked with. She pursed her lips as she slowed her pace, her brows furrowed at the messages.

It was embarrassing how much she'd tried to get in touch with Elliott. Someone might even think that she was crazy, obsessed. That's what *he* had told her after her third call a few weeks ago. She'd had a few too many glasses of wine, and after four years of being in a relationship together, it felt like he should've been more reachable.

But maybe it's time to rip the Band-Aid off. Shelly let out a short breath as someone's heavy boots thudded past her. The streets were never all that crowded at that time in the morning, and she didn't look up from the phone as she deleted the text messages— and then, with a sigh, Elliott's number. It was time to move on and find something else to worry about. Maybe if she couldn't access him, it would force her to move forward. Or something like that.

Raindrops hit the top of her worn umbrella with a little more oomph, and the summer rain left her skin feeling sticky as she stuck the phone back in her pocket. The moment left her feeling a little lighter, though she wasn't all that sure why. It wasn't like deleting the texts would remove them from Elliott's phone. No, he would still probably think she was desperate... and crazy.

But then, the sound of a shriek stopped her dead in her tracks, her head jerking upward toward the strange, ominous wail. Squinting through the rain, a few blocks up ahead, she could barely make out a figure in a *trench coat* quickly moving to the northwest. Whoever it was carried a large black umbrella and the trench coat had a hood, making it almost impossible to make out anything about the figure at all. It was little more than a dark blob in the dreary morning light.

But where had the cry come from? Shelly didn't immediately

start moving from where she stood, not until she spotted a crumpled body on the ground.

"Oh no!" Her voice caught in her throat as her heels clacked against the pavement, unable to tear her gaze from the blond hair spilling over the cement. Her urgency only grew as she watched the woman's body convulse, the blond hair plastered to her face.

Shelly dug out her phone, fumbling with it as her umbrella thudded to the ground. She was no longer concerned about the rain ruining her morning, her old umbrella that needed replacing, or Elliott. No, all she could see was the woman lying on the ground, convulsing and jerking. By the time she made it to her side, the woman had stopped convulsing and her body was still.

"Miss? Miss, are you okay?" Shelly dropped to her knees, ignoring her now-soaked dress pants. She reached out and shook the woman's shoulder, her heart pounding. *Heart attack? A seizure? Do people lose consciousness after a seizure?* She racked her brain as her trembling fingers tapped in the numbers.

"Nine-one-one, what's your emergency?" The dispatcher sounded distant in her ear as she continued to shake the woman.

"I... I... I don't... There's a woman... She fell and now, I don't know." Shelly couldn't get the words out as her own blond hair fell into her face blocking her view.

"Where are you located?"

Shelly glanced up and around as her stomach churned. "Um, Eighth Street. I don't know the exact address. I'm on West Eighth, near... near Market Street." She finished, embarrassed. She'd worked around there for nearly three years and couldn't recall where she was in her panic-stricken mind.

"Please stay where you are. I'm dispatching paramedics to your location right now. Is she breathing? Have you checked for a pulse?"

Shelly heard the dispatcher, but her eyes were fixated on the woman's face. "She's so young..." she whispered. *And dead.* She knew by the blueish lips and faded color of her skin.

"Ma'am?" the dispatcher said. "Are you still there?"

Shelly nodded, though it didn't tell the operator what she wanted to know. She pressed her fingers against the woman's wrist, too scared to touch her face. "There's no pulse. I think she's... I think she's dead." *Well, I know she's dead.* But Shelly pushed that nagging thought away. No one cared about her past or the things she had seen. Right now, it was just about this woman.

At the sound of the ambulance in the distance, Shelly leaned away from the woman. Part of her wanted to hold her hand, but she knew if she did, it would more than likely grow cold in her grasp, and that wasn't a feeling she wanted to experience... again.

"The paramedics are here," Shelly said robotically into the phone before hanging up. She shoved the phone into her pocket and rose to her feet, her gray slacks soaked from the knees down.

"What happened?" one of the two EMTs asked as the other rushed to the woman, circling her and pushing Shelly and the other nice, young EMT out of the way. She was grateful for the added distance; her stomach was churning.

"I... I don't know," she answered, shaking her head in disbelief. "I was walking down the street"—she gestured back in the direction from whence she came—"and I heard someone cry out. I looked up and there was this figure in a trench coat walking quickly... and then I saw the woman on the sidewalk."

"Did you see her fall?"

Shelly considered the question but shook her head. "No, no I didn't see her fall. I didn't see anything like that, really. The man —er, person—in the trench coat was blocking my view." As she spoke a blue and white police cruiser pulled up behind the ambulance, and a uniformed officer stepped out. She turned to continue talking to the EMT, but by then he was helping the other EMT with the woman.

"Are you all right, miss?" a deep voice asked from behind her.

She turned to see a young, dark-haired officer with bright blue eyes looking seriously at her.

"I'm... I'm fine. I just... I think something bad happened to her. I think someone..." Her voice trailed off as she watched them lift the young woman onto a stretcher.

She felt a hand on her arm; it was a gentle touch. "Ma'am, I know it can be traumatizing to witness something like this, but do you mind if I ask you a few questions?"

Shelly turned quickly to face the officer, ignoring the small crowd that had now formed around them. She hadn't noticed them. She'd been too lost in her own thoughts.

She nodded and said, "Of course."

"You called nine-one-one. Is that correct?" he asked, taking a small notebook from his pocket.

"Yes," she replied.

"Did you see what happened?"

"I told the EMT," her voice wavered. "There was someone in a trench coat. I couldn't make out much about them, but they had to have walked *right* by her..."

The officer nodded but didn't say anything. He just looked at her expectantly, his pen poised over the notebook. She was fairly certain that he probably thought she was crazy. After all, what did some shadowy figure have to do with a medical emergency?

"Did this person you saw attack her?" he asked, finally. "Did you see them do anything other than walk past her?"

Shelly Seward thought back to the moment, one that was already becoming a blur in her mind. "I don't... I don't know. I looked up as they walked past, and then I saw the woman on the ground." She repeated herself, her mind replaying the scene. The person didn't attack the woman, not that she had seen, anyway.

But still, something felt very off about it.

"So, you didn't see him physically attack this woman?" The sound of the ambulance doors slamming shut nearly drowned out his voice.

Shelly looked him right in the eye and paused. "No, I didn't, but there was something about what I saw that wasn't right. I *know* something is wrong with that person… I felt it in my stomach… and the woman's scream. It was eerie and painful. I don't know how other people on the street didn't hear it. I wasn't even paying attention and I heard it. It was horrible, a terrible screeching noise."

The officer paused, scratching the light stubble on his jaw and his expression unreadable. "Well, I'll pass this on. I'm sure someone will want to talk to you again. Can I have your contact details, please?"

Shelly blinked a couple of times, fighting the urge to argue… But for what reason? She knew how it sounded, some mysterious trench coat-clad figure rushing away down Eighth Street like a ghost, dropping a woman dead. It even sounded crazy, and with her history… no one would second-guess that's exactly what she was. Yes, for now, she would keep her suspicions to herself.

"My name is Shelly…"

2

Wednesday, June 22, 7:45 a.m.

"COME ON, SAMSON. IT'S TIME TO GET TO WORK," I SAID TO MY panting canine in the back seat as I parked my unmarked cruiser in the lot behind the police department building.

He tilted his head as if to say, *Waiting on you, Kate.*

I pushed open my driver's side door, sucking in the morning breeze. The humidity was heavier than I'd expected, even though I'd breathed it in only twenty minutes earlier. It was going to be a warm day, maybe not enough to cook an egg on the sidewalk, but enough to break a sweat just stepping outside.

"The countdown to fall begins," I joked, opening the back door for Samson. I unbuckled him and gestured for him to join me. "At least it's not raining."

He raised his eyebrows at me, hopped down, and together, we headed to the building. As I opened the door I racked my brain, trying to remember if I had anything pressing, but nothing came to mind. Thankfully, things had been mostly quiet lately... well, quiet as it could be. There was always *something* going on, but nothing that had my mind twisting and churning. I knew the break wouldn't last long though. Over twenty years in law enforcement had taught me that.

I stepped through the doors and welcomed the drier air. Samson let out a sigh beside me. We were on the same page as usual; we were almost always on the same page. My mysterious canine partner's past was unknown, his training a puzzle, but we'd been working together long enough now to know each other. In fact, I think Samson knew me better than anyone else.

I'd opted for a pair of black flats that morning, my knees aching from a long run the previous evening. I don't know if my age was starting to catch up to me—I'd be forty-five in a couple of months—or maybe it was just the extra few miles I'd picked up, but regardless, fifty was a milestone that was getting closer and closer, though I did my best not to think about it too much. And, in short, I would soon be given the perfect distraction.

We took the elevator to the second floor and walked the seventy-five feet or so across the situation room to my office.

As soon as my hand connected with my office door, I stopped. The blinds were closed, but the light was on inside. *Surely, I didn't forget to turn it off?* I pushed the door open and froze.

"Good morning, Kate," Chief Johnston greeted me with his usual gruff voice, though I thought my boss looked a little less friendly than usual. Not that he ever really looked friendly, and it was unusual for him to visit me in my office. Most times, I'd receive a cryptic call to join him in his office.

Ugh, I hope it isn't another silly speech I need to make!

Police Chief Wesley Johnston is... I guess the word I'm looking for is imposing: five-eleven, broad-shouldered, always impeccably dressed, his uniform crisp and sharp, his head shaved. And that unusual mustache; think Hulk Hogan. He's a humorless man, a martinet, if ever there was one, but fair, if a little ruthless at times.

"Close the door behind you," he said sharply.

Well, that's not a good start to the morning, I thought as I did as he asked. Samson lazily made his way to his bed under the window. Chief Johnston never got to Samson. No one ever bothered that German shepherd unless they were a bad person, in which case, they very much bothered him.

"What's going on?" I asked, keeping my tone light as I eyed the coffee maker in the corner of my office. I'd upgraded it a week or so earlier and was already wearing it out. And I would've liked to have had a cup before starting my impromptu meeting with the chief.

Chief Johnston let out a sigh that caused me to frown. "There's something I want you to look into," he said, "but I want to keep it under wraps until we figure out whether there really is something to be concerned about."

"Okay…" This was shaping up to be an interesting morning. "What happened?"

He leaned against my desk, preventing me from making my way to my much-needed caffeine machine. "Madison Lombardi dropped dead on the street on her way to her offices last Tuesday morning. Right in the middle of Eighth Street. It was ruled a medical event."

I frowned. "Madison Lombardi? As in Madison Lombardi the defense attorney?"

"Yes, that one," he replied dryly.

I nodded, not sure I was grasping the purpose of an investigation. "Doc Sheddon deemed it a medical event?"

He shook his head. "No, it was a state autopsy technician that did the initial examination. Her husband isn't having it. He reached out to Doc himself."

"Wow, bold move," I commented, glancing at Samson, who was sitting up on his bed, seemingly listening to our conversation. "So, when did Doc get involved?"

"Yesterday," Chief Johnston answered me. "And you can imagine, since the husband is putting pressure on Doc, he's putting pressure on me, too."

I folded my arms, my body chilled from the air conditioner blowing down on me. "Do you know him, the husband?"

"Loosely, I suppose. Tony Lombardi is a wealthy stock investor. He's always at the city's events, showing face."

"Hmm," was all I said. I knew the prominent type. "So he doesn't think his wife simply died of a heart attack."

"No, and in his defense, she has no medical history that's remotely indicative of impending death."

I nodded. "But even marathon runners drop dead... occasionally."

"Seizures," he replied.

"What?"

"According to the sole witness, she was having a seizure prior to her death. The woman said she was convulsing on the sidewalk, among other things."

"Cardiac arrests can sometimes cause seizures." The comment was out of my mouth before I processed the latter part of his statement. *What other things happened at the time of death?*

Chief Johnston sighed, and I realized quickly my constant reasonings might've begun to irk him.

"Just look into it Gazzara..." he growled. "Look, I'm not saying we have to make it into something that it's not, but you know how these types are. He's going to keep knocking on my door until we provide him with some sort of an acceptable answer."

"Right," I said, inwardly rolling my eyes and shaking my head. "I'll get with Doc Sheddon... but first, I'll start with the witnesses. It's already been more than two weeks. We need to pick their brains before memories start getting too fuzzy."

"Well, you only have one brain to pick," Chief Johnston said with a chuckle. "There's only one witness. Shelly Seward is the woman's name. She works at an insurance firm off Eighth Street. Here..." He handed me a slip of paper.

I nodded, making a mental note. "Were there any uniformed officers there after the fact?"

"Yeah, Officer Barron responded, a newbie from Nashville. He thinks the witness is a crackpot."

"Great," I muttered, not even recognizing the name of the officer. The more the city grew, the more I realized I was losing touch with the uniforms. It was hard to keep track of them. "Is he in right now?"

"No, he has today off, but he'll be on duty tomorrow."

"Noted." I fished out my notebook and wrote down a reminder to hunt him down the next day. "I'll see what I can come up with."

"Let me know what you've got by the end of the day. I'm sure Doc will be able to shed some light on the situation. Hopefully, we can wrap this thing up in a quick report and move on. Otherwise, we might have something high profile on our hands." He gave me a weary look.

"I'll see what I can do," I told him as he pushed off my desk, standing up straight again. "And I'll report back as soon as I know something, or by the end of the day."

"Good. I'll be waiting for you," he said, passing by me and reaching for the door. I took a deep breath as I watched him leave. I never liked it when Chief Johnston was *waiting for me.* That typically meant we needed to have something substantial— and by the end of the day. And I already had a feeling it was going to be easier said than done.

As soon as Chief Johnston slipped out, I saw a familiar face through the glass window in my office door. My partner had the same look on his face as I had on mine when I saw Chief Johnston waiting for me. He gave the chief a greeting and a nod before stepping into my office and closing the door behind him.

"Well... I'd tell you good morning, but..." Corbin shot me a wonky grin, followed by an overexaggerated shudder.

I shook my head at him, not in the mood for jokes as I finally made my way to the coffee maker. "I have a feeling we have a big day ahead of us," I said, without much enthusiasm, as I started the machine.

"I can only imagine," he replied. "What's it this time?"

As I waited for the coffee to brew, I briefed Corbin on what I knew about Madison Lombardi's death, which wasn't much. And by the time I'd finished, I could tell by the expression on his face that he was on the same page as I was.

"I guess we start with the witness, then?" Corbin asked as I finished. "Seems like it's either that or Doc, but if he got it only yesterday... Well, he's going to need more time."

"If I know him, he'll be good by this afternoon," I said, finally taking a sip of the bitter yet refreshing liquid. "We should be able to wrap this thing up before the end of the day, I hope. Sometimes young people do die, you know. It's not all that rare."

"But she was only in her late thirties," he said. "I do find that pretty rare. You want to brief the rest of the team or see where the day takes us first?"

I pressed my lips together as I mulled it over. "You can send them a message while we're on the way to visit Shelly Seward. If something comes of it, we'll look into it. Right now, it's small scale, and they have other things to do."

"For now," Corbin hummed.

3
___

Wednesday, June 22, 9:50 a.m.

"Whew! It's warm today," Corbin remarked as we stepped out of my car.

"Seems to be the theme for my thoughts today, and I'm not just talking about the weather," I said as I opened the rear door for Samson.

The sun was already pounding down on the back of my head, warming my exposed neck. My hair was up in my usual ponytail, but with the hot sun, my hair being down would've been much worse.

"So this is where it happened," Corbin said as he gestured to the area just ahead. I took in the scene, though there wasn't much to be said about it. The streets were clear, other than the inevitable bike rental stations. It was a picturesque area, and Chattanooga was attempting to turn it into a trendy place. I had walked Market Street and Eighth Street more than enough times, and usually, there were plenty of pedestrians, which had me thinking...

"So why only one witness?" I thought aloud, frowning as I

took in the sidewalk that bounded the ten-story office building and the restaurant at street level.

"Well, a lot of these businesses wouldn't have been open at that time in the morning," Corbin commented as we turned south onto Cherry Street, heading toward one of the small office buildings where the Mickelson Insurance Company was located. "Maybe there just wasn't anyone else, and you said it was raining, right?"

"Yeah, I guess that could've prevented people from paying much attention. Most would have had their heads down. But according to Johnston, there's more to it than that."

"Guess we'll find out soon enough, won't we?" Corbin smiled at me as he pulled the door open for Samson and me. We slipped through the opening, and I glanced down at the dog, whose nose was already twitching at the new smells. He might be as poised as ever, but he was almost always investigating, and I couldn't help but smile.

"Can I help you?" a woman greeted us with a glassy smile as we stepped into the foyer. She glanced at Samson, as people always did. However, he was suitably dressed in his harness and badge.

"I'm Captain Gazzara, Chattanooga Police," I said by way of introduction. "This is Sergeant Russell. We're here to talk with a Miss Shelly Seward."

"Oh, that's me," the woman said, pushing back from her desk and rising to her feet. She pushed her light blond hair away from her face and smiled. And I couldn't help but think how young she was. She had to be nearly twenty years my junior, putting her somewhere in her mid to late twenties.

"Is there somewhere we can chat privately?" I asked, eyeing the cubicles and curious gazes we were attracting. As much as I was for gathering as much information as possible, I wasn't a fan of having an audience. It never served the witness well.

"We can go into the break room," Shelly suggested, motioning down a narrow hallway to the right. "There won't be anyone in there right now."

"All right." I nodded, and we fell in step behind her. I didn't miss Shelly stealing several glances over her shoulder at Samson. She seemed wary of him, though he paid her little attention. He was busy taking in the scene, and the fact he didn't find her to be all that interesting was a good sign.

"Here," Shelley said, opening a plain white door.

We stepped inside, and it looked just like what you'd expect a break room to look like. A couple of vending machines in the corner, a half-dozen tables and chairs, a coffee maker, a microwave oven and one leather couch that looked like it had seen much better days.

I chose to stand while Corbin took a seat opposite her at one of the tables closest to the vending machine. Samson sat down beside me, quiet but alert.

"You're here about that woman, aren't you?" she asked.

"That's correct," Corbin said. "Why don't you tell us what happened that morning when you found Madison Lombardi on the sidewalk?"

Her brows raised. "That was Madison Lombardi?"

Corbin and I exchanged glances, but I spoke first. "Yes. She worked at a law firm just a block from here. Very high profile. We thought you might've recognized her."

Shelly shifted in her seat. "No! I know who she is... was, of course, but I didn't know her. I don't pay much attention to people. Not really. I saw that man, well, person, rushing away, and I thought something was... off."

"Can you describe exactly what happened?" Corbin asked in his unreadable tone and expression.

"Well, I already told one of you people about it," she huffed, her button nose scrunching up. "It makes me feel uncomfortable to keep talking about it. Look, I'm not crazy, you know. I just went through a bad breakup, and then I started taking Prozac, but that was only because I'm the type of person who gets anxious in my alone time."

I nodded, though internally, I began to question her reliability. "Let's get back to what happened that morning. Can you describe what you saw?"

"Right, right. Sorry." She let out a squeaky giggle but then continued. "I was walking to work like I always do. I had my umbrella up because it was raining. I heard a scream and looked up, and there was this man—well, I assume it was a man. Whoever they were, they were taller than me—though most people are. And he was wearing a trench coat with a hood. I couldn't make out anything else. But I *swear* when he passed that woman, that had to have been when she fell."

"Were the streets crowded?" I asked, wondering if maybe someone else had seen this person during their morning commute.

Shelly shrugged. "Not really. It was raining pretty hard. I mean, I know how it sounds, but there really was something off about the guy. I know there was."

"We believe you," Corbin reassured her. "We're just trying to cover our bases."

She eyed the two of us. Her blue eyes seemed icy, but her smile was warm enough. "I don't know what happened to her," she continued. "I felt terrible. I was probably half a block away? Something like that. And then I looked up, and there she was, crumpled on the sidewalk. I think by the time I got to her, she was already gone."

Samson yawned and snapped his jaws, startling her. I reached down and gave his head a pat as I asked, "So did you actually *see* this person walk past her?"

Shelly hesitated. "Well… I… I saw him walking quickly away from her, but I guess I didn't see him physically pass her, no. But I know that he did. And I know the timing had to have been right.

I *know* it. I had been checking my phone, but it was just for a split second."

Corbin nodded, and I watched from behind as he shifted in his seat. "And was there anything else you saw that morning that seemed suspicious to you?"

"No, not that I can think of. As I said, it was raining, and my umbrella is the worst," she answered with a sigh. "I know what it probably sounds like to you, but I know that the guy had something to do with it, and then he just disappeared afterward. And there's nowhere to go, either."

I paused what I was writing down in my notepad. "What do you mean?"

"Well, he would've kept down Eighth Street, but I'm not sure where he could've gone from there. I guess he could've ducked into a building? I feel like I would've seen him if he would've been moving at a normal walking pace… He had to have been running."

"We'll see if we can get some security footage of the area."

Shelly cackled, startling Samson so that he jumped sideways and sat down on my foot. "None of the security cameras are working down here. They've been down for maintenance for nearly three weeks now."

"Oh?" I raised my eyebrows, wondering if the timing could have something to do with Madison Lombardi's death. But then again, that would be admitting that I thought this whole thing was something more than a medical emergency, and this woman did not have me convinced that it was.

"You can ask, of course," Shelly said quickly, looking first at me and then at Corbin. "I was just telling you what I know. The camera system is unreliable at best around here. That's all I was saying…"

"And thank you for the information." Corbin's tone was soothing, and once again I was reminded of his ability to bend to a level of understanding for the people he was interviewing. It was an admirable trait, and it was working well in this instance; Shelly visibly relaxed.

"Is there anything else you'd like for us to know?" I said, making a mental note to check on the cameras before the day was over. If there were working cameras, it could answer the question of the mystery figure Shelly swore she saw.

"I don't think so. Look, I have to get back to work," she said as she rose to her feet, eyeing Samson.

He eyed her back, but his level of interest was less than enthusiastic.

"Well, let us know if you think of anything," Corbin said, also rising to his feet and handing her a card.

She nodded, took it from him, glanced at it, and then walked to the door, opened it and stepped out into the corridor where, unsurprisingly, there were several bystanders loitering around.

"You all are so nosey," Shelly snipped at them as we passed by. Part of me wondered if we should ask them if they saw anything, but it was already clear that no one other than Shelly saw what happened. I wasn't even sure she saw what happened. There were blanks in her story, and I was hoping that Doc Sheddon would be able to write this whole thing off for us.

Hopefully, we wouldn't have to go chasing after her mysterious hooded figure.

4

"IT ALMOST SEEMS LIKE A NOVEL, DOESN'T IT?" CORBIN REMARKED as we headed down the sidewalk. "Think about it. A mysterious, hooded figure walks past a woman on the street and she drops? That's the stuff of urban legend."

I pressed my lips together as I caught a whiff of one of the restaurants already starting lunch. "It does, and it feels like a reach. I don't know how someone could just *walk past* another person and make them drop dead."

"Magic," Corbin joked, shrugging before coming to a stop outside of Hello Monty's. "You ever tried this place?"

I shook my head, though I wasn't sure if I was in the mood to try something new. "I haven't, no." I glanced down at Samson. "Think they'll let you in, buddy?" I gave him a smile, and he seemed to smile right back up at me.

"Well, we're right here," Corbin said. "And I missed breakfast this morning."

"Sure." I checked my phone just in case I'd missed a call from Doc Sheddon. I hadn't, which irked me a little. I was more than ready to hear from him. I was hoping he would wrap this thing up and we could put it behind us. Something about it was making me feel a little off.

We headed into Monty's, a nice modern restaurant, and sat down at a table out on the patio. It would've been nice to enjoy the air conditioning, but it was much easier to keep Samson—and the staff—happy if we stayed outside. We ordered burgers and settled in.

"I'll send Cooper a text to have him check on those security cameras while we wait," Corbin said as he typed on his phone.

I nodded, and as we waited for our food to show up, I stared at the area where Madison had died. Corbin was right. It was indeed probable that there would have been no one around at the time of death to witness what happened. It was, however, still hard to believe that Shelly Seward was the *only* witness.

There could've been more, I thought. *Maybe they just didn't want to get involved. It happens all the time.*

"What are the odds d'you think that the cameras aren't working?" Corbin's voice drew me from my thoughts. "It's hard to believe that the cameras down here would've been shut down for maintenance."

"Stranger things, Corbin," I said as the waiter brought our orders. "Stranger things.

I gave Samson his. He finished it off even before I had time to pick mine up, then looked up at me. I shook my head and dropped him a couple of fries.

"You still enjoying a house instead of the apartment?" Corbin asked, then took a bite of his burger.

"Oh yes," I replied. "More every day. It's more work, but it's worth it. It was time for a change."

Corbin was about to reply, but my phone began to ring. I dug it out of my jacket pocket and was relieved to see Doc's name on the screen.

Chapter 4

"Hey, Doc," I said. "I was just thinking about you. What d'you have for me?"

"So you were expecting my call then, huh?" He chuckled his usual gimpy laugh. "Madison Lombardi! When I got the call about this one, I have to admit I was thinking it was probably a waste of time."

"Tell you what," I stopped him before he veered off on one of his tangents. "Why don't Corbin and I meet you over at your office in about thirty minutes? You can give us the rundown then."

"Fair enough. But don't get too excited." And he hung up before I could ask about the comment. Knowing him, though, it could have meant just about anything.

We finished our lunch. I paid the check and we headed to my car.

"Coop just texted me," Corbin commented as I started the drive across town to the medical examiner's office. "Shelly was right. The cameras were down. They were replacing the entire system, so there is no footage of the incident."

I sighed. "You know," I said, not bothering to hide my frustration. "For all the security systems in the downtown area, it seems that more than half the time, they're useless. I often wonder why they even bother with them."

Corbin chuckled. "I think that's the trend. Murphy's law, right?"

We continued our discussion for the next fifteen minutes or so until I pulled into the lot at the front of Doc Sheddon's forensic center.

"Well, let's hope we can wrap this thing up here and now," Corbin said as he pushed the car door open. "My wife is making lasagna for dinner, and I don't want to miss it."

I shot him a look. "It's not even one o'clock yet. I don't think you're going to miss your dinner."

"You know how long-winded he can be." Corbin gestured to

Doc Sheddon's name on the front door. I shook my head and smiled. Doc Sheddon did love to talk.

But I liked him, and over the years, we'd developed a good relationship. It was a luxury, and one I tried never to take for granted.

"Come on, Samson," I coaxed my canine awake. "You can nap inside."

He yawned hugely as I unclipped him from his restraint and clipped his leash to his harness, and he hopped down onto the pavement.

"You can get your beauty sleep tonight," I said to him, and I swear he glared at me. I laughed and together we joined Corbin at the front door.

"Here we go," Corbin said as he opened the door for us.

Doc Sheddon was just inside the empty reception area, a cup of coffee steaming in his hand.

"Well, look what the cat dragged in." Doc Sheddon shot us a wink. "And you've brought the dog, too, I see."

"Officer." I gestured to Samson's badge.

"Oh, yes, of course he is." Doc stared at us over the rim of his silver wire-framed glasses. He was a stubby man, but his brain far exceeded his height. "And you want to discuss the Lombardi case?"

"I do," I replied. "I'm hoping we can wrap it up, but that depends on you, I guess."

"I wouldn't count on that," he said dryly. "Though I will say that the examination itself was not all that remarkable." Doc took a sip of his coffee. "That being said, I did find a strange rash around her nostrils. I did a couple of extra tests the state's autopsy tech didn't do. Not a very thorough job done there, I'd say. Must have assumed cardiac arrest; not surprising, though, considering the circumstances."

"That's the reason you're the best," Corbin said, grinning at him. "What do you think caused the rash?"

Chapter 4

"Not sure. I sent it all to the lab. I did put a rush on it, though. Tony Lombardi has called my office multiple times."

I raised a brow. "That's interesting."

"Not really." Doc chuckled. "I think he's the kind of person who's used to getting his answers quickly. He doesn't like to wait. I'll be glad to have him off my back though."

Chief Johnston feels the same way, I'm sure, I thought.

"Anyway," he continued, "I'm pretty sure cardiac arrest is the primary cause of death, though what caused it is, at the moment, anybody's guess. But there's more..." He trailed off, his brow furrowed, and he said, almost as if to himself, "She seemed to have damaged her lungs somehow. It's an odd one. The preliminary toxicology results are in, but they didn't show anything untoward, and you know how I feel about those."

I nodded. "So... Any chance the lung damage isn't related?"

He gave me a lopsided grin. "There's always a chance, but the damage appeared to be quite recent."

"Still, the cause of death *was* cardiac arrest, correct?"

"That is correct." Doc nodded. "In fact, if the in-depth toxicology report comes back clean, then I would say this is just a devastating loss of a young, healthy woman. Her husband gave me a solid twenty-minute spiel about just how active and healthy she was... But you know how that goes, athletes drop dead on the field from cardiac arrest more often than anyone wants to admit."

"Right." I glanced down at Samson, ignoring the lack of relief Doc's words brought me. For some reason, he didn't sound as sure as he usually did, and that was creeping around under my skin.

"So that's it?" Corbin's brow furrowed. "She had a heart attack?" he repeated.

"I just said so, didn't I, sergeant?" he said with a smirk. "But, as I also said, with the strange rash and lung damage, I wouldn't write it off just yet. I'll need to see the results of the tests."

"And when will you have them?" I asked, already knowing the answer.

"Well, with the rush I put on them, *maybe* three weeks? But that's saying the lab listens to my appeal. Everyone wants to rush results these days."

I sighed, hoping the cardiac arrest answer would be enough to stave off Tony Lombardi and appease Chief Johnston. "Let me know when you have something, please, Doc."

Doc Sheddon smiled at me. "Oh, you know I will."

5

IT WAS JUST AFTER FOUR THAT AFTERNOON WHEN WE ARRIVED BACK at the office. I finished up some paperwork that had been gathering dust on my desk and then readied myself to speak with Chief Johnston. He'd been out when we returned. I was just about to get up from the desk to go make my appearance when he made his. There was a sharp rap on my door. It opened and he stepped inside.

"Captain! I was just passing by," he lied, "and thought I'd drop in to see what you have for me. Tony Lombardi has called me twice today. Couldn't even have a nice lunch with my family."

I raised my brows at him, surprised. "He's that eager?"

"Persistent is the word," he replied.

"Well," I said, after taking a deep breath, "Shelly Seward didn't have much to add to what you told me this morning," I began, pushing back from my desk and rising to my feet. "Other than a figure in a trench coat and hood... that's it."

Johnston's icy look didn't change. "I see," he said with an edge to his voice.

"Yes…" I looked at him and then delivered the rest of the bad news. "All of the security cameras were down, too. We have nothing."

"No other witnesses?"

"That's the way it looks," I said.

"And what did Doc Sheddon have to say?" His tone was now as icy as his look.

"Cardiac Arrest—" I stopped before I continued, glancing over at Samson. He perked his ears at me as if to nudge me onward. "There may have been a contributing factor, but we won't know for sure until he gets the tests back from the lab. Apparently, she had a rash on her face and some lung damage. That's it. He said he'll be in touch as soon as he knows something."

"Gather your team and meet me in the conference room in say…" He looked at his watch. "Fifteen minutes." His voice dull and heavy. "Maybe there's more to it."

I couldn't hide my surprise. "You think? I know the lung damage and the rash are a little out of the ordinary, but… Homicide? I don't think so."

He shook his head and said, "Maybe not, but I think we should at least send someone to talk to the people at her law firm, and the husband."

"Very well," I said, nodding. "Then, by all means, let's brief the team."

And with that, he nodded, then turned and left, closing the door behind him.

Me? I called Corbin and had him gather the troops, then I made myself a mug of coffee and motioned for Samson to follow me to the conference room.

"I guess we're going to dig deep then?" Corbin whispered as he took a seat beside me.

I nodded. "Looks like it."

"Then we shall do it." He chuckled, leaning back in his chair. He was in an unusually uppity good mood, and I had to smile.

Me? I was feeling like... I was more than a little fatigued and ready to call it a day. But it wasn't just that. I was still struggling to see the point in starting an in-depth investigation into something where malicious intent seemed unlikely... Unless, of course, you believed that a hooded figure could walk by and cause someone to drop dead of a heart attack.

"Does this have something to do with those security cameras?" Cooper asked the moment he plopped down on one of the chairs. "I texted Corbin to let him know the system wasn't working."

"Yeah, it does," Chief Johnston spoke for me. Cooper nodded in reply but didn't say anything else as the rest of the group funneled in. Hawk, Ramirez, Jack, and Anne Robar took a seat at the table, and once they were settled, Chief Johnston took it upon himself to conduct the briefing.

That was a first, and it struck me as a little weird that he was so invested in the case, but then again, if he was feeling pressure from Tony Lombardi, maybe he was just determined to nip this one in the bud and as quickly as possible. I, on the other hand, still didn't see the point in engaging my entire team in something that I still considered the proverbial storm in the teacup.

"So... She had a heart attack?" Anne Robar echoed at the end of his briefing. "And we have a shadowy figure who... we assume... what? And that's it?"

"I guess it's time for some good old-fashioned police work. We need to canvass the area; go door to door, so to speak. See if anyone saw or heard anything."

There was a groan from around the table. "Geez, there must be several hundred offices and businesses in that area," Cooper moaned.

"Then the sooner you get on with it, the better," Johnston snapped.

"We can start first thing in the morning," I said, glaring at Cooper.

"Surely, someone other than our witness must have seen a person in a trench coat and hood," Anne said.

"If he was there," Hawk added flatly. "But it sure seems like a reach."

"Or maybe he was just someone trying to stay out of the rain," Anne added with a chuckle. "I know I can look pretty rough when it's pouring outside."

"Whoever canvasses can also stop in at the law office. Talk to her partners and staff," Johnston said. "But Kate," he added, looking at me, "I want you and Corbin to talk to Tony Lombardi. Find out what he was up to when this thing happened. Persistence in and of itself is not always suspicious, but he doesn't have a sparkling background."

"Oh?" I asked. What he said was news to me.

"He has ties to the Lombardi family in New York, I bet," Jack said, grinning. "I did a little digging on him when he donated a large sum at one of the community galas—just a Google search, but still..."

"Mob ties?" Corbin sounded intrigued. "That's an interesting twist."

"Anne, Hawk, Cooper, and Ramirez," I said, "I want you to start canvassing the area first thing in the morning. Before you start talking to people, be on the street from seven until eight. Be looking for this... this... I dunno, ghost in a trench coat." I looked at the chief and continued, "Corbin and I will drop in on Tony Lombardi and see what he has to say for himself, but..."

"But what?" Johnston asked.

"I think we'd better tread carefully with him," I said. "If there's nothing to this... I'm not even going to call it a suspicious death, then—"

"Call it what you like," Johnston said. "Let's just make sure we cover all the bases. I don't want any blowback. Understood?"

I nodded. Once again, my tongue had gotten the better of me.

"In the meantime," Jack said brightly, "I'll do some deep

digging into Lombardi. Any time there might be a mobster in play, you know I'm interested."

Not me, I thought.

"Let's keep this quiet while we work out the details," Chief Johnston said, closing out the meeting. "We all have our opinions, but it is what it is. We'll investigate it thoroughly until we're absolutely certain it was just a medical event."

I eyed Corbin as I rose to my feet. He gave me a shrug, and with that, we all went our separate ways.

Me? I couldn't wait to get out of there. It was nice to be out of the office at a normal time, and I was hoping that Samson and I might have a chance to go on an evening run. But I have to admit, I was feeling more than a little antsy, what with everything that'd happened that day—and I blamed it on my creative mind and an enigmatic figure in a trench coat in the rain.

You'd think I was dreaming up a frickin' ghost, I thought ruefully.

I shook my head to clear the images of Jack the Ripper I'd conjured and bid the team a good evening, clipped Samson's leash to his harness, and headed out to the car.

"Maybe not a run tonight," I told him as I unlocked the vehicle and swung open the back door for him. "It's unseasonably warm today. Maybe we should get takeout and watch a movie."

He wagged his tail in response, and I buckled him in. He was the closest thing to any immediate family I had. And a boyfriend wasn't in the picture... Not that I wasn't interested in that. I was, but my job... well, it wasn't conducive to romance. Only once before in my life had I... Well, that's another story, and that was years ago. Friendship made much more sense for Harry and me now...

And speaking of Harry Starke, I couldn't help but wonder if he *might* be the right person to give a call about the Lombardi case. Hell, he might know something I didn't about the Lombardi family. After all, there were *many* things that Harry knew that I didn't. He was able to wade into unknown territories, being a private investigator and all. I picked up my phone and dialed his number as I pulled out of the parking lot.

"Kate," Harry answered, his voice bright and airy. "How the heck are you?"

"I'm good, Harry. How about you? I must say, you don't sound all stressed out and worked up." I laughed. "Must be an easy day for you at the office today."

"Not a lot going on right now," he replied, "but you know how it is. I could be flying across the country tomorrow. But to what do I owe the honor of this call?"

"What d'you know about Tony and Madison Lombardi?" I asked.

There was a long silence, long enough that I actually checked to make sure the call was still connected. "Harry?"

"Sorry, you caught me a little off guard there. Tony Lombardi is a catch, if you know what I mean."

"Mob?"

He chuckled. "I don't know about that. No, I don't have a clue about the mob, but I do know that he's in the top one percent here in Chattanooga. The man is wealthier than most. His wife is a hotshot defense attorney who works out of a private practice off Eighth Street."

"Correct, and she's dead," I added flatly.

"Yes, I heard."

"She died last Tuesday morning. Dropped dead on the sidewalk. Tony Lombardi thinks it was more than a heart attack and is putting pressure on everyone to find out what happened. He's called Doc and the chief multiple times already—but I don't see it. The cause of death, according to Doc, was cardiac arrest."

"Huh, okay... So what's the problem? There's always a reason, even if it's merely denial. Sometimes people can't cope with grief and they... But you know that. I'm preaching to the choir over here."

"Well, the witness," I began as I turned onto my neighborhood street, "the only witness said she saw a shadowy figure in a trench coat and hood walk past Madison Lombardi right before she died."

"So what? Someone zapped her with a magic wand and gave her a heart attack?"

I chuckled as I parked the car inside my garage. "Well, I don't know about that, but Doc Sheddon also found some lung damage and a strange rash on her face."

"Drugs?"

"I don't know," I replied. "He's still waiting for the test results."

"That means he doesn't know the answers." Harry sighed. "And that in and of itself *is* a call for an investigation. I wouldn't let it simmer too much though, Kate. She could've simply come into contact with something she was allergic to, sneezed, and it gave her a heart attack."

"She sneezed herself to death," I said, smiling. "That's one for the books, even from you, Harry... But what about the lung damage?"

"Oh hell, more people have lung damage than they probably even realize."

"Right," I muttered as I let Samson out of the car and through the garage door to the backyard. "Maybe I'm overthinking it."

But something in my gut told me I wasn't and that there was more to come.

6

Thursday, June 23, 9 a.m.

I DIDN'T SLEEP WELL THAT NIGHT AND WAS UP EARLY. I THOUGHT about going for a run. But my head just wasn't in it, so I sat and watched the news over a cup of coffee, made some breakfast, then showered and dressed. At eight-thirty, I stood at the door with Samson on his leash, knowing damn well that I'd missed something. What it was, I didn't know, but I dropped the leash, rechecked the locks on the doors and windows, and made sure I'd turned off the gas stove. That done, I grabbed Samson's leash and headed out to my car, still with a daunting feeling that something was amiss.

Corbin was waiting and watching for me in the PD front lobby when I arrived. He ran out and jumped into the passenger front seat and we headed straight over to Tony Lombardi's office on West Eighth in downtown Chattanooga.

"You think he had something to do with it?" Corbin asked as I parked on the second level of the nearby multi-story parking facility.

I shrugged. "I don't know. I would think if he killed his wife, he'd be keeping a low profile. But he's the one pushing for this investigation. And how the hell he could have pulled it off is beyond me. All we have is a heart attack."

"And the strange rash and lung damage," Corbin added.

"Right," I said with a nod as I pushed open the car door and made my way to Samson in the back seat. "So let's go pay Mr. Lombardi a visit; see if we can rattle his cage a little."

We took the elevator to street level, walked the couple of blocks to the high-rise office building, and then rode up to the top floor.

Corbin nudged me as we stepped out of the elevator on the penthouse level. I glanced at him and nodded. Luxury was the operative word, and the suite of offices occupied by Lombardi Financial Solutions could easily have been confused with something on Wall Street.

"Man, I never would've thought he was doing *this* well," Corbin leaned in and whispered to me as we headed through the lobby to the reception desk. The woman at the desk was a dark-haired beauty in her mid-twenties.

She stood, looked us up and down, made a face at Samson, and said, "Um, I'm afraid animals aren't allowed."

"He's a police officer," I said flatly, not even attempting to give her another option. "And I'm Captain Gazzara, Chattanooga Police Department. This is my partner, and I need to speak with Tony Lombardi."

"I'm afraid he's busy all day," she said, her voice having a sharp edge to it.

In my three-inch heels I was a good four inches taller than she was and I looked down at her, then took a moment to read the name plate on her desk.

Lucille Weller.

"Is he now?" I said. "Then perhaps you'd better interrupt him and tell him that we're here to discuss his wife's recent demise."

Her eyes widened as if something had clicked in her brain,

and she reached for the phone in the corner. "Let me just call him."

"Thank you," Corbin answered and then glanced at me. I wondered if he was thinking the same thing I was—that maybe she'd been told to always turn away law enforcement. I mean, if the guy was really mafia material, that might be standard protocol.

Lucille cleared her throat. "He'll see you now. It's the office at the end of that hallway." She gestured to a dark opening to her left, away from the wall of windows. "I'm sorry for my initial knee-jerk reaction."

"Not a problem," I told her before falling into step behind Corbin. I forced a light smile in her direction but had to admit I wasn't really feeling it. The entire office was empty, and why have such a large space if you're not filling it with employees? It seemed like a waste, but then again, I was more practical than most.

As we walked the dimly lit hallway, the black door at the end swung open, and a tall, broad-shouldered man with jet-black hair and equally black eyes stepped out to meet us. His elongated nose and olive skin were indicative of his Italian heritage, but I passed no judgment on the somewhat handsome man.

"Good morning. It's good to see someone show up to actually sit down with me and chat." His accent was strong Little Italy New York City, and a low growl rumbled at the back of Samson's throat. I looked down at him. His hackles weren't raised, but he was obviously on the alert.

"Thank you for seeing us," Corbin said, taking his offered hand and shaking it. "I'm Sergeant Russell, and this is Captain Gazzara."

Lombardi's gaze held mine for a few tense moments. I knew when someone was sizing me up; this was one of those times.

"Please," he said, eventually, after a moment of awkward silence. "Come in and take a seat."

He stepped aside and motioned to a couple of black leather armchairs in front of his desk. The south wall was floor-to-ceiling windows. The office was lavishly furnished, complete with a full bar and lounge area. His desk was... I can only describe it as a sea of burnished walnut.

Excessive, I thought as I took a seat, Samson parking himself beside my feet. He still looked wary, but I patted his head and he settled down and put his head on the carpet between his front paws. *So far, so good,* I thought. *It wouldn't do for him to attack the guy before we had a chance to talk to him.*

"Thirsty?" Lombardi asked before taking his seat at his desk.

"I'm good, thank you," I answered.

"I just had coffee," Corbin added. "Why don't we, uh, just go ahead and dive right in?"

"Fine by me," Lombardi grunted, sitting down in what could only be called a throne. "I suppose you'll know I'm aware you probably think this investigation is a waste of your time, but I know that my wife didn't just keel over dead on the street; there has to be more to it than that."

I nodded. "What makes you think that, Mr. Lombardi?"

"She'd had a routine cardiac stress test just a week before she died." His voice was curt. "And she passed it with flying colors. Don't you think it strange that a week later, she's dead from a heart attack?"

I had to agree with him on that one. It was a fact that we hadn't been aware of, and now I was second-guessing the likelihood of her passing from a heart attack. Having said that, there could have been unknown underlying health conditions. *Hmm.*

"Very well," I said. "Let's suppose you're right. Can you think of anyone who might have held a grudge against her, who might have wanted to harm her?" I asked, setting my phone to record and placing it on the desktop between us. "You don't mind if I record the interview, do you?" I asked, taking it for granted that he would but wouldn't have the cajónes to say no, but I had a pretty strong feeling he wouldn't like it.

Lombardi glared at the phone, then at me. I smiled at him. He hummed as if he was mulling the question over, then said, "Not really. At the same time, she *did* represent some pretty scary characters. But she was the best at what she did, and I can't remember the last time she had a problem with one of her clients."

"What about her coworkers?" Corbin asked.

"Lawyers always act like they hate each other," he replied. "Things can get tense in court, as I'm sure you well know, but no. I don't think so. She seemed to have a close relationship with most of her colleagues. Same goes for friends and family. We don't have any family that lives around here, and Madison lived and breathed her job. She didn't have a lot of friends."

"I'd like a list of those friends," I said, squinting in pain as Samson sat up and put all his paw and most of his weight right in the middle of my shoe. It was almost as if he was urging me to ask a question. But you know, he couldn't talk.

"I can do that," Lombardi said as he grabbed a sheet of paper and began scribbling names.

"How was she that morning?" Corbin asked. "Was she happy, in a good mood, feeling... sick? Anything out of the ordinary?"

He shook his head. "No, nothing. It was a Tuesday, just like any other. As far as I can recall, she was in a good mood."

"So why don't you tell us how that day went for you?" Corbin leaned back in his chair and stared at him. His tone, though still professional, had an edge to it and I wasn't sure if that meant he wasn't buying what Lombardi was saying.

"Uh…" Lombardi's voice trailed off as he slid the paper across the desk to me. "It was just an average day. She left around seven to go to the office, and I came straight here like I always do. We parted ways at the front door."

"So you were here when it happened?" Corbin pressed him.

Something shifted in Lombardi's demeanor as Corbin asked

the question. "Where the hell d'you think I was?" he snapped. "*Yes*. I was *here* when it happened. Lucille can vouch for me. If you're insinuating that I had something to do with—"

"We have to ask," I said, cutting him off. "It's standard procedure. It's how we eliminate you from our inquiries."

I looked at Corbin. His eyes were narrowed and he was staring at Lombardi. Not good! The last thing we needed was for this meeting to turn confrontational.

"Listen," Lombardi said, a little more easily. "I don't want to believe that my wife was *murdered*. But I'm not an idiot, and I know that she was in good health. Maybe this is my way of coping with the tragedy. I just want answers so I can lay her to rest and try to pick up the pieces."

"And I hope we can provide you with those answers, Mr. Lombardi," I said, allowing a pinch of sympathy to slip into my voice. "But again, we have to cover the bases. I have my entire team on it. We have detectives on the street and at her law offices this morning."

"Make sure you vet them good," Lombardi muttered. "If anyone knows anything, it'll be them." Something in his voice piqued my curiosity.

"Why d'you say that, Mr. Lombardi?" I asked quietly.

Tony leaned toward us, his hands clasped together in a single fist. "Let me put it to you straight," he snarled. "Those guys knew my wife better than I did. That's for sure—and I wouldn't be surprised if they knew she had enemies that I am unaware of."

I nodded, suddenly questioning their relationship. "What about your marriage? Were you... doing well?"

"Of course," he said, waving his hand as if to dismiss any concerns. "Just because my wife was invested in her career didn't mean that we weren't fine. We had our ups and downs, but that's just life, isn't it? Things aren't always sunshine and roses in any marriage." As if on cue, his phone began to ring, and he stopped talking and took it from the inside pocket of his suit jacket. "I'm sorry. I need to take this."

"We'll see ourselves out," Corbin said as he rose to his feet and nodded toward the door. "Thank you, Mr. Lombardi."

Lombardi gave us a wave and then answered his phone, his voice hushed. We didn't wait around to hear the conversation. Instead, we took the elevator to the ground floor and walked out of the cool building into the heat of the morning.

We paused for a moment on the sidewalk and looked around. It was a busy scene, but I internalized little of it, thinking that as much as Samson didn't seem to be a fan, I could find little to dislike about Lombardi.

7

Thursday, June 23, 2022, 12:15 p.m.

I UNWRAPPED THE FOOT-LONG SUBWAY SANDWICH ON MY DESK, ignoring Samson's longing gaze and said, "You can have the leftovers, but ladies first." I gave him a pat on the head and then took a bite. We'd picked up the sandwiches on the way back from interviewing Tony Lombardi but, unfortunately, when I arrived back in my office, I'd gotten swamped in paperwork.

I wasn't sure what Corbin was doing, but as far as I knew, the rest of my team hadn't returned from canvassing the incident area. But I knew they'd drop in whenever they made it back.

I glanced at the clock, and seeing how long they'd been there, I couldn't help but wonder if they were making any progress.

"I don't know what I expect them to find," I mused to Samson before taking another bite. What we were doing really didn't make a lot of sense, which became a recurring theme in the endeavor. I was, at that point, just about convinced we were dealing with a case that would turn into nothing. But there was that little niggling at the back of my brain that was telling me *something* was off with it.

Absently, I tossed Samson a chunk of my foot-long then looked at him and said, "What do you think, Sammy? Do you think Madison Lombardi was murdered?"

Samson gobbled up the hunk in one snap of his jaws and then looked up at me, his head tilted at an impossible angle. "You have no idea, do you? You just want my sandwich. Well, you can forget it. If you're a good boy, I might save you some."

He straightened his head, clamped his jaws shut, turned and ambled over to his bed. Clearly, he wasn't in the mood for more conversation. *Hah! Maybe he's just as confused as I am.*

I finished my sandwich, saving the last few inches of bread, meat, and cheese to feed my four-legged partner, and then grabbed the Lombardi file. But that was as far as I got before my office door swung open.

"They're back," Corbin said, the creases around his eyes looking more pronounced than ever. "I told them we'd meet here in fifteen and discuss."

"Yeah, I'd like to hear what they found," I said, then added dryly, "if anything."

"I hear you," he said, his tone curt.

I narrowed my gaze and stared at him. "Something bothering you today, Corbin? Seems like ever since we got done with Tony Lombardi, something's been eating at you."

Corbin shrugged. "I just didn't like the guy."

I crumpled up the sandwich wrapper and tossed it into the trash. "Yeah, I could tell by your attitude. Samson wasn't a fan either."

He nodded. "I know, but there wasn't a real reason not to like him. He didn't give us anything that swayed my feelings about this case one way or the other. It was just... *him.*"

"I think that might be the first time you've ever said you didn't like someone," I said, smiling at him.

"There's something about him that doesn't gel for me," Corbin continued. "I can't put my finger on it, but I think he's hiding something."

"Well, given the way the receptionist gave us the cold shoulder," I said, "I wouldn't be all that surprised if he was up to all sorts of no good. Let's face it. When you're handling other people's money, as I'm sure he is, the opportunities for grift are more than plentiful."

"That's true, I suppose," he replied thoughtfully.

One by one, the team filed in and sat down at the table. Jack was, as usual, the last to arrive, and when he did, Corbin also took a seat at the table. Me? I stood up, stepped around my desk, parked myself on the front edge of my desk and folded my arms.

"So, who'd like to begin?" I said, looking at the collection of upturned faces. None of them appeared all that excited, so my guess was they'd come back with nothing.

"Well, after some research into Tony Lombardi," Jack began, "I can't really tie him to anything. His family is from New York; that's true, but it appears that it's his cousins who are involved in the family business, which is a polite way of saying, the mob. He appears to be self-made. He's in good standing with everyone, has a triple-A rating with the Better Business Bureau and has a credit score of eight hundred and two. He keeps up with his taxes and, in my humble opinion, is a pillar of the local community."

"What did you get from the interview with him?" Anne asked me, a curious expression on her face. "Because he seems to be the only one who thinks his wife didn't die from a heart attack."

"He says she was in great physical shape," I replied, "and that she had a cardiac stress test a week before she died, so there was nothing wrong with her heart. That seemed to be the driving factor behind his insistence that we investigate." I glanced at Corbin, then continued, "He also said she had no enemies, and he had an alibi for the time of death. What did you find?"

"Not much of anything," Hawk said. "We canvassed the area,

and most people said they saw the emergency lights, but nothing else."

"Except for one person," Ramirez added. "A woman, Nila Gregario, was finishing up a night cleaning shift when she saw a man in a trench coat and hood walk past."

"So now we do have confirmation of the shadowy figure," I said. "Do you have the time on that?"

"She said it would've been between seven-fifteen and seven-thirty."

I nodded, checking the box in my head. "But other than that, no one else saw anything?"

They all shook their heads.

"And what about the coworkers?" I asked.

"Yeah, that was fruitless, too," Cooper said, shaking his head. "We only got to talk to a couple of interns, a Barbra Edmonds and a Nathan Shaw. They ranted and raved about how much they liked working there, and they said that the whole team of attorneys were very close."

"Hmm," I said. "Closer than they were to their spouses, is what Lombardi said."

"They pointed out that Madison wasn't the life of the party. She took her job seriously, and didn't take much time off," Anne Robar continued where Cooper left off. "I don't know what we're digging for, but no one seemed to think anyone would want to harm Madison. She doesn't have many clients—none that were recently released—and everyone was generally happy with her."

"*Generally* happy?" I said. I couldn't help but pick out the phrase. It wasn't something that Anne ever said, and it sounded *very* lawyer-like.

"Yeah, that's what they told us," Anne clarified. "I'm assuming they meant that there were no issues at the office."

"How long have the interns been there?" Corbin asked.

"Barbra has been there for…" Anne glanced down at her

notes. "Four months. Nathan Shaw had only been there for about a month and a half."

"Wow, not very long," Corbin commented. "That makes it difficult to trust their input."

"The rest of them were in court," Hawk answered. "But the interns did say that Madison's death had been talked about thoroughly, and that everyone seemed to be grieving. Especially David Mitchell, who apparently worked closely with her for years."

Interesting. I'd heard the name before, and I was certain David Mitchell was one of the hotshot criminal defense attorneys our prosecutor had gone up against—and hated when they did. Still, I made a mental note of the name, just in case it came up again.

"I wish the cameras would've been working," Ramirez said, running her fingers through her hair. "It would've been nice to get an actual picture of what happened that morning."

"I agree," I said, "but I think our best shot at finalizing this one is Doc Sheddon's pending report. That should put this thing to bed once and for all." I paused for a second, then said, "Okay, that's it for today. I'll see you all in the morning, bright and early." That last was said as I was looking at Jack. He just smiled and nodded.

And with that, I wrapped up the meeting, somewhat relieved that nothing was going to keep me up tonight. I did my best not to take work home with me, but after everything I'd experienced in my time as a homicide detective, there were any number of cases that haunted me—but not this one. At least not yet.

"Well, buddy, it looks like a whole lot of nothing," I told Samson as the door closed behind Corbin, who was the last to leave. "So maybe this one will close out before anything crazy happens."

He perked up his ears and looked sleepily at me, and that's when my phone started ringing in my pocket. I dug it out and checked the number on the screen—one I didn't recognize. "Gazzara," I answered.

"This is retired detective Thomas Drews." The voice was deep, the accent southern. "I was calling you to see if you had a moment to chat about the Lombardi case."

I blinked a couple of times, struck by the interest in what I was almost sure was an open-and-shut case. "What can I help you with?"

"Well, I just wanted to chat about the circumstances. I worked as a detective for fifteen years before turning to investigative journalism."

Nope. Not doing this. He's just a nosey reporter.

"Sorry, I'm not at liberty to discuss this right now."

"Well, but I was wondering—"

I hung up on him and tossed my phone to my desk. Chief Johnston made it clear he wanted to keep this quiet, and I knew he'd have my guts if I talked to anyone in the media.

8

Tuesday, June 28, 12:30 p.m.

IT WAS ALMOST A WEEK LATER, LUNCHTIME, AND I WAS ALONE IN MY office with Samson.

"It's been too quiet," I told him as I tossed him one of the three junior whoppers I had gotten from Burger King. I really shouldn't have been eating fast food, but it was the first time I had done so in almost a week. Plus, I'd gone for a long run the evening before, so that had to count for something, right?

I shut the Madison Lombardi case file and pushed it off to the corner of my desk. It had been more than a week since her death, and so far not much had materialized. And by not much, I meant *nothing*! I had written a brief report and left it on Chief Johnston's desk the evening before. It contained nothing new, and we were just waiting for Doc Sheddon's final report, which was still a couple of weeks away.

I leaned back in my chair, looked out the window, and took in the rain. It was the kind of day that made me want to finish up right then, go home with some takeout, and find a mind-numbing TV show to get lost in while I hung out on the couch with Samson. I yawned, and I suddenly found myself battling to stay awake.

Geez, something needs to pick up around here, I thought. Most days, the quiet was welcome, but things hadn't been too eventful in the last week and I was ready for something to happen. And then my office door swung open and Chief Johnston stepped in. I knew my wish had been granted.

"How's the Lombardi case coming along?" he asked.

I sat back in my chair and raised my eyebrows at him. "It's not. We're still waiting on Doc Sheddon's report to close it out, but I put that report on your desk last night before I left." I wasn't usually up for pointing out things like that, but I really didn't have anything else to say to him about it.

"Yes, I know, and have you spoken with anyone at the firm today?"

I shook my head, unsure of where he was going with it. "I haven't."

"Well, then, here's a surprise for you, Gazzara." He chuckled as he said the words, but there was no humor in his voice. None at all. Whatever he was about to say, was *not* going to be good.

"Oh...kay?" I said warily.

"David Mitchell dropped dead about a block from his office... *this morning.*" Johnston was no longer smiling.

"No!" I retorted. "You can't be serious."

"Oh, I'm serious. You'd better believe I am."

"Not another heart attack?" I said.

"That's what the EMT's initial report said, yes," he replied. "Doc Sheddon has the body. He's promised to do the autopsy ASAP."

There was a moment of silence after that, and I wasn't sure if he was waiting for the news to sink in—or if he was insinuating that I wasn't on top of things the way I should be. Whatever, it left me stunned.

"It can't be a coincidence," I said slowly.

Harry Starke had long ago taught me that there were rarely any coincidences when it came to investigations. Occasionally, there would be a strange happenstance or two, but they were few and far between.

"Maybe they're all using the same drugs to get through the long nights?" I said, not knowing what else to say. The thought came from nowhere, but as I looked up at Chief Johnston, he shrugged.

"That's not too much of a reach, I think. They were both working in the same place and maybe had access to the same substance."

"But that would've led to the preliminary toxicology report containing something," I added, shaking my head.

"Maybe," Johnston agreed. "But maybe not. We won't know for a while, but once Tony Lombardi catches wind of this—or the media for that matter—it's going to bring up a lot of questions. I need to be ready with answers, Kate."

I nodded. "I'll get the team together and we'll get to work on it. I don't know… I don't know what this could mean, but it can't be a coincidence, not two lawyers working in the same office; that would be a stretch."

"You're right, and you need to talk to Officer Barron. He worked this scene too."

Right, the newbie I haven't met yet.

"Is he still here?" I asked as I stepped away from my desk, poured myself a fresh cup of coffee and took a sip, prepping for the mess of a case that we were going to be wading through. "I'd like to chat with him, now, if possible."

"He gets off at two today, so you better hurry." With that, Chief Johnston turned, left my office and disappeared across the incident room.

Me? I did my best to gather my scattered wits. I wanted to chat with Officer Barron before I did anything else. He'd been present at the scene both times and if there were any witnesses, he would know.

I made my way to Patrol on the other side of the building, stopping along the way to peek into the lounge. Several officers were sitting at the tables. "Any of you Officer Barron?" I didn't pretend to know who I was looking for. We were a big department.

A younger man with jet-black hair turned and stood up. "I am," he said.

"I'm Captain Gazzara. You have time for a quick chat?" I asked.

He nodded, and I nearly laughed at the rookie look of concern on his face. The others sitting there with him did laugh, but I ignored them, taking Barron to one side.

"What can I do for you, ma'am?"

"I need to know what happened this morning over on Eighth Street."

"Uh, it was a pretty routine call. I heard the medics being called to the scene, and I responded, as I did several weeks ago. It was right around seven-thirty. Though I'd have to check my report to be sure of the exact time. A gentleman had some kind of medical episode on the sidewalk there outside of the law firm."

"Anyone see anything?"

"Not that I know of. No one offered anything. There's always bystanders though, people who want to see what's happening."

"You know who called it in?"

He shook his head. "I believe someone found him and called it in. He was deceased before they called, so I understand."

"Okay." There wasn't much else I could say to that. If no one saw the event occur, then no one could even make a guess of what his cause of death was. I'd have to contact Doc Sheddon—or he'd have to get in contact with me. Whoever got to it first.

"There was something strange though," Officer Barron spoke up, catching my attention again. "There was this... I don't even know how to describe it... But it was like the skin on his face was burned? I don't know. That sounds weird, doesn't it?"

"You mean like a rash?" I asked. Now he had my attention.

"Yeah, I guess you could call it a rash." Barron nodded his agreement. "I mean, at the time, I thought it looked more like a burn, but a rash is probably a better description. He also had some white foam around his mouth. I only noticed that because the woman—the woman a couple weeks ago—had the same weird film. The EMT told me it was due to a seizure."

I should've talked to this man sooner.

"And did anyone mention seeing someone in a trench coat and hood this morning?"

Officer Barron's eyebrows shot up. "Ah, you must've talked to Shelly Seward, too. She was real adamant about that, you know. But not a single other person said they saw anything like that, and no one did this morning, either. I couldn't find a single witness."

Hmm, I wonder if the cameras are working now, I thought.

"Thank you, Barron," I said. "If I need anything else, I'll let you know. In the meantime, if you think of anything else, anything at all, even if it seems insignificant, call me."

Barron took a deep breath and exhaled sharply. "I don't... I mean... I will... I will tell you this; there were some familiar faces standing around, but I couldn't tell you who they were or even if I could recognize them again. I'm sure they were just people who work in the area."

I nodded, mentally noting that we'd need to canvass the area again—and maybe work a little harder at prying information out of people. Someone had to have seen something or maybe know if there were any odd happenings going on at that law firm.

"I think the whole thing is weird," Barron continued at my silence. "I've never heard of two people in good health dying right there on the sidewalk. It seemed off-kilter to me, if that makes sense."

"Yeah," I said. "Me, too!" I gave him a nod and dismissed him and then went back to my office.

"You know what, Sammy?" I said to the dog as I walked in. "I have no idea what the hell is going on, but I know one thing is for sure, if this *is* a coincidence, it's one hell of a big one."

Tuesday, June 28, 1:00 p.m.

IT WAS TIME TO GET TO WORK AGAIN, TIME TO GATHER MY TEAM.

I picked up the phone and called Corbin. "Hey," I said when he answered. "We need to talk. Have everyone meet here in my office in fifteen minutes."

"What's happened?" he asked. "Something bad. I can tell by the sound of your voice."

"We'll talk when everyone's here," I replied. "Fifteen minutes, okay?"

"Fifteen it is," he said and hung up.

"Is this about the Lombardi case?" Hawk asked as he dropped down on his chair at the table. "I thought that was wrapped up until we got the toxicology report."

"It was…" I replied, "but it's happened again. We have another dead, high-profile attorney. He dropped dead this morning, in virtually the same spot as Madison."

"No shit?" Jack said, shocked.

"A heart attack?" Anne Robar gave me an inquisitive look.

"Looks like it," I replied.

Barely had I uttered the words when my door opened and Chief Johnston walked in.

I pursed my lips, not sure how I felt about his heavy presence in my investigation. It wasn't something I was used to.

"I just wanted to drop off this list of David Mitchell's family and friends," Johnston said as he handed the paper to me. Then he turned to the group and said, "Listen up, all of you. We need to get a grip on this thing. It takes top priority. Got it?"

There was a murmur around the table. Hawk sat back in his chair, folded his arms and stared at the chief.

Me? I merely nodded and glanced at the list.

"There aren't many names here," I said thoughtfully. I don't know why I was surprised, but an attorney of Mitchell's standing typically had a vast reach. "Who gave this to you?"

"His wife. And I expect you to have someone pay her a visit this afternoon, yourself, preferably."

"Sure, I'll take Sergeant Russell with me." *And Samson.*

He nodded, eyeing the rest of the team each in turn. I thought for a moment that he might say something more, but he didn't. Instead, he turned, walked to the door, paused, turned and gave me one last *you better get this done* kind of look.

"David Mitchell is one of the most well-known criminal defense attorneys in the city," Ramirez said, frowning. "And he just fell over dead, just like that. It can't be a coincidence."

"And he worked at the same firm as Lombardi," I said.

"Now, yes," Jack said. "But I ran his background. He'd also been a partner at Tooly and Watts for almost ten years. He only recently went to work with Lombardi."

"I need those details, please, Jack," I said. At this point, I wasn't going to discount anything, no matter how irrelevant it seemed. "We also need to know which cases Mitchell and Lombardi worked together, if any. And, if these two deaths are indeed homicides, there has to be a connection between them, and I want to know what it is."

"So, you really think this is something more than a couple of bad hearts?" Hawk said skeptically.

"I'm not sure yet," I admitted. There was no point in feigning knowledge I didn't have. "All I know is that it's just too… I don't know, weird, to be a coincidence. Whatever it is, we need to get to the bottom of it—even if it is just two coinciding medical events. So, for now, we're treating this as a case of multiple homicide."

"So, I guess we get to canvass the area… *again?*" Cooper said, rolling his eyes.

I ignored the eye roll and said, "Not exactly. I want you and Tracy to pay a visit to their law firm, but this time, you need to push a little harder. Talk to the interns again, but I also want to hear from the lawyers. So, wherever they are, hunt them down and question them. Be tough but respectful. These are the people in the know. We need to talk to them." I looked at Tracy. "You with the program?"

She nodded. "Of course."

"You think they're avoiding us?" Corbin asked, frowning.

"That's another question I don't have the answer to."

"We should also stop in and talk to Doc Sheddon," Corbin said.

"We will," I agreed. "But not today. I doubt he'll be done with the examination. I'll drop in and see him on my way to work in the morning."

"Hawk and I can work our way through that list of family and friends." Anne nodded to the list still in my hand. "And I guess that once we're done, we can start recanvassing the area. Maybe we'll find a witness or two. It's worth a shot."

"Jack," I said, "I want you to do a deep dive into both Mitchell and Lombardi. If there's a connection, we need to find it. Get their phone records. Look into their case histories. Okay, so that's it for now. Let's get to it."

"You think I should also dig into their emails?" Jack asked. "Or do I need to try to get a warrant for that?"

Would a judge grant us a warrant? I wondered. I could see a judge throwing a fit about digging into emails over what might only be cardiac arrest—but then again, maybe I just needed permission from Mrs. Mitchell or Tony Lombardi... Or did I? There might be problems with attorney-client privilege. What we really needed was their computers and laptops, and for that, we did need a warrant.

As far as I could see, I had two options: I could call in a favor from Judge Henry Strange, or I could call Harry Starke. His ability to wade into the gray was... legendary.

"Hold off on the emails for now. I'll think about what I can do about getting laptops and passwords. Concentrate on the phone records and the background checks."

Jack nodded. "Okay, got it."

"You're going to find a lot," Ramirez said. "Mitchell's been involved in some major cases—many more than Madison Lombardi. He was a challenge to go up against in court."

Lots of stress, then, I thought. *But yet he died of a heart attack—or did he?* I was already leaning more toward the *or did he* at that point. I learned long ago that it's never good to make assumptions, but my gut was telling me something was seriously amiss. *I mean... two prominent attorneys, both from the same office, both dropping dead in the street and within a couple of weeks of one another? Come on! Think about it, Kate. How likely is that?*

Inwardly, I shook my head, then pursed my lips and said, "Let's get on with it, people. We're going to need some answers, and this is going to be a long day."

Corbin pushed back from the table and rose to his feet.

Anne stretched her arms over her head, already looking fatigued. If we weren't so pressed for time, I'd have checked on her. Instead, however, I made a mental note to keep an eye on her. I needed my team to be in tip-top shape. They were damn near like family to me. If something was off in their life, I wanted to know and do what I could to help.

But maybe she just didn't get enough sleep. I knew that problem all too well, and while lately it hadn't been a challenge for me, I had a feeling it was coming.

Everyone filed out of the room with the exception of Corbin, who stayed back, waiting for me.

I grabbed Samson's leash and clipped it to his harness.

"Well, let's go pay Mrs. Mitchell a visit," I said to an unusually quiet Corbin. He was never the most talkative guy on my team, but he did usually have *something* to say.

"Yeah." His short answer caused me to pause again.

"What's going on with you?"

He let out a heavy breath. "I wonder what kind of mess we're about to get into. You know, if someone can kill a person without so much as even touching them—that's some pretty high-level stuff."

I shrugged. "Unfortunately, these days, all it takes is a few Google searches and you've got all the techniques right at your fingertips."

"You're not wrong," he agreed, though his expression stayed unchanged. "But considering they're both defense attorneys, I think we should be looking into any losing cases they had. Nothing pisses off a felon more than getting charged with a crime they thought they were going to get away with. And then there's the thought that maybe someone was *wrongly* convicted because of a weak defense. That could lead to a revenge situation."

"All good points," I commented as we walked together across the situation room to the elevator, headed out of the station. "Anything's possible, but right now we have nothing, so we stick to the basics."

"Nothing but that mysterious hooded figure," he muttered as the elevator doors closed.

IT WAS a little after two thirty when we stepped out into the hot afternoon sun. I grimaced at the intensity. The storms of the early morning had moved on, and the excessive moisture had filled the air with an almost palpable humidity. By the time we made it to the car, the back of my neck was already coated with a thin layer of sweat.

"Wow, wealthy attorney," Corbin muttered as he glanced at the screen of my GPS.

"It's a fancy neighborhood then?" I hadn't heard of it, which wasn't surprising considering it was outside our jurisdiction.

"Yeah, probably one of the nicest in Hamilton County. My wife has a friend who lives over there. It's tough to get in there."

"Great," I muttered, pulling out of the parking lot.

It was busy for a Tuesday afternoon, but I hardly noticed as I drove across the city, all the while thinking about the hooded figure. "You really think that person in the trench coat has something to do with it?" I glanced sideways at Corbin. He turned his lips downward, frowning.

"Who dresses like that in June? Yeah, it was raining," he said thoughtfully. "But it was also warm, hot, and sticky, you know? Not the weather for a trench coat. Most people would just use an umbrella or make a dash for it."

I nodded. "But then again, maybe whoever it was, was just making sure their clothing didn't get wet?"

"Maybe, or maybe not. Maybe they didn't know the cameras weren't working. I don't know, Kate. The whole idea of covering up like that…" He trailed off.

I smiled at him, then glanced up at the rearview mirror. Samson was sitting up, watching me in the mirror. "What do you think, buddy?" I asked.

He merely tilted his head, then laid down.

10

Tuesday, June 28, 3:40 p.m.

"CAN I HELP YOU?" THE SECURITY GUARD GLARED AT US AS IF WE were a couple of vagrants.

"We're here to see Mrs. Sarah Mitchell," I answered coolly, showing him my badge. "I'm Captain Gazzara, and this is Sergeant—"

"Yeah, that's enough. Go ahead," he snapped, cutting me off.

I raised my brows at the rude greeting but chose to roll up my window instead of engaging.

"How does a defense attorney afford a mansion like one of these?" I wondered aloud as I weaved through the upscale subdivision, marveling at the multimillion-dollar mansions. We could have been in Beverly Hills; not that I'd ever been there, but still.

I wonder if Tony Lombardi lives in a place like this, I thought. *After all, didn't someone say he was one of the wealthiest men in the city?* I took in the new money style homes, each having its own unique concept, some like castles, some colonial, some English Elizabethan.

"There," Corbin said, pointing to one of the castle-like homes, complete with gray stone walls and a rounded tower. "Geez, did you ever see anything like it? It's massive."

"Maybe he's in someone's pocket," I said.

"More like multiple someones if that's the case," Corbin replied.

"Maybe he's just a great attorney," I said as I exited the car and went to the rear door to let Samson out. I hooked his leash to his harness. I had no idea if Sarah Mitchell was going to be happy entertaining my canine partner, but I never liked to leave him behind and certainly wouldn't leave him in the car on a hot day, so she was going to have to put up with it.

I'd parked at the bottom of a flight of at least a dozen steps that led up to a huge open porch and a pair of heavy wooden doors. We were about to mount the steps when one of the doors opened, and an attractive woman I estimated to be about my age stepped out. And she certainly looked like she belonged in the neighborhood. She was tall, slim, blond, smooth-skinned and—to me—appeared too heavily Botoxed. I couldn't take my eyes off her lips.

"Good afternoon, ma'am," Corbin said. "I'm Sergeant Russell with the Chattanooga Police Department, and this…" He glanced at me. "…is Captain Gazzara. We're—"

"You're here about my husband." She cut him off. Her tone was sharp, her voice hard. "I thought you might come, though I'm not sure how I can help. I'm busy trying to arrange his funeral. He was much loved by this community."

"I'm sorry for your loss, ma'am," I said quietly. It was clear that she was on guard, though why, I wasn't sure. "We have a few questions, if you don't mind."

She pursed her Botox-filled lips as she looked me up and down. "Well, I suppose you'd better come in," she said, sounding tired. "Though, as I said, I don't know how I can help."

"Thank you." I took a step forward.

"And, umm, is the dog coming too?" She curled her lip as she looked down at Samson.

Samson smiled up at her.

I patted him on the head. "Yes, ma'am, if you don't mind. It's too hot to leave him in the car."

"Very well, then. If he must, he must." And, without a second look at any of us, she spun on her stiletto heel, and we followed her into the house, Corbin leading the way. We stepped through into what could only be described as a magnificent house, one that could've easily passed for a museum. The centerpiece of the huge foyer was an abstract glass sculpture, but we had no time to admire it. Sarah Mitchell walked ahead as if she was on some kind of a mission, leading us eventually into an ornate—what she described as a—chat room.

Photographs and paintings of her and David were everywhere —on the walls, on the matching antique sideboards. There was not a picture anywhere that was *not* of the two of them. It was as excessive as the house itself, an in-your-face kind of excessive as if they were determined the world should know they were a happy couple—but I had seen it all before, many times.

They were probably not *a happy couple at all,* I thought bitchily.

"Can I offer you something to drink?" she asked us, looking first at Corbin, then at me. "I have coffee, tea, and water."

"I'll have a coffee. Thank you," Corbin said.

"Coffee for me, too," I said. "Black. Thank you."

"Same for me, black," Corbin said.

She nodded with a tilt of her head. "Make yourselves comfortable. I'll be right back," she said, her voice flat.

"This is kind of intense," Corbin muttered, almost a whisper.

"The pictures?" I replied, eyeing the biggest one on the wall. It was the two of them on their wedding day, the dark-headed, slender attorney holding the blond woman in a mermaid-style gown tightly in his arms. The two looked happy—as if in a fairy-tale—but we all knew that a picture was worth a thousand words… words that weren't always true. "Yes, kind of blatant, isn't it?"

We were seated together on a large sofa. Samson was sitting quietly at my feet. The coffee table in front of us was large and out of keeping with the antique décor.

Five minutes later, she reappeared bearing a silver tray with three cups of coffee thereon and set it on the glass coffee table top.

"Please, help yourselves," she said as she took a cup for herself and sat down on the armchair to Corbin's right.

"Now, you say you have questions," she said before raising the cup to her lips and taking a small sip. It was a statement rather than a question.

"Yes. How long have you and David been married?" I said, starting the conversation carefully. She didn't come across like a grieving widow, but some people were stoic cannons, and if you said the wrong thing, they'd explode. "Oh, and by the way," I continued, "I'll be recording the interview, if you don't mind."

I set my digital recorder on the coffee table in front of her.

"Is that really necessary?" she asked.

I nodded. "It just makes things a lot easier, but Sergeant Russell can take notes instead if you like."

Sarah shrugged but didn't object further. She took a deep breath, not a single crease or line showing on her glowing face. "How long have we been married? Almost twelve years. And now… he's… gone. Sorry." She looked down into her cup. "I'm still trying to process it."

"That's all right," Corbin said softly. "What can you tell us about your husband? How was his health?"

"Good," she answered without thinking. "His last appointment at the cardiologist went very well. He did have high blood pressure, but it was being treated. He'd never skipped a beat, if you know what I mean. He was extremely active, healthy, and felt well. He went for a run most mornings, and he played golf at least twice a week, sometimes more. He was in very good shape."

I nodded. "Do you know of anyone who might have wanted to hurt him; anyone who has some sort of grudge?"

She raised her eyebrows at that, though the question didn't appear unexpected. "Well... that's not an easy question to answer. I don't know of anyone like that who would want to harm him, but he did work with some very unsavory individuals. And I'm sure that, doing the kind of work he did, he made some people unhappy. He was very good at what he did, you know."

"Can you think of any instances in particular?" Corbin said, then took a sip of his coffee.

She shook her head. "No, not really. It wasn't all that uncommon for him to mention some sort of confrontation at work, but he left out specifics, of course. Personally, I thought he could be a little overdramatic about his work. I work from home as an IT specialist, and he was out in the world, making waves. He was a bit of a bragger, I'm afraid."

Hmm. Interesting...

"Anything recent?" Corbin pushed her, raising his eyebrows.

"Well, there was... I think he was having a bit of a problem with one of the interns. Nathan... Nathan something? But it wasn't anything out of the ordinary. He just missed a lot of days. I think the kid was really sick, but you know, David thought he was playing hooky." She waved it off, rolling her eyes. "He would run those poor interns right into the ground. There was always something with him."

"And what was his relationship with Madison Lombardi like?" I asked, careful to keep my tone conversational.

Her upper lip twitched, and I noted a brief moment of discomfort flash across her face. "They were colleagues. I don't know anything beyond that, really. I think they got along well enough."

"They worked together?" Corbin said. "So they must have seen quite a lot of each other."

"He was working there, and she was working there. That's all I know. He didn't talk much about his work. A lot of it was confidential." Her voice was strained, and I wanted to press. However, before I could, my phone rang in my pocket.

"Were there any colleagues that your husband mentioned often?" Corbin asked as I dug out my cell phone. Anne Robar was calling.

I held up a finger. "If you'll excuse me for a moment, I have to take this." I rose to my feet, leaving Samson with Corbin. I slipped out of the room and went back to the foyer as I answered. "What is it, Anne?"

"I think David Mitchell and Madison Lombardi were closer than we initially thought."

I frowned. "They were colleagues. What are you telling me? How much closer could they be?"

"They were having an affair," she replied.

Well, that just blew the lid off. I rubbed my forehead. "Who told you?"

"Both of the interns and one of the other lawyers, Lauren Lewis. She said she knew they'd been having an affair but said she was *almost* certain it had ended. There's no way to be sure of that, Kate. Not many other people really knew about it. They kept a pretty low profile."

"Okay, did anyone mention if either of the spouses knew?"

"Lewis said she was pretty sure that Sarah Mitchell knew."

"Anything else?" I asked.

"No. We're still waiting on Colton Rhodes, another lawyer here. He's in court right now, but they say he'll be back before five."

"Okay. Thanks for the information, Anne," I said. "If you hear of anything else, you call me."

"I will," she said, and we hung up. I made my way back to the chat room and took my seat beside Corbin.

"Mrs. Mitchell…" I paused as I saw her tense. "I'm sorry, but I have to tell you… I know your husband was having an affair with Madison Lombardi, and I think you knew he was. Why don't you tell us about it?"

She blew out a deep, pained breath, and then she put her hands to her face and began to cry.

I turned to Corbin who looked at me, his eyes wide.

11

Tuesday, June 28, 4:35 p.m.

WE WAITED FOR SARAH MITCHELL TO CALM DOWN, AND AFTER I'D handed her several tissues from the box on the coffee table, she finally took a deep shuddering breath, dried her eyes and looked at me. She looked pathetic, and no wonder.

"I'm sorry," she sniffled, wiping the smeared mascara from her eyes. It only made her look worse, but I wasn't about to point that out. "It's been a horrible day, and I knew this would eventually come up."

I nodded. "I know it's a painful subject, but we have to talk about it. Please... What can you tell us?"

I glanced again at Corbin, who was obviously still processing the news I'd so casually dropped on him.

"Well, it's over. It has been for a while. The affair is water under the bridge," she said, still dabbing the tissue under her eyes. "It's painful when I really think about it, but it was just a bump in the road for us. Once Tony Lombardi found out, he made Madison end it with David. I know she obeyed him, too. He's a powerful man."

"Before we talk about that," I said carefully, "what about you and David? Let's focus on the two of you. How did you handle it?"

"It was hard. I found out through his emails." She looked away from us and shook her head. "That was probably the worst part—the finding out—but after that, we decided that it wasn't worth ending our marriage over. That was…" Her voice trailed off as her eyes squeezed shut. "That was two and a half years ago. It happened right about the time that he started at the firm. They'd been working on a case together, and it went from there. A lot of late nights. You know how that works, I'm sure. It didn't help that David and I weren't getting along, either. I wanted children. He didn't. I eventually decided that it was fine… Oh, I don't know. They ended the affair a long time ago."

Corbin nodded. "But they weren't still seeing each other?"

She shook her head but paused. "Not in the way you think. If they were, they were very secretive about it. I checked his emails and texts regularly. That's how we built our trust back in our marriage. There were no signs of him doing anything wrong."

"Do you have his laptop and cell phone?" I asked. "If so, I'd like to take them with us. We'll return them, of course."

"I don't have his cell phone. I believe that's with him—wherever he is."

"He's at the medical examiner's office," I said. There was no point in skirting around that fact. "So, do we have your permission to take his laptop, then? It would be helpful."

"Of course," she said, rising to her feet. "I'll go get it for you. I'll be right back."

As soon as she was out of earshot, Corbin turned to me. "Well, this is a major development."

I nodded. "There's always something, and, at this point, if what she says is true, we can't even be sure that it means anything. People have affairs all the time; most of them don't end in murder."

"True enough," he said, "but still—"

"I never expect anything, Corbin. That way I'm never disappointed." I chuckled, reaching forward and grabbing my coffee. It was lukewarm after having sat for most of the interview, but my mind had been too busy to worry about my caffeine intake.

Mrs. Mitchell appeared back in the room carrying a laptop bag. "Here's his computer. There's a notebook in the front pocket that has all of his passwords. Like I said, our marriage was fine, but we were still maintaining that transparency."

"Okay, thank you." Corbin pulled out his card and handed it to her in exchange for the computer. "Now, what can you tell us about Tony?"

"Ha!" She laughed, tipping her head back. "Tony Lombardi is a snake of a man, but that's about all I know about him. He had Madison under lock and key, and I think the reason she slept with my husband was solely out of spite for her husband. Everyone knows he has ties to some really shady characters."

"And David didn't have any such ties, right?" I asked. At the time I was thinking about the house that cost more than most people make in their lifetime.

"No, and if you're wondering how we paid for all this," she said and waved her hand in the air, "I'm the one with the money. I received a large inheritance after my father passed. That's how we can afford this house and our lifestyle. It's me, not him." There was something snarky in her voice, like she needed validation that she was the wealthy one, not her husband.

"You said Tony Lombardi was in with some shady characters," I said. "Do you have any names?"

"No," she replied. "It's just what I heard... mostly from David. He said it was common knowledge, but I didn't involve myself in that type of gossip. I'm sure there are plenty of people who'll confirm it, though. You'll just have to ask around."

"And one last question," I said. "Where were you this morning between seven and nine?"

"I beg your pardon?" she said, obviously outraged by the question.

"It's just routine," I said. "So that we can eliminate you from our inquiries."

"Eliminate me? So you think someone killed him?"

"At this point, no," I said. "But we're still waiting for the medical examiner's report."

"I was here working," she said.

"Can anyone corroborate that?" I asked, thinking I knew the answer.

"My boss can. We were in a video meeting," she said, surprising me. "As I told you, I work from home."

"Is there anyone who can verify that you were here at home? Maybe a maid... or..." I shrugged.

"They don't come in until after ten," she replied haughtily.

"Well," I said as I picked up my recorder and rose to my feet. "Thank you for your time, and for answering our questions. We may need to talk to you again, and I'll be sure to return the laptop as soon as we've finished with it. And, again, we're very sorry for your loss."

"Thank you." She sighed, her face softening slightly.

Samson yawned obnoxiously, and Sarah glanced down at him. "He's a very well-behaved dog, isn't he?"

He smiled up at her, and I shook my head. He was always a charmer, and I often wondered if he understood every word that was being said to him.

We headed out of the house and made our way back to the car. Sarah took a step back and shut the door, disappearing back into her lonely mansion... *alone.*

"That has to be a depressing way to live," Corbin muttered as I started the car. "All alone in that big house with a husband who's sleeping with his coworker. Not a good scenario."

"No, but she doesn't seem like the type to murder her husband, either."

"You sure?" Corbin made a face at me. "I could see it. She's got that kind of thing about her. You know, she's stoic until suddenly she's not. She could go into a fit of rage, poison the two of them… or something."

"Something? Hah! Why not just kill Madison?" I countered as I backed out of the driveway. "Wouldn't that have solved her problem? She seemed *very* into the marriage."

"Maybe she just wants us to think she was happily married."

"Maybe," I agreed. "That coffee wasn't all that great, was it?"

"She could've poisoned us." Corbin winked at me and laughed. "Really though, I didn't think it was all that great either. Let's swing by and get some fresh. I bet we can catch Doc before he closes up for the day if we hurry."

I looked at my watch. It was already after five-thirty.

"We can give it a try," I said.

"What do you think then, Kate? Where's this thing going? And what about Tony Lombardi? Maybe we should pay him a visit before we go diving into Doc Sheddon's report." I had to admit that he had a point.

"Okay," I said. "Tell you what: you call Lombardi's office and I'll call Doc. That way we'll know where we go this evening and where we go in the morning."

"Deal," he said, and I pulled into a parking spot in front of Starbucks.

"I'll step out to make my call." Corbin pushed open the door and climbed out while I set Samson's pup cup in the holder on the back seat. He dug in, and I called Doc.

"Kate Gazzara," Doc greeted me on the second ring. "I was hoping that you were going to give me a call before I left for the day."

"Oh yeah?" I replied. "I take it you have something for me? I was hoping to get your opinion on David Mitchell. I know there might not be much yet, but anything will help."

"Captain, I think I can do more than just give you a little help. I can paint you a picture."

I liked the sound of that. "I take it David is cut and dried; maybe less mysterious than Madison Lombardi."

Doc laughed. "Oh, not at all, Kate. If anything, I'd say his case is much more complex than Madison's, but I now have no doubt they were both killed by the same individual."

"Really! Geez, Doc. What does that mean, exactly?"

"Well, as I said, I think they were murdered, Kate, and I'll tell you the rest when you get here." With that, he hung up, and I groaned in frustration. I swear, he liked to make me stew, and that's not something I enjoyed; not at all. I had to put up with enough of that without Doc playing havoc with my mind.

But they were murdered. That had my mind spinning. My assumption had been wrong all along. Someone had targeted them, and my guess is that Doc now knew the *how*. We just had to figure out the *who* and the *why*.

"Tony is out for the day," Corbin said as he climbed back into the passenger seat. "I hope you have better news than me."

"Oh, I do, Corbin. I really do. We're going to see Doc… to learn just how our two victims were *murdered*."

His mouth dropped open as he hurriedly shut the door and buckled up. "I guess we have two homicides on our hands then?"

"That we do," I said as I put the car in drive and pulled out onto the street, tires squealing.

12

I DROVE AROUND TO THE BACK OF THE FORENSIC CENTER AND parked outside the rear doors, noting for the umpteenth time the road sign that proclaimed: Dead End.

Samson followed along beside Corbin as we made our way into the building and down the corridor to Doc's office where, luckily, he was at his desk waiting for us.

"Good evening, you two," he said, an impish smile on his face. "You got here quickly. Someone light a fire under you?"

"You did, you old reprobate," I replied. "You made me curious. What d'you have for me?"

I looked down at Samson. He looked on edge. I don't think he liked Doc's little shop of horrors any more than I did, and no wonder; it was full of dead bodies, and while I'd seen my fair share of those over the years, it never got any easier.

"Hah!" he said. "Well then, sit yourself down and we'll chat. I finished the autopsy more than an hour ago, so you missed that and will have to make do with photos."

"I'm more than okay with that," Corbin muttered under his breath from beside me.

I smiled, shaking my head. Corbin had a weak stomach ever since I'd met him. But I had the feeling something else was bugging him, so I made a mental note to talk to him about it later.

I looked expectantly at Doc, waiting for him to begin.

"Here." He set his cup of coffee down on his desk and shuffled through some of the files, retrieved several photographs and laid them out side by side. One was of Madison's face, the other of David's.

"That's quite a rash," Corbin commented, leaning forward to get a closer look.

"Looks like a burn to me," I said. "What is it, acid?"

Doc shook his head. "Good guess, Kate. But no! I would've been able to tell immediately if it was. What I find intriguing, though, is that if you look at Lombardi, her rash is not nearly as pronounced as Mitchell's."

I looked closely at the photo of the blond woman and nodded. "It's not as widespread, or as angry-looking, and it's only around her nose. It's more widespread on his face."

Doc clicked his tongue. "Yes, you're right, and I had difficulty figuring out what had caused such a violent reaction. One might've thought she'd been snorting something caustic that had caused the rash... But Mitchell..." He paused and shook his head. "He shows classic signs."

"Of *what?*" I asked and looked up at him.

"Cyanide poisoning."

I blinked, then said, "Cyanide... on their faces?"

He nodded. "I'm afraid so. Yes. Via an uncommon route to be sure, but lethal, nonetheless. So, based on those findings, I believe someone threw cyanide in their faces. It would've caused an almost instant reaction, and they would've died within minutes of inhalation."

"Wow," Corbin said. "I've never heard of such a thing. Wouldn't it leave traces of powder—it was powder, right?—on the skin, though?"

"I'm sure you haven't," Doc said, "and most likely it would have been powder; it's easier to inhale. The rain would have washed away the residue." He leaned back in his chair and laced his fingers together over his ample stomach. "It's an oddity; quite uncommon, which is why it took so long to come to the conclusion. Lombardi's reaction was quite mild compared to Mitchell's. It was his reaction that pointed me in the right direction. I'm still waiting on the toxicology report for confirmation, of course, but I sent the images to a couple colleagues. They're in agreement with me."

"So..." Corbin said, "someone tossed a handful of cyanide—"

"Oh, much less than a handful," Doc cut him off. "It was probably just a small amount in Lombardi's case. Quite a bit more in Mitchell's. I'd say whoever did it to David was... quite angry."

I nodded. "That beats all," I said. "It's a new one on me too."

"Understandable," Doc said, nodding. "I know of only one other case." He paused, picked up the photos and slid them back into the folder. "It involved a mafia hitman. I believe he was known as the Iceman. He'd kill his targets in like manner. He'd walk by and toss a little cyanide in their face. It was damn near impossible to accurately ascertain the cause of death; most were ruled cardiac episodes."

Corbin shuddered. "And almost impossible to trace."

Doc continued, "Well yes, unless there happen to be security cameras. The killer still has to have some sort of interaction with the victim. It's not something most investigators would catch. But you're not most investigators, are you?" He winked at us, and I chuckled.

"And you're not like most medical examiners, either," I replied.

"I'll take that as a compliment, Kate," he said, picking up the file. "I've already emailed my findings to you and my pre-toxicology report conclusions, including the amended conclusion for Madison Lombardi."

"Thank you. I'm sure Chief Johnston will be interested to see them." I said it with tongue in cheek. I didn't even want to think what his reaction would be when he found out there was a killer on the loose... *throwing cyanide in their victim's faces. Geez, what will they think of next?*

"I'll let you know when the official report comes back, but I'm pretty certain I have it right. It's the only explanation."

"Well..." I said and paused, trying to decide what this new information meant for the case. "At least we have something to work with now." I said it, but I was less than confident. This new information was spinning around inside my head. At that point, I really didn't know what it all meant, except that we were now dealing with two homicides, though all we really had was a cause of death. Good to know, but not exactly helpful.

"Thanks for that, Doc," I said rising to my feet. "I have to get back to the office and prepare something for the chief. I'll call you if I have more questions... and I'm sure I will. This is... crazy."

Doc stood, offered his hand, and said, "I agree, and I will say this. Be careful, Kate. This person is extremely dangerous."

"Thanks again, Doc," I said as I shook his hand. "I will."

WE STEPPED out into the evening, leaving Doc to his gruesome work. It was warm and humid as ever, and Corbin mumbled something I didn't catch as we walked to my car.

"This is a weird one," he said as I buckled Samson into the back seat. "I don't think I've ever heard of anything so... *sinister.*"

I didn't answer. I was deep in thought. My mind was racing. We were only two blocks from the police department and I would soon be heading home. But the thought foremost in my head was that walking on the sidewalk would never be the same.

"We need to find the guy in the trench coat," Corbin said as I backed out of the lot. "It has to be him."

"Or her," I said absently.

"True. You don't think… Tony Lombardi could have done it, do you? He has ties to the mafia."

"He has an alibi," I said. "Though, I'm sure that secretary would say whatever he asked her to." The thought made me frown. He was also extremely wealthy and could have hired someone to do it.

"I was thinking about the rashes," Corbin said. "I mean, Madison's wasn't that bad, but David's was much worse. It could be happenstance, but wouldn't Tony feel more rage toward David for sleeping with his wife?"

"I suppose," I said. "I guess David would've died quicker." I glanced back at Samson in the rearview. He seemed unenthused by our conversation, watching out the window as we pulled into the parking lot.

Corbin unbuckled his seatbelt. "I don't know. I think we need to pay him another visit tomorrow. He didn't mention the affair when we spoke to him."

"Neither did Sarah Mitchell," I replied. "Maybe the two of them are working together." I smiled at the thought as I stepped out of the car.

"Maybe! At this point, I don't think anything would surprise me," Corbin said as we headed inside.

I'd already received texts from the team letting me know they'd left reports of their findings on my desk. Now, I had to sort through them and pass along the information to Chief Johnston. I knew he was going to have a field day with Doc's findings. And I also knew we were going to do everything we could to keep the new findings out of the media.

The more I thought about it, the more concerned I became. *If it ever gets out that someone's walking around and tossing cyanide into people's faces... there'll be hell to pay.* I shook my head. *I just hope this is an isolated event... two events. Geez, one more and...*

It didn't bear thinking about.

13

Tuesday, June 28, 8:15 p.m.

"I'm beat," I told Samson as the garage door closed behind us. He yawned beside me on the front seat. I think he preferred the passenger seat—*who doesn't?*

I pushed open my door and let Samson jump across the console to exit the vehicle. His paws pattered on the concrete, and he headed for the interior door, whining.

"Ready for dinner, huh?" I said as I unlocked it. I turned the knob and pushed the door in, the heady scent of home rushed out to greet me. The vanilla and sandalwood had become relaxing. Home was my haven away from the chaos of work and the city, and I hoped it always stayed that way.

Samson followed me to the kitchen where I picked up his bowls and filled one with fresh water and the other with his kibble. I was late feeding him, and the fact that he wolfed it down was evidence of that. I dug through the fridge, searching for something easy to make for myself.

I didn't feel like cooking but hadn't been in the mood for takeout either. Corbin and I had burned through nearly an hour finishing up the report for Chief Johnston, and I wanted to sit on my couch and chill.

"I need to tell everyone that we'll meet after lunch," I thought aloud. Samson paused over his bowl and looked up at me, his ears perked. "We have to talk to Tony Lombardi in the morning." I'd already arranged to meet Corbin in the PD lot at nine.

Samson went back to licking his bowl.

I settled for leftover chicken, rice, and vegetables, heated in the microwave. By the time it was ready, I was just about done in. I grabbed the food and what was left of a bottle of red and went to the living room, determined to find something to watch to distract me from the bland dinner and the rigors of the day.

"What should we watch?" I asked Samson as I flopped down on the couch and turned on the TV. "Something funny? Adventurous?"

Samson climbed onto the other end of the couch, circled round and round, then let out a deep, shuddering breath and collapsed. I waited for him to get comfortable before scrolling through the programs. Nothing looked all that appealing, and it didn't help that my mind kept returning to trench coat man.

"What do you think about it, Sammy?" I said, looking at my sleepy-eyed pup. "You think Tony did it? Revenge on his cheating wife and her lover?"

If a dog could shrug, I swear Samson did. I shook my head and laughed at him, thankful for the companionship.

I settled on an episode of *Friends*. I'd never spent much time watching it back in the day, but it was a good distraction, even if the jokes didn't make me laugh. I ate my dinner, wishing that I'd taken the few minutes to get takeout. Then, just as I set my empty plate down on the coffee table, my phone rang.

Oh, terrific, I thought. *Not another homicide, please.* I picked it up and looked at the screen. *Oh no. Not again...* I hadn't saved the number, but I knew who it was. *That pesky investigative journalist.*

I hit the reject button and rolled my eyes. Some people never know when to quit.

I glanced at Samson. He was giving me one of those head-down frowny looks. "What's that for?" I laughed. "It's an active investigation. I can't talk to the media. You know that."

He didn't raise his head from between his paws, but he did raise his eyebrows and looked at me as if to say, *Rejecting someone's call isn't good etiquette.*

I ignored him and went back to *Friends*. It wasn't too long after that when fatigue began to tug at my eyes. I did my best to ignore it. I wasn't quite ready to turn in for the night, though I supposed my body could've used the extra rest. However, before I gave it a second thought, my phone rang... *again.*

You have to be kidding me. This is one determined guy. I blew out a breath, scooped up my phone, ready to reject the call, but as I read the name, I quickly changed my mind.

"Hey, Kate," Harry greeted me. "I was calling to see what happened with that lawyer. For some reason, I haven't been able to get it out of my mind."

"Harry. This is an unexpected surprise. You mean Madison Lombardi? Yes, well, there's been a development. Did you hear about David Mitchell?"

"Uh, no, but I know him. He's another defense attorney; a devil in the courtroom."

"He was," I replied, "but you're not going to have to worry about him anymore." I reached out with the remote and paused the TV. "He dropped dead this morning, early, on the sidewalk, same manner of death."

"Geez, Kate," he said. "That's one hell of a coincidence."

"It's no coincidence, Harry. They were both murdered. Cyanide poisoning."

He was silent for a few moments. "Like the Iceman."

"Doc Sheddon mentioned him," I said. "Mafia hitman."

"A cold-blooded serial killer. The guy enjoyed his work, but yeah, he had ties to the mafia. You have any suspects?"

I shrugged—like somehow Harry could see me doing so through the phone. "No, not really. Lombardi and Mitchell were having an affair. But that ended a couple of years ago, supposedly. Corbin suggested Tony Lombardi, but he has an alibi for his wife's murder, though it could have been coerced."

"So you're thinking revenge?" he replied. "I dunno. Two years is a lot of time."

"Unless they were still seeing each other," I said. "These days, people can hide just about anything. You know that better than anyone."

"You're not wrong. It is surprising the lengths some people will go to. So okay, let's say the two of them were still seeing each other. They both have spouses, right?"

"Yes," I said, nodding. "Tony Lombardi and Sarah Mitchell. We've spoken to them both, but Tony never told us about the affair. We're going to talk to him again in the morning."

"And Sarah?"

"She admitted to the affair, but only after we brought it up. We didn't know about it when we talked to Tony. Sarah said it was water under the bridge, and she reacted more to it being brought up than she did to her husband's death."

"Funny how things affect people differently," he said thoughtfully. "It could've been that bringing up the affair made her feel the pain again, especially with the loss of her husband."

"True," I said. "She said that their marriage was good now. That they'd worked through it. She gave us his laptop, and I'm waiting on Jack to go through it."

"I see," Harry replied. "Well, only time will tell with that one. But you never know when someone is lying."

"You're right, Harry." I sighed and then continued, "Some people are snakes. They can charm you into thinking one thing while leading you down a totally different path."

"It's quite a coincidence, don't you think, that cyanide was once a mafia technique and you have a mafia-connected spouse?"

"Maybe," I replied. "My brain's telling me Tony, but my gut's telling me no."

I thought about it for a long moment, my lips pursed. I never spent too much time in the early days of an investigation thinking about my gut feelings, but at that point, I was way down the rabbit hole. I'd thought it would be a wash, but it wasn't. We were in the middle of a double murder investigation and I had nothing to work with.

"I guess you'll just have to talk to the guy," Harry said, interrupting my thoughts. "Does he have any real connections to the mob?"

"I don't think so," I said. "From what we've learned so far, it's distant. Cousins. You know?"

"Hmm."

"Yeah, tell me about it." I laughed, shaking my head. "I don't have a clue, and while I think the affair is a big twist and a potential lead, it might not mean anything at all."

"Well, as you well know, murder is usually motivated by a half dozen things: greed, love, hate, money, sex, revenge, jealousy, rage, even just plain fun. Or it can be a mixture of any of them. An affair would be motivation enough. You never really know what's going to cause someone to snap."

"True enough, but these killings were premeditated, well planned and thought through."

"Of course," Harry agreed. "Well look. If you need anything, you let me know. You know I'm always happy to help when I can."

"Of course," I said. We said our goodbyes and I hung up. "Well, shall we go to bed, Samson? I'm ready."

He looked up at me as if to say, *I thought you'd never ask.*

14

I WOKE EARLY THE FOLLOWING MORNING, AS USUAL, AND WE WENT for a quick three-mile run through the neighborhood.

On return, I showered, dried my hair, put it up in a high ponytail, and then dressed in a beige leather jacket over a black blouse, and a pair of dark blue jeans. I spoiled myself with two fried eggs on two slices of toast and a couple of cups of coffee before Samson and I piled into the car.

We took a detour through the McDonald's drive-thru: coffee and a couple of sausage biscuits for Sammy—yes, I know. They're not good for him. The trouble is, he thinks they are.

It was a little after nine when I picked Corbin up in the PD parking lot.

"Hopefully we get some answers this morning," he said as he settled into the passenger seat. "I didn't sleep well last night. How about you?"

"Me? I slept like a dead dog. Harry called. I talked it over with him. Didn't get anywhere, but it was good to talk to him... This case is really bothering you, isn't it?" I commented as I pulled out onto Amnicola and headed toward downtown Chattanooga. "I can tell."

Corbin nodded. "I don't know why, but it is; it's bugging me. It's like it has invaded my mind, and I can't get it out. I do know one thing, though. I really don't like this Tony Lombardi guy."

"I get it," I said as we passed the Boat House, one of my favorite restaurants on the river. "But what gets me is the cause of death. You have to admit it's unnerving to think there's someone walking around out there flinging cyanide into people's faces."

"Yeah, and I wouldn't be surprised if it was Tony Lombardi or one of his hired hands."

We spent the rest of the ride in silence. We parked the car in the multi-story ramp and took the elevator to the ground floor in silence. We walked from the parking garage to the high-rise office building, also in silence. Maybe it was the anticipation of what was to come. *How will Lombardi handle the news we're fixing to drop?* I wondered.

"Good morning," Lucille greeted us as we stepped once again out of the elevator onto the top floor. "I take it you're here to see Tony again?" She was more pleasant this time, but I wouldn't say particularly amicable. Her upbeat attitude seemed... forced, but I took it for what it was.

"That's right," I said. "Is he in?"

She picked up the phone. "Those two detectives are here to see you, Mr. Lombardi."

She listened for maybe a couple of seconds, then hung up and said, "You can go in now." She gestured back to the dark hallway, and we made our way to the office at the end of the hall. The door was open, and I could see Tony seated at his desk, a cup of coffee in hand.

"Ah, so you're back," he said as we stepped inside. Samson again was on full alert, as he was last time. His reaction put me on edge, though I didn't show it.

"Please, take a seat," he said with a wave of his hand.

"Thank you," I said as I sat down. Samson sat on my foot again. *What is it with him?* I wondered. It was as if he was trying to protect me—*by sitting on my foot? That's going to slow me down, boy.*

"I figured you'd be back after David passed. Sarah called me with the news yesterday."

"Mrs. Mitchell?" Corbin didn't hide his surprise. "Are you two friendly?"

Tony looked hard at Corbin, his eyes narrowed to mere slits, then he let out a long, slow breath before downing the rest of his coffee and setting the cup on the desk. "I wouldn't call us *friends*. More of an... acquaintance, I think, and less than pleasant, given the circumstances."

"And why is that?" I asked, extending the offer for him to tell us, rather than me telling him.

"Oh, don't play coy," he scoffed. "I'm sure you already know that my wife engaged in an extramarital affair with Mitchell. I told you she lived and breathed work, and apparently enjoyed some extra benefits, too."

I couldn't tell if he was bothered or not by what he was saying; his voice was emotionless, his expression stony.

"So you knew about the affair?" Corbin said.

"Duh, yes! Of course, I knew about it."

"Sarah told us you all worked through it," Corbin said.

"Yes," he said as he nodded. "We did, but I won't lie and tell you it was easy. It was an extraordinarily painful process, and she refused to leave the firm, as I asked her to. I wanted to start over somewhere else, but she didn't want that. She wanted to stay here. And work with *him*."

There was no missing the resentfulness in his voice. Maybe the affair had been over, but it was obvious to me that Tony Lombardi was *not* over it at all.

"Anyway, it's water under the bridge now, isn't it?" He looked away, his eyes drifting toward one of the many windows. "Things like that happen all the time," he continued absently. "They ended it when she knew I'd found out. She wanted to stay married to me."

Corbin nodded slowly. "Because you loved each other?" he asked skeptically.

Tony's eyes narrowed again. "I don't know what you're trying to insinuate, sergeant, but *yes*, I loved my wife. She loved me, too. People make mistakes, and the affair was hers. It wasn't as if we hadn't both made mistakes. No one is without fault."

"That's an admirable way to look at it," Corbin commented. "Where were you between seven and eight yesterday morning?"

Tony's eyes narrowed even further. "Are you trying to accuse me of having something to do with either of their deaths?" he snapped.

"We're just trying to cross the names off the list," I said lightly. "We're not accusing you of anything."

But Tony's face continued to flush. "I would *never* have killed my wife, or David, for that matter. I didn't even blame him for the affair. It was Madison who initiated the affair. I read the emails. I saw her flirting and pushing herself at him. It was *her* fault. Not his."

Noted. And I had to wonder what we'd find among Mitchell's emails now that we had his laptop.

"I hated that she did it," he continued, "and I don't like to talk about it. That's the problem with affairs. They hurt like hell and they leave scars, regardless of if you move on past them. We were doing a lot better, and that's why I didn't even bother to bring it up. It was irrelevant."

"When did it end?" Corbin asked.

"More than two years ago," Tony answered, looking at me.

I nodded. That corroborated what Sarah had told us, and for that reason, I was pretty sure I believed them. Of course, there was always the chance that everyone involved was lying.

"Who else knew about the affair?" Corbin asked. "Anyone else who might have had a problem with it?"

Tony shrugged. "That whole damn office knew about it—and supported it. I'm not exactly the most well-liked fella when it comes to them. I think she must have bad-mouthed me... a lot; more than I deserved."

"What did she say about you?" I asked, trying to figure out their dynamic. I couldn't decide if Madison was the victim or Tony.

"I don't really know," he replied. "All I know is I got dirty looks and whispers when I dropped by." He stared at the empty coffee cup "Everyone seemed to think I'm a bad guy but..." He looked up at me. "Look, I may not be the greatest, but I'm not the worst either. I loved Madison. I never gave her anything other than a good life. I worked hard to provide for her while she went through law school, and since. We've been together a long time."

"And then she cheated on you," Corbin said flatly. "And that had to hurt. I could see you wanting to get even."

Tony shook his head. "It wasn't worth it. I decided that if I caught her at it again, I'd leave her. She didn't want kids anyway, and I did. I'd had her sign a prenup when we got married, but I would have looked after her financially. There was no reason to make a big scene about it."

I had to admit to myself that this guy wasn't sounding like a killer to me. "So where were you yesterday morning?"

"I had an eight o'clock meeting with a client. You can check the books and call him if you'd like. After that, I was here."

"And where exactly was that meeting?" I asked.

"Just up the road, on the Northshore," he replied. "At Michael Prince's law offices on Frazier. I can give you the number if you like."

I nodded, and he did.

Inwardly, I shook my head as I tried to work the times out in my head. Did he have time to pass by the law offices before work? It just took a simple toss to bring David Mitchell down. In the end, though, I figured it might be doable, but barely. But that didn't mean that he couldn't have hired someone to do it for him.

"I don't know what you want from me, but whatever it is, let me know and I'll do my best to comply. I'm not calling a lawyer. I don't need one. I'm an open book." Tony put his hands up in a low surrender position.

"We appreciate your cooperation," Corbin said. "I think you already have our card, but if you think of anything, let us know."

"You should know…" Tony paused and looked again at his empty coffee cup. "You should know I roughed him up; Mitchell," Tony said as we stood up. "I mean. When I found out, I was so pissed off, I went to the office. I made a big scene. The people down there saw it. There were a couple other lawyers there— Colton Rhodes and Paul Gerrick. Madison was close to them as well, though not in the same way. And there were the interns…" He trailed off, frowning. Also," he continued to ramble, "Judy, the secretary. She's full of the latest gossip. You might want to chat with her."

I raised my brow at the unexpected information. "Okay, thank you."

"Just figure out who did it."

"We'll do our best," Corbin said as he turned toward the door.

"Just one more thing, Mr. Lombardi," I said. "Do you have Madison's laptop? If so, I'd like to borrow it. It could be helpful."

"It's at home," he replied. "I'll have it sent to you."

I thanked him and walked to the door, but then a thought struck me: we hadn't told him his wife had been murdered, or the cause of death. But, on thinking about it, I had the impression he already knew. Could he have guessed, based on our reappearance? Or did he *already* know?

I half-turned to ask him, but he was on the phone, his back to us.

Hmm. I guess I'll just have to keep that one in mind.

15

Wednesday, June 29, 11:05 a.m.

IT WAS JUST AFTER ELEVEN THAT WEDNESDAY MORNING WHEN WE made it back to the PD. Corbin went around the incident room, telling everyone to gather in my office.

I brewed a fresh pot of coffee, still working through the details in my mind. Tony Lombardi and Sarah Mitchell both stood out, though they did have alibis. However, while Sarah's was concrete, Tony's was... well... not quite.

"What do you think?" I asked Samson as he curled up on his bed under the window. The skies were growing overcast, and I chided myself for not watching the weather. I probably should've. But then again, what would have changed?

"I think it's going to rain again, Sammy," I said, more to myself than to him, but he perked his ears at me anyway. I grinned at him and took a seat behind my desk, hoping for a few minutes of silence while I enjoyed my coffee.

I stared at Samson. He hadn't liked Tony. I could tell, but it was kind of a passive, wary thing, and it wasn't evidence of Tony's guilt... nor even an indicator.

"Something's wrong, though," I muttered, shaking my head. I was stating the obvious, but it felt like it was a mystery. Had Shelly mentioned the height and build of the person in the trench coat? Would she remember now if I asked her? I wasn't sure, but I scribbled it down on a notepad to have someone reinterview her.

"Captain," Hawk greeted me with a nod, grabbing my attention. He was the first to step into the room, followed closely by the rest of the team. I saw Jack was carrying David Mitchell's computer and my immediate thought was that we might be about to get some answers.

They were quiet as they took a seat at the table. Me? I stood up, stepped around my desk, parked myself on the front edge of it and sat with hands gripping the edge. I was already beginning to feel a little antsy; about what, I didn't know.

"All right," I said. "Who wants to go first?" I folded my arms.

"Me, I guess," Ramirez said. "I wish we had more than we do. I feel like we're just going round and round with those people at the law office. None of them were forthcoming."

"They're lawyers." Hawk snorted. "What else do you expect?"

"You have a point," Anne agreed. "Though I did get to speak with Colton Rhodes. He seemed visibly shaken over the deaths. David and Madison were his friends."

"Did he mention anything about the affair?" Corbin asked.

"No. Not at all," Anne said. "I asked him about that, but all he said was that what they did in their personal life was their own business. No one wanted to talk about it."

"Except Judy Constance," Cooper perked up. "She talked about it. In fact, it seemed like it was all she wanted to talk about. You'd have thought it was still going on from how she went on and on about it."

"You think maybe she was just gossiping, or d'you think they were still seeing each other?" I asked.

"I tried to get her to be specific," Cooper replied, "but she just rambled on. She mentioned late nights and the, uh, *longing looks*, as she put it."

I made a face and said, "Well... all right then. Maybe we should bring her in for a formal chat. If the affair was still going on, it opens up a whole new line of investigation."

Everyone seemed to agree with that, and from what they said, it appeared Ramirez was right. There was little to be learned from the lawyers. They were intent on protecting their own.

I turned to Corbin and said, "Why don't you brief them on what we learned from Doc Sheddon?" I went back around my desk, sat down, picked up my rapidly cooling coffee and listened as Corbin thoroughly explained Doc's cyanide theory. As usual, he went on a little too long, but I didn't interrupt him. I was gathering my own thoughts.

"That's some off-the-wall stuff, right there," Hawk said skeptically. "Don't you think this is enough to get a search warrant for the Lombardi residence?"

I hesitated. "I don't think so. We don't yet have the results, so no confirmation. If Doc says it's cyanide poisoning, that's good enough for me, but not for a judge."

"Not even your buddy, Henry Strange?" Jack quipped.

"Not even him," I said.

"But Corbin said Tony roughed David up?" Anne said. "Wouldn't that be enough probable cause? Maybe?" She seemed to be second-guessing, which was unlike her, and again, I thought I might need to have a quiet word with her.

"I think it's worth looking into Lombardi a little more," Corbin agreed. "After all, Samson didn't seem to like him..." He trailed off and looked at me. I shook my head.

Samson sat up at the sound of his name and cocked his head to one side.

"That, in and of itself, is a reason for a search warrant," Ramirez said.

"We have no good reason to search his place," I said. "He was cooperative, and I was inclined to believe him. The fact that Sammy was wary of him... Well, I can't go to a judge with that. I'd get laughed out of the building."

"But you have the incident with David," Ramirez argued. "You also have the affair and the fact that neither of his alibis are exactly airtight."

I shook my head. It was minimal at best.

At that point, Jack jumped in. "You also have a plethora of emails," he said. "Mitchell sent multiple emails to Madison telling her he thought Tony might kill him for sleeping with her."

That got my attention. "He did? Why didn't you say something earlier, Jack?"

"I was waiting for an opportunity," he replied dryly as he opened the laptop. "They're all old, more than two years old, and I had to dig into the hard drive to find them, but they are there."

"Let's hear it," Corbin said, leaning forward and resting his hands on the table.

"Just give me a minute, will you, sarge?" He tapped the keyboard... and we waited until, finally, "So, this is the first one. It's dated March twelfth of twenty-twenty. 'You need to get your husband under control before he hurts someone. He showed up here again yesterday while you were at your doctor's appointment. I'm tired of him constantly berating me for something that's already over.'"

"Okay, so he was pissed off about his wife sleeping with a coworker." Hawk shrugged. "So what? I would be, too."

"It gets worse," Jack answered. "March twenty-third, same year. 'Maddie, please. You have to convince Tony that it's over. He showed up at my house last night and threatened to break down the door if I didn't come out and talk to him.'"

"Geez," I said. "That's a revelation. He really was upset, wasn't he? But again, that was more than two years ago. I'm not so sure it has anything to do with the here and now."

"Maybe they'd started up the affair again," Anne said. "If so, it could have been enough to make Lombardi lose it entirely."

I nodded, then shook my head, pursed my lips, and blinked several times as I thought it over, then said, "I think those emails might be enough to get a warrant to search the Lombardi house. It might not be such a bad idea—but it needs to be done *quietly.* The last thing we need is a big stink in the media over this. He's already raising Cain over the fact that we haven't yet done anything about Madison's murder. Now if we're investigating him for it, he's really going to be angry. And it sounds like he doesn't do well with anger management."

"I agree," Corbin said. "And we need to be prepared to take some flack over it. The captain's right. Lombardi's not going to take this very well. In fact, I'll bet he'll quit cooperating the moment we turn up with the warrant."

"Well... it's nothing personal," I said reluctantly and glanced at Samson, wishing I could ask him what it was about Lombardi that bothered him.

I thought for a minute, then nodded my head and said, "Okay, let's do it."

"I'll run it by Chief Johnston, then," Corbin said, pushing back from the table. "It might be better coming from him, right?"

I nodded and then drummed my fingers on the top of the table. "I'm still not convinced that these deaths have anything to do with him."

"Maybe not, but we have nowhere else to go," Cooper said. His words hung heavy on my shoulders. He was right; we didn't have anything else, but that in and of itself wasn't a good reason to invade the man's life and property, and I knew the moment we made the move, Tony Lombardi would see us as the enemy.

And that would not be good.

16

Wednesday, June 29, 4:45 p.m.

SAMSON AND I SPENT THE REST OF THE AFTERNOON MOSTLY AT peace, picking through the files and sorting through the paperwork. I grabbed a turkey, Swiss, tomato and lettuce foot-long from Subway for lunch and fed half of it to him, telling myself the veggies would be good for him, but knowing I was going to have to do better.

Chief Johnston had approved the request for a search warrant, albeit reluctantly. We were still waiting to hear from the judge—not Henry Strange—and I knew it could take several days. And by three that afternoon, I convinced myself that the emails wouldn't be enough.

But, as it turned out, they were. At fifteen minutes to five, Corbin rapped on my door, opened it, stuck his head inside and said, "It's go-time, Kate. We got a warrant for the residence and his office."

Oh boy, Tony is going to be livid, I thought, then took a deep breath and nodded. Samson and I would have to have a late dinner. "Give me a minute, Corbin. We'll split up. You take the lead. I want half the team to go to the residence and half to the office."

"Where do you want to go?" Corbin asked.

"The residence. I've been to the office enough for one day. We'll let fresh eyes see it." I rose to my feet, tisking at Samson to get up.

I stood for a moment and looked out the window. The weather was turning ugly again; another summer storm was on the way. But that wasn't what was bothering me. It was the storm we were going to raise when we arrived at Tony Lombardi's home.

"Let's go," Corbin urged as I shrugged into my jacket, wishing I had an umbrella in the car.

Samson and I followed Corbin out and to the parking lot. "I'll follow you there," I said, not feeling like chitchatting. I wasn't happy about what we were doing. My gut feeling was that we were on a loser to nothing.

"I think we're making a mistake setting our sights on Tony," I said to Samson as I followed Corbin out of the lot onto Amnicola.

Samson gave my arm a nudge with his nose, as if he were trying to reassure me. I smiled at him, but I didn't feel reassured; not one bit. And I'd already made up my mind I was going to let Corbin take the lead on this one. However, by the time we parked in Tony's driveway, I could already see the problem... Tony Lombardi was standing out front in the yard, seemingly facing down Corbin.

"What the hell d'you think you're doing?" he erupted as Samson and I stepped out of the car to join Corbin.

"We have a warrant to search your home and your office," Corbin said, his voice calm.

It was then that Ramirez and Cooper arrived with a half dozen uniformed officers, including Officer Barron.

"I don't know why you're doing this," he snapped, "but you're making one hell of a big mistake. You're trying to point the finger at me, but you seem to forget that it was me who instigated this investigation. I'll have your job for this, *Captain!*"

"It's nothing personal, Mr. Lombardi," I said. "You know the protocol. Thirty-four percent of the murders in this country are committed by an intimate partner. We're just covering all the bases, which is what you, as the intimate partner, would expect us to do. Isn't that correct, Mr. Lombardi?"

He stared at me but didn't answer, so I continued, "We found evidence that you had a real beef with David Mitchell. You were showing up at his place of work and his home."

I glanced at Corbin. He nodded toward the house.

"Why don't you go ahead and oversee the search," I said. "I'll stay out here with Mr. Lombardi."

Corbin nodded, then turned and walked away toward the house, taking the rest of the team with him.

I looked down at Samson, who was seated beside me. He seemed to be relaxed, which seemed a little strange, considering that he hadn't been a fan of Tony the two previous times we'd met with him. I reached down and patted his head, looking up at Lombardi as I did so.

"I thought we were on the same team, Captain," he said, exasperated, his guard dropping suddenly. "Look, I admit I overreacted when I found out about the affair, but that was *years* ago. I don't care about it anymore. I got over it. Like I said, I'd already made up my mind that if it happened again, I was going to leave her. I told you that!"

"I know," I said quietly. "And if that's the truth, then this search won't turn up anything that you need to be concerned about."

"I need to call my lawyer," he said, looking around. "I can't believe this is happening. As if I'm not going through enough pain and suffering already."

He shook his head, then turned and walked quickly away,

taking his phone from his pocket as he went. And inwardly, I groaned, because I knew that whoever would be representing him would be the best of the best. It would be one hell of a problem to interview him from here on out.

"You look stressed," Officer Brenham, an older uniformed officer said to me. "I wouldn't worry about the guy. We'll keep him under control if you wanna take a peek inside."

I nodded, tugging on Samson's leash. "Yeah, I think I'll see what's going on in there." I took a pair of latex gloves from my pocket and snapped them on and, together, we entered the house, knowing that if Tony was hiding anything, we'd find it.

I walked across the foyer of the seven-thousand-square-foot house, eyeing the furnishings and décor. It was different than the Mitchells' house. This one appeared more lived in. The art and décor were more... *simple.*

"Interesting," I muttered to myself as I stepped into what I assumed was Tony's study. Officers were riffling through the desk drawers and sifting through papers. I walked on, my lips pursed.

I'd made it as far as the kitchen when Corbin came rushing in.

"They found something," he said, obviously excited.

Me? I was skeptical. "What did they find?"

"In the utility room, Barron found a package of a white substance. It's consistent with cyanide."

"How d'you know that? I hope he didn't taste it. If he did, he's a dead man."

"Nope... at least, I don't think so," Corbin said, his forehead furrowed.

"If he did and he's not dead, it's not cyanide," I said. "Show me." I followed him through the kitchen and into a mudroom where a couple of officers were sealing a Ziplock bag containing what looked like a small amount of white powder into an evidence bag.

I stood back. Barron held it up. I looked at it. It could've been anything. But it did give me pause to think: maybe we were barking up the right tree.

"Be careful with that," Corbin said to Barron. "We don't know what it is."

Officer Barron nodded. "Looks just like the stuff that was under the victim's nose."

"Or something Mitchell might have put *up* his nose," I said. "It could also be rat poison, or even powdered sugar. We won't know until it's been tested."

I gave Barron a half-smile and then turned back to the kitchen. If this was as simple as it looked, we'd have the case buttoned up and ready for the prosecutor in a couple of days.

But I didn't think so; it didn't feel right to me.

"I think we ought to take him down to the station right now," Corbin said. "See what we can get out of him. There's a chance if he knows we found something, he'll start talking."

"Corbin," I said, more than a little exasperated. "He called his lawyer. He's not going to talk, and a bag of unknown white crap isn't justification to haul him downtown, and you know that. You don't like him. I get it. If we're lucky, they might agree to an interview with his attorney present, but…"

"You don't think we're going to be that lucky."

I shook my head. "We've poked the bear, that's for sure. If he's guilty, we did the right thing, but if he's not, we may have just made him an enemy."

"We've had plenty of them in the past," Corbin said. "He'd just be one more." Corbin chuckled at that. "You're right, Kate. I don't like him. He's sleazy, and sleazy usually means bad guy. *You* know that… I wonder if they've found anything over at the office."

"I don't know," I said, running a latex-covered finger across the counter in the kitchen. *Dust.* "I don't think he's here all that often."

"Or maybe he just doesn't clean," Corbin pointed out. "Plenty of people don't keep up with regular cleaning, especially when they're living alone."

I shook my head, staring down at the grayish dust on my fingertip. "My best guess is that he spends most of his time at the office, or maybe he just doesn't use his kitchen."

"What're you thinking, Kate?" Corbin said, giving me a funny look. "You have that perplexed expression on your face again, and that's never good."

I pressed my lips together. I didn't really know what I was thinking, other than this was not where I'd expected this case to go.

It was then that we heard shouting coming from the front yard. We rushed out of the house into the front yard where I saw two uniformed officers holding Lombardi back.

"You can't take my work computer!" he shouted. "I need that. You take that and I'm going to lose business!" The officers took no heed and continued loading his things into the two SUVs.

"Let's take him to the station," Corbin said.

I nodded. People—neighbors—were gathering on their front lawns. "All right," I said, unhappy with the way things were developing. I'd wanted the search to go quietly, but Tony was making it difficult. And I had a feeling he would continue to do so.

And boy, was I ever right.

Wednesday, June 29, 8 p.m.

ON THE WAY BACK TO THE STATION, SAMSON AND I HIT McDonald's for the second time that day, and I swore to myself that I wouldn't do it again.

I handed a junior burger to Samson and took a bite of my own, thinking how I needed to start watching what I ate. I ran often enough, but I couldn't help feeling guilty that I was living mostly on fast food. I needed to do better.

By the time we arrived back at the police department, Tony Lombardi was already in the interview room, sitting next to a slender redheaded, middle-aged woman. I recognized her and cringed. Allison Weaver. She was indeed the best of the best.

I took a deep breath, looked down at Samson and said, "I think you're going to have to sit this one out, boy." I patted his head, took him back to my office, gave him some fresh water and made sure he was comfortable.

I hadn't been there but a minute when Corbin poked his head in and said, "Ready?"

"Ready as I'll ever be for a face-off with her," I muttered. And we made our way back to the interview room.

"You want to go in together?" Corbin asked, staring at the pair through the observation room window.

"Might as well," I replied. "She's not going to let him say much, but it's worth a try, I guess."

I reached for the handle, opened the door and let Corbin enter first. Corbin took a seat opposite Tony and Allison. Me? I decided to stand, so I went to the back of the room, facing them, leaned against the wall and folded my arms.

"You're wasting your time," Tony said. "You're going after me because I'm the easy choice. Well, it won't work."

Allison cleared her throat, silencing Tony. "You have no reason to detain my client."

"We're not detaining him," Corbin said coolly. "We'd just like to ask him a couple of questions about the item we found in his home."

His eyes narrowed and he frowned. *Was that a flash of concern?* I wondered.

"What could you have possibly found?" he asked.

"We found a baggy of a white substance in your utility room, Tony. You want to talk about that?"

I was watching him closely. He looked confused. "I have no idea what you're talking about."

"You don't keep any dangerous substances in your home?" Corbin tapped his fingers on the table. I continued to watch in silence, noting the discomfort in both Tony and Allison. Did they know what we were talking about?

"Listen, a *white substance* can be anything," Tony snorted. "How about washing machine powder, or detergent? Madison used to make her own. You're a damn fool, sergeant." He looked at me, then continued. "And you... you should know better."

If that's what it was... It was really going to make us look stupid.

I bit down on the inside of my cheek. No, I didn't like how

this was feeling right now; not at all. In fact, I wished I could slip out of the room, grab my dog and go home. I knew the search warrant wasn't a good idea. I should have nipped it in the bud before it got started. Then again, I reminded myself, that even if this turns out to be fruitless, we have to cross Tony off the list. And that would leave us... what, nowhere?

I didn't like that answer. Not one bit.

"Look," Tony said, a little more reasonably. "I get it. It looks bad for me. I told you guys this morning that I overreacted to the news of the affair, but it was *years* ago. My wife and I were fine. I'm grieving her loss. I *miss* her."

"I think we're done here," Allison said. "You're causing my client undue stress. He's been more than compliant. Either charge him with something or we're out of here."

Oh, shove it. I thought. "We're trying to do everything we can to get to the bottom of these murders, Ms. Weaver. All we're trying to do here is eliminate Mr. Lombardi as a suspect."

"My home is being ransacked," Tony mumbled. "You've taken my computer. I can't work without it. What am I supposed to do?" He paused, seemingly lost in thought, then continued, "And quite frankly, it hasn't felt like home since I lost Madison. I'm selling the place—"

"Tony," Allison said, sharply, cutting him off. "That's none of their business."

He took a deep breath and then looked me straight in the eye and said, "You have to believe me. I didn't hurt my wife. I didn't do anything to her. I don't even know how she died. I have *no* idea *what* happened to her!" He slammed his fist down on the table and Allison jumped beside him. Tony Lombardi had a temper, but again, that didn't exactly line up with him being a poisoner.

Poisoning took patience. It took thought. Tony was the type of guy who struck me as a fist or knife fighter. Geez, I was really torn about this.

"What's the white substance we found in your house, Tony?" Corbin repeated himself as the interview door swung open.

Chief Johnston stuck his head in. "Captain Gazzara, a word, if you please."

Uh-oh. I nodded and walked quickly out of the room, into the hallway.

"What is it, Chief?" It was after nine, and he should've been at home, and the fact he was still meandering around the building made me feel uneasy.

"Forensics did a simple test on the substance you found, one that could easily have been done in the field. It tested positive for cocaine."

"Cocaine?" I closed my eyes. *Son of a bitch! I should have known.*

"Yes, cocaine, and they just wrapped up the search. They found nothing else. They still have to process the computer, of course, but that will take time."

I nodded. "So he's got drugs."

"Less than a gram. Enough for personal use, I'd say." His expression was difficult to read, and I couldn't tell if he was happy with the search or angry. But then again, I never could tell.

I shook my head. *So it's a bust. And it's my damn fault.*

He continued, "Other than a misdemeanor drug charge, that's all you've got. I think you'd better charge him and then let him go; don't you?"

Johnston thought for a minute then said, "Or maybe we let it hang over his head and wait for him to slip up. Worst case scenario, we're wasting our time, and that's exactly what I think we're doing, Gazzara."

I bobbed my head slowly. I wasn't going to admit that I was thinking the same. "Chief, for all we know, that cocaine could've been Madison's." I hated moments like this.

"Wrap it up," he said. "I don't want a lawsuit from that malicious lawyer you've got cornered."

"Got it," I said and turned away.

I closed the interview room door behind me, went back and took my place against the wall, looking Tony in the eye. "Looks like all we found at your home was your stash of cocaine."

"What?" Tony shook his head and laughed. "I don't have any drugs in my house. I don't do drugs."

"Testing shows otherwise," I said curtly, folding my arms. "It's cocaine, and it was found in your utility room. Maybe your wife wasn't making laundry detergent after all."

He swallowed hard, his face a mess of barely controlled emotions. He looked down at his hands. "Did I even know her?" he mumbled, his voice trembling.

Corbin turned and looked at me, and I shrugged. There wasn't much we could do for the guy. If this wasn't a cover-up for his own use, then it probably was a slap in the face for him. It must have been a shock to find out your already cheating wife was also using drugs.

"So, you'll be charging my client with possession, then?" Allison said, her face flushed with anger.

"Not today," I replied.

"Good," she snapped. "Then I think it's about time we left. Surely, you can see that he's not in the best state of mind. He's a grieving husband, and now… he's facing drug charges?"

Corbin and I watched as they rose to their feet. I was watching Tony. He really did look downtrodden, though I wasn't convinced if it was because we'd found the drugs or if it was because he truly thought they belonged to his wife. There was also the question that he *still* hadn't asked us how his wife had died.

"Tony," I said, catching them before they left. "Don't you want to know what happened to your wife?"

He frowned at me, his eyes narrowed. "She was murdered. What more is there to know? I don't need to know the details."

"You're not curious?" I asked as I watched his face harden.

"Captain Gazzara, you know about my relations in New York

City. That was where I was raised. I saw a lot of death during my formative years, including my mother, who suffered a heart attack and died... alone. On the sidewalk. I don't want to know *what* did that to my wife. I just want to know *who* did it. Now, if you don't mind, I want to go home, so I can spend my evening *alone* and try to pick up the few pieces you've left me with. And I can promise you this, you'll be hearing from Ms. Weaver, and soon."

I didn't answer him. I merely stared at him for a moment before I nodded to Corbin.

Two minutes later, they were gone, leaving me certain of only one thing.

We'd made an enemy of Tony Lombardi.

18

Thursday, June 30, 7:15 a.m.

SLEEP DIDN'T COME EASY THAT NIGHT. THE SEARCHES OF TONY Lombardi's home and offices had turned up nothing but a small amount of cocaine. It's true we could have charged him with possession, but Chief Johnston wasn't keen on that idea. And really, I didn't blame him. The charge probably wouldn't have made it past the DA, not with Tony's prominent position in the local community, his squeaky-clean record and powerful attorney.

Not worth the effort, I thought as I flipped on the coffee maker and peered out into the early morning mist. *Raining... Again. Geez!* I shook my head. Rain is almost always a good thing here in the South, but it didn't feel that way that morning. I heard a whine and turned toward the kitchen door to see Samson, looking at me with sleepy eyes.

"Need to go out?" I asked him, nodding toward the back door.

He turned and headed for the door. I smiled and let him out into the backyard. He wasn't out there for more than a minute or two, seemingly as unhappy with the rain as I was. And who could blame him? I let him in. He shook himself violently, his feet skittering on the tiled floor.

I wasn't sure what the day would hold, given that I knew we were going to have to come at the Lombardi and Mitchell case from a completely different angle—and, at that point, I had no idea what that angle might be. After a little thought over a cup of coffee and a couple of slices of toast, I decided to get the team together and do some brainstorming, though my brain felt as if it was filled with concrete.

"I think we messed up going after Tony Lombardi the way we did," I said to Samson as I pulled my hair back into a ponytail. "He could've been an ally, but now... I have a feeling he's going to go after me."

Samson was seated in the open bathroom doorway, his head tilted to one side. But he didn't seem to agree, because he lowered his head, turned and walked away into the bedroom, his tail swishing from side to side.

"Well okay," I said. "Be that way. I just think it *feels* like we made a mistake."

But feelings don't matter when it comes to solving crimes. I sighed as I smoothed out my cream-colored blouse and slipped my belt through the loops of my black jeans. I stood for a moment, staring at myself in the mirror, trying to get inside my own head but, in the end, I simply shook my head, went to the closet, took out a tan leather jacket, went downstairs, slipped on my shoulder holster and then the jacket.

"Well, Sammyo, let's go see what the day holds for us. It's a little early, but what the hell? Maybe we can go for a run this evening."

He seemed good with the plan, and we headed to the garage. I buckled him in, climbed in and then sat for a moment, checking my phone—something I should have done earlier. *Damn it, why can't you leave me alone?* I thought when I saw *another* missed call from Thomas Drews.

"And, I forgot my damn coffee," I muttered as I backed out of the driveway. I hit the brakes and considered going back. But, instead, I watched the garage door close and resigned myself to a trip through the McDonald's drive-through, where I ordered a large black coffee for me and a sausage biscuit for Samson. The thought of breakfast made my stomach turn.

Even with the extra stop, we made it to the police department a good fifteen minutes early.

I flipped on the lights, glanced at the two whiteboards, and sighed. Samson settled in his bed under the window and the rain continued to fall. It was a gray, gray day and, the rain aside, I had a sinking feeling it wasn't going to get any better.

I went to my desk, sat down and texted everyone, letting them know to convene in my office as soon as they made it. In the meantime, I flipped through the reports from the day before, seeing a note from Hawk that the cameras, yet again, weren't working on Cherry Street. *Great.* I shook my head and refreshed my memory, hoping *something* would jump out and grab me. It didn't.

"Good morning, Cap," Corbin said as he walked in, coffee in hand.

"Hey," I said. "Good morning. You have a good night?"

"Not bad," he replied. "Yesterday was a mess, wasn't it?" I looked up at him. He had a smile on his face, but it looked... forced.

"You could say that," I replied. "I don't think Mr. Lombardi is going to be much help."

Corbin pulled out a chair and sat down, and I joined him at the table. "Was he ever that much help, anyway? I don't know that losing his cooperation is that much of a loss, Kate. You're beating yourself up for nothing."

I hope so, I thought, but I just shook my head and waited as the rest of the team filed in, one by one. All of them looked somber, except for Jack, of course. Nothing ever seemed to bother him.

"Where do we go from here?" Corbin asked.

"Are they going to charge Lombardi with possession?" Hawk asked, leaning back in his chair and folding his arms. "I think they should."

"I don't," Corbin replied. "It wouldn't do anything but make him even more hostile than he already is."

Hawk muttered something I couldn't understand, but I let it go. Corbin was right.

I looked at Jack and said, "You find anything on Tony's computers?"

Jack shook his head. "No. At least not as far as his business goes. If he's up to anything shady, he knows how to cover his tracks. As far as his personal life? Well, I found a few old emails complaining about his wife's affair, but they were nothing like what we saw in Mitchell's email."

"Why am I not surprised?" I said. I set my cup of coffee down on the table and looked around at everyone. "I think we should dig a little deeper into Sarah Mitchell, for starters."

"I can take on that," Anne Robar spoke up. "Cooper and I can focus on following that lead."

I nodded. "I think we should also consider the fact that the affair between David and Madison ended years ago and so has nothing to do with their deaths."

"I agree," Tracy said, nodding. "But there has to be a connection. Something they did, or didn't do, made them targets. I mean, they were both defense attorneys, so it's not a stretch to assume they screwed up somewhere along the line and there's a disgruntled client out there somewhere bent on revenge. The affair is just evidence of their character."

"I'd like to visit with Judy Constance again," Hawk said. "She had plenty to say about the affair, but she might know if something else was going on there."

"Good idea," I said. "Why don't you invite her to come in here for a chat?" I suggested.

"Speaking of which," I continued, "I'd like to get anyone who might have information interviewed away from their comfort zone. A good shake-up might get them talking."

"I can work on arranging that," Ramirez said.

"Good," I said, nodding. "Now let's talk about the cyanide and how one might get ahold of it. See if anyone at the law firm has purchased any."

"I'll work on that today," Corbin said.

"I'll keep working on Lombardi's computers," Jack said, "and I'll look into their past cases. There might be something there."

I nodded. "Good, and Hawk, you and Tracy work together. See if you can get Judy in here and talk to as many of the rest of the staff as you can. It might take a couple of days to see them all but that's okay."

I looked around the table and said, "Okay. I think we all know what to do, so let's get to it. If any of you need anything, come find me."

"I think we can pretty much assume these were not random events," Corbin said. "What are the chances of two random attacks on two lawyers who work together and have been fooling around? It would be a reach. Don't you think?"

"Agreed," I said. "So, let's see what the day brings and hope that something breaks."

They all nodded and pushed back from the table. I watched them go, but I didn't get up; not until they were all gone and the door was closed. Only then did I rise to my feet, stretching my arms over my head. Corbin was right. It was one hell of a reach, and I was wondering if we'd need to bring in some help to get it wrapped up.

I frowned, rounded my desk and sat down. I couldn't shake the feeling that the affair had to have something to do with their deaths. But then again, most of the time, murder comes within months of the spouse finding out, when the emotions are still running high. To kill them years later, after the marriage had been repaired? It didn't make a lot of sense.

But if it's not that, then what is it? I wondered as I looked over at Samson. He was out cold, snoring gently. I watched him for a long moment, the seconds ticking away as my mind meandered this way and that, trying to analyze what little we had, and failing miserably.

I shook the meandering thoughts from my head and looked out the window. The rain had lightened up some. I stood up, grabbed my umbrella and said, "Come on, Sammy. Let's go take another look at Cherry Street and Eighth. Maybe a fresh look at the crime scene will jerk something loose."

Samson yawned and rose to his feet. He stuck his behind in the air and stretched his front legs, then walked over and nuzzled my hand. I smiled down at him and hooked his leash to his harness, and we headed out the door toward what I was already sure would be a waste of time.

19

Thursday, June 30, 10:30 a.m.

THE TRAFFIC THAT MORNING WAS FAIRLY LIGHT, SO THE DRIVE OVER to the law court area of Chattanooga didn't take long. I parallel parked at one of the metered spaces on Cherry Street, noting the emptiness of the area. There were plenty of cars around, but not many people on the sidewalks.

I got out of the car and went to the rear door, feeling just a tiny bit antsy. I put it down to the fact that someone had walked these streets and, with just a flick of the wrist, had killed two people.

I fed the meter and said, "Let's go take a walk, Sammy."

We strolled past the Chattanooga Billiard Club, a place I'd never been to, and continued slowly onward to the law office taking in the sights along the way until I spotted an alleyway I hadn't noticed before.

I tugged Samson's leash and we crossed at the intersection, backtracking down the other side of the street. I stopped at the opening of the alleyway. *Hmm... someone could easily slip down there and out of sight. It looks like it leads around to the back of the law offices... and other buildings.*

Why not? I thought and led Samson down the alleyway. It was just big enough for a car to drive down. When I reached the back of the buildings, I could see that there were indeed a number of vehicles parked back there.

"Hey," someone shouted from behind me.

I stopped, slipped my hand under my jacket, and turned slowly around to see a man standing about ten feet from me. He was tall, even taller than me in my three-inch heels. He had to have been at least six-feet-four. He was strikingly handsome... and that's saying something, considering I rarely noticed such things. I figured him to be in his late forties, his dark hair peppered with gray.

"Can I help you?" I asked, taking in his casual appearance: he was wearing jeans, a black T-shirt and a rather ratty-looking blue suit jacket. He didn't look like a lawyer. *Maybe he works at the billiard club*, I thought.

He looked at Samson, then at me and said, "Are you by any chance Captain Gazzara?"

I narrowed my eyes, my hand on the grip of my Glock.

He took two steps closer.

I checked Samson's demeanor, but he didn't seem bothered by the man. In fact, his tail was wagging. I shortened his leash.

"What can I do for you?" I asked.

"I've just come from Lewis, Scone and Petty," he said and gestured back behind him. "I saw you and your dog take off down the alleyway, and I thought it might be you."

My eyes narrowed. "You've been looking for me? If so, you can call the police department."

"Well, I've been trying your cell," he said and laughed, his voice deep, his tone light and easy. I wasn't sure if it was unnerving or intriguing.

"I'm Thomas Drews," he said.

Of course, you are. I shook my head and took in a deep breath. "With all due respect, Mr. Drews, I'm not at liberty to discuss this or any other case with you. You need to find someone else to talk to." And I turned and walked quickly away back down the alley. I had no desire or authority to entertain a reporter, nor did I want to spend another moment giving him the idea that I might.

"Look, if you could just spare a few minutes." Drews charged after me. Samson stopped, almost causing me to trip.

"Samson," I scolded him. *"Come on."*

But he didn't budge. My jaw tightened with frustration as I eyed my car, which was a hundred or so feet away.

"Captain, I promise I'm not going to waste your time," he said in a breathy tone as he stepped into my ten-foot bubble.

"I cannot discuss the case," I snapped, finally budging Samson from where his paws seemed to be glued. I must have looked stupid as I damn near dragged him out of the alleyway onto the sidewalk.

"I might be able to help," he called after me as I darted out across the street. I wasn't in the mood to entertain him for another minute. There were way too many people who wanted to play detective, and I wasn't in the mood to listen to some off-the-wall conspiracy theory he'd put together using Reddit and Web Sleuth.

"Get in," I snapped at Samson as I opened the door.

I glanced back at Drews, who was standing on the other side of the street shaking his head. His shoulders slouched. The man looked defeated, and that didn't bother me one bit. Maybe now he'd finally get the message and leave me alone. People have taken out restraining orders for less.

That thought made me chuckle to myself as I pulled out onto the street. It was nearly lunchtime, and I had a hankering for a good burger. *I wonder what Harry is up to? Maybe I could pick his brain again.* I picked up my phone and hit the button beside his name. He picked up on the third ring.

"Ah, Kate," he said lightly. "Are you finally going to ask me to help solve your case?" he joked.

"No, but I wouldn't mind discussing it if you're up for lunch. I'll buy." And inwardly I chuckled as Thomas Drews dwindled in my rearview mirror.

"Uh-oh." He laughed. "It's not often a case gets Kate Gazzara's head in a twist. When do you want to meet up? I have about an hour."

"Fifteen minutes?" I suggested, eyeing the clock on the dash.

"Sounds great."

We decided on Burger Republic and met up about fifteen minutes later as planned. I had to backtrack to get there, but I avoided the area where I'd left Drews, not really sure why, but I did.

Fifteen minutes later, Samson and I stepped out of the car at the same time Harry came walking over to join us, looking as dapper and as young as ever, *and he's two years older than me*, I thought snarkily.

"You look like you didn't get much sleep last night." Harry chuckled, and I shot him a warning look.

He held up his hands in surrender, though he didn't stop laughing. "You know me. I just call it like I see it, Kate."

"I'm aware," I muttered, guiding Samson toward the entrance. We were ahead of the lunch rush, though it was still pretty crowded.

"You know this place was ranked one of the best burgers in Tennessee?" Harry threw out the random fact like I really cared.

"Good for them," I said as we entered and took a seat. I slid into the chair as Samson sat down beside me.

"You ever heard of Thomas Drews?" I asked.

"Who?" His brow creased.

"Never mind," I said, shaking my head. I really wasn't in the best of moods.

He looked at me with concern as the waiter filled our water

glasses. We both ordered a simple cheeseburger and fries. I wasn't feeling all that adventurous, but I was hungry and needed something I was sure to enjoy.

"Okay, so what's got you all bent out of shape?" Harry said and took a sip of his water. "I have to admit that your case is a bit of a head-scratcher, even from the outside."

I sighed. "We searched Tony Lombardi's home and offices last night and came up empty, except for a small amount of cocaine—not enough to even tempt the DA to charge the man with possession."

"Okay..." His tone suggested that I keep going.

"When we mentioned the cocaine, the guy actually looked... wounded. I don't even think it was his."

"You think it was Madison Lombardi's?"

I shrugged. "Possibly? I feel like we've hit a dead end, Harry. The team is digging their heels in and searching for connections, but I don't have high hopes."

"Ah, Kate Gazzara is on a downer," he said. "Have you looked into Mitchell's wife? I wouldn't write off the affair, though I do have to admit that I think it might just be a thing of the past. You might do some digging into the cases they've worked on together. Maybe someone is out to get even."

I nodded. "We're working on that, and we're about to start picking that law firm apart. You know how those people are. They go through interns like they go through plastic sacks at Walmart, and maybe there could be some bad blood among the rest of the staff, too."

"Right, could be," he said, leaning back in his chair and folding his arms. "So why did you want to meet with me? You seem to have things well in hand. I don't think you need me at all, Captain."

I blew air out through my lips and shook my head. "I think I'm just frazzled with it, Harry. I just needed somebody to talk to, I guess."

He raised his eyebrows. "Maybe it's about time you took some vacation time? You'd be surprised. It can do wonders for you."

"Says the man who rarely takes a day off."

"I have to run my own business," Harry pointed out. "And I *have* taken some time. Amanda and Jade are quite happy enough with me. We spend a lot of family time together."

Something tugged at my insides, but I ignored it. "Samson might enjoy a vacation," I said, feeling a little stupid.

Harry nodded slowly. "He might, at that... So, you mentioned a Thomas Drews? Is this a new... dating interest?"

I laughed. "More like a thorn in my side. He's an investigative journalist who's trying to pin me on the Lombardi case. He's as annoying as hell."

"Ah, the best ones always are," Harry replied.

20

Thursday, June 30, 5:30 p.m.

THE DAY WENT BY WITHOUT MUCH OF A HITCH, AND AS THE TEAM dropped off their information for the day, none of it was all that helpful. Sarah Mitchell's family was staying firm, and her alibi was solid—with video proof of her whereabouts: the Zoom call was logged.

Judy Constance had been sick but promised to come to the station when she was feeling better. And finally, cyanide...

"As it turns out, cyanide is easier to get ahold of than I thought," Corbin said as he leaned against the doorframe to my office. "Jack and I did some digging into purchases over the last six weeks, but the problem is some of them are masked."

"What do you mean?" I asked as I gathered my things, Samson eyeing me as I grabbed his leash. "They're selling it as something else?"

"Kind of," Corbin said. "If you want the good stuff, you have to go to the dark web, and on there... Well, there's plenty of it for sale; no questions asked."

"Disturbing," I muttered, shaking my head. "You find any sales to anyone we know?"

He shook his head. "We're still working our way through it. It feels like we're grasping at straws." He sighed and rubbed his jaw. "Once we found out about the affair…"

I stopped him. "We've beat that idea into the ground, Corbin. I think we're on the right track by extending our reach. Are we doing anything with the cases they worked on together?"

"There's a lot of them, Kate, and nothing strikes a chord so far. We'll keep digging into them. But here's the thing: they haven't worked on anything together in almost two years. Since the affair ended, in fact."

"Keeping their spouses happy, huh?" I commented, shoving my phone into my jacket pocket. "Well, for now, keep digging into possible suspects related to their work as lawyers, I guess."

Corbin nodded, and we walked together out to the parking lot. The rain had passed, leaving the air sticky and cloying. Not that I cared. I was more than a little preoccupied.

Corbin and I parted ways, and I loaded Samson into the front passenger seat and then slid into the driver's seat.

"I don't know about you," I said to Samson as I headed toward home, "but I'm starving. Maybe we should do DoorDash. What d'you think?"

I glanced at him. He was panting, looking straight ahead through the windshield. He seemed to be happy enough.

"So that's what we'll do then," I said as I blew through an orange light. The closer I got to home, the more ready I was to flop down on the couch and do some research. I hadn't had a chance to dig into Thomas Drews, but I fully intended to do it that evening.

When we made it to the house, I quickly changed into a pair of leggings, a tank top, and my running shoes. As much as I wanted to skip the run, I had already skipped too many. So

Samson and I blew through four miles without much effort, though the humidity was almost unbearable.

I took a quick shower, ordered some Chinese takeout via DoorDash, and then finally settled in on the couch with my laptop. I wasn't sure what I was looking for, but I knew that there had to be something about Drews somewhere. *What's his game, I wonder?* When someone goes sticking their nose into my business with his kind of tenacity, it often means there's a connection, and I was wondering if there was more to it than just curiosity.

I started with Google. I typed his name into the search bar and clicked enter, and then waited for the results to load. And boy, did they ever...

"Wow," I said aloud, catching Samson's attention. I had already fed him his kibble for the evening, but he was, as usual, sitting at the far end of the couch watching me. "He's got a lot of accolades." I tilted the laptop so Samson could see, and then shook my head. Sometimes I forget my dog is, well... a dog.

I scrolled through Drews' achievements, wondering why in the world he ever quit his job as one of Nashville PD's top detectives. His career was impressive, but why become a journalist? I squinted at the screen as I clicked on another article.

Thomas Drews Blows Cases Wide Open on His Podcast, Finding Truth: The Hunt for Answers on Unsolved Cases. I read the title and frowned. I didn't know much about the fad, but I did know that people were more interested in True Crime than ever and, apparently, Drews was making a boatload of money off of it. I looked up his podcast and was amazed to see he had more than ten million views.

"Well, you're not going to put my case on your show," I muttered.

It was at that moment that my doorbell rang. I sat the laptop to one side and went to the door. I gave the Door Dasher a wave and scooped up my brown paper sack filled with containers of fried rice and sweet and sour chicken. It wasn't my usual choice, but I'd fancied a change and it sounded good.

Samson was sitting up, watching me. He licked his lips as I tore the bag open. Laughing, I set out the containers on the coffee table, no longer thinking much about Thomas Drews. His credentials were impeccable and reading them had lessened my unease, though thinking back on it, I wasn't sure I was ever really that uneasy around him. Mostly, I was just annoyed that he was digging into my active case.

I popped open the box of rice and, wouldn't you know it, my phone began to ring, vibrating noisily on the glass coffee table top. I pursed my lips as I scooped it up. It was an unfamiliar number, but still local.

"Gazzara," I said, not hiding my irritation, hoping it wasn't Drews using another phone.

"Uh, yeah," a male voice said. "I hope I'm not bothering you, but I'm Paul Gerrick. I worked with David Mitchell and Madison Lombardi."

I set the chopsticks down and sat up straight. He had my full attention. "Good evening, Mr. Gerrick. What can I do for you?" I'd heard his name but knew little more of him.

"I was just…" His voice trailed off. He didn't sound much like the savvy, professional lawyer I knew him to be. "I was, um, wondering if we could chat about… about them and… and what's happened to them."

"Yes, of course," I said. "Why don't you come to the police department first thing tomorrow morning? We can talk then—"

"Have you found out who did it?" he blurted, cutting me off.

I frowned. "As I said, why don't we meet tomorrow morning? We can talk about it then."

I wasn't about to divulge any information we did or *didn't* have. Paul Gerrick sounded nervous and antsy, and I wanted to gauge his reactions face to face. I wasn't sure if anyone had spoken with him yet or not, but based on his tone and obvious agitation, I figured he might know something.

"Um, okay. I can meet up tomorrow. But not in the morning. I have a busy day. I'm free for lunch if that works for you?"

I pursed my lips, wishing I could have him come straight to the office. But if that made him uncomfortable, I was willing to go along with it. "All right," I said. "How about an early lunch, say eleven? Before the rush. It will be quieter then and we can talk."

"Yes, that will be fine. We're on Market. You can look it up. There's a sandwich shop right next door. I'll meet you there."

"All right," I said, "eleven it is. I'll look forward to it."

Gerrick hung up and I went to the kitchen, grabbed a pen and paper, scribbled down the information, and stared at it, thinking. "Well, now, isn't that interesting?"

I went back to the living room and sat down again, still thinking about the call. I looked at Samson. He whined at me, tilting his head and slapping his tail against the couch. I chuckled and then popped open one of the containers, picked out a piece of chicken and tossed it to him.

"You really shouldn't beg for food, Samson. It isn't gentlemanly."

He looked sideways at me as if to say, *But it works, doesn't it?*

I shook my head at him, shut my laptop, grabbed the remote and turned on the TV.

I flipped through the channels until I found another old episode of *Friends*. Then I texted Corbin and let him know about my plans to meet Gerrick. He acknowledged and wished me luck.

"And we need all the luck we can get," I muttered as I exchanged my cell phone for the container of chicken fried rice and chopsticks.

Friday, July 1, 7:00 a.m.

I HAD ANOTHER BAD NIGHT, TOSSING AND TURNING THROUGH MOST of it. Just about the time I finally fell into a deep slumber, my alarm went off.

I lay there for several moments, wondering if I was alive or dead, finally making up my mind it was the former and rolled out of bed, landing on my knees. I rested my arms on the bed for another long moment then hauled myself upright and staggered to the bathroom where I took a long, hot invigorating shower.

Fifteen minutes later I was dressed, downstairs and in the kitchen, the coffee maker doing its work.

Two cups of coffee and a plate of scrambled eggs and I was ready for the day, barely.

But I sat for a moment at the table, nursing a third cup of coffee, thinking. It seemed that was all I ever did, think and drink coffee. *You need to get a life, Kate,* I thought.

But, you know, something in my gut was telling me today was going to be different. It was Friday, and I was looking forward to a weekend of peace and quiet. It was a stretch—I knew that—but maybe Harry was right. Maybe it was time to think about going on vacation.

It was almost eight o'clock when Samson and I made it to the office; early, for sure, but not early enough, so it seemed, for no sooner had I stepped inside than my door opened and in walked Chief Johnston.

We hadn't spoken much since the abortive search of Tony Lombardi's home and offices, and I knew I wasn't at the top of the chief's popularity list.

"Any news for me?" he asked, without preamble.

I hated that question. "I'm meeting Paul Gerrick later this morning. He's—"

"I know who Paul Gerrick is," he cut me off, his expression stony. "He doesn't work at the Lombardi firm."

"No, but he said that he's worked with both our victims in the past and he wants to talk. And I gotta tell you, Chief; at this point, I'll talk to anyone if it will advance the investigation." *Except pesky Thomas Drews, of course.*

Chief Johnston nodded. "Not much else other than that, then?"

I shook my head. "No, sir. Afraid not. Lots of questions, no answers. We should get the toxicology report soon, though I'm thinking it will only confirm what we already know."

He gave me a stony look. "After that search fiasco, something needs to break, and soon. We can't have a crazy idiot going around throwing cyanide in people's faces. Get it done, Kate."

"Of course," I said, seeing him glance sideways at Samson, who was sitting beside my desk staring at him.

"Keep chipping away at it," he said, his tone a little more reasonable. "You'll figure it out. You always do." And with that and a final nod, he turned and walked quickly out of the office, leaving me alone with my thoughts.

I, too, nodded at his back, taking the compliment, a rarity coming from the chief.

Chapter 21

I glanced up at the clock and decided to go pay my team a visit. Maybe they'd have something already in the works. I called for Samson and slapped my thigh. He was instantly on the alert. I smiled at him. He looked at me, a goofy expression on his face.

"Let's go," I said, and we walked out into the incident room where I spotted Hawk and Robar at their desks, facing one another, talking together.

"Good morning," I said as I approached the desk.

"Morning, Cap," Anne said.

"Mornin'," Hawk muttered.

"What are you two working on?" I asked as I looked down at a long list of names on the desk in front of Hawk; its twin in front of Anne.

"This is the list of the interns that have worked at the same firm as Lombardi and Mitchell over the last three years," Hawk began, picking up the list and holding it out to me. "We requested it yesterday, but they didn't send it over until this morning."

I nodded, noting the highlighted names. "What are these highlighted names?"

"Those are the interns that have criminal records."

"What?" I said, frowning as I stared at the list. "They shouldn't be working at a law firm if they have a record."

"Right, which is why they no longer work there." Anne chuckled. "In fact, one of the interns got fired *because* he was convicted while working there."

I nodded. The information piqued my interest.

"When was this?"

"The guy's name is Victor Williams," Anne answered, bringing up the information on her screen. "He worked there for nearly a year and was fired four months ago."

"And *no one* mentioned this?" I asked, perplexed.

"No," Anne said, shaking her head, "but that's probably because they assumed he was in jail awaiting trial, but he's out on bail."

"What was the offense?" I asked.

"Aggravated stalking," Hawk said.

"Wow… So who was he stalking, and why?"

"Well…" Anne paused and looked at Hawk, then continued. "It's not a normal stalking case—not that any of them are, but… Well, it's kind of strange."

"Elaborate," I urged, wishing suddenly that I had thought to bring a cup of coffee with me.

"Oh, it's a doozy," Hawk said. "Apparently, this guy has been stalking random people since he was young—and I'm talking like sixteen—and this obsession grew through college and then peaked at his internship at the law firm."

I frowned. "So, he just picked random people?"

"Men and women, ages ranging from teenagers to elderly. Diverse backgrounds, ethnicities—you name it. It's like the guy just picks someone at random and then makes their life a living hell. He went undetected for years."

"And then, he escalated?" I asked.

Anne nodded. "His final victim—the one that led to the charges—was a woman named Mattie Vilago. She's in her mid-forties. Never married. Victor taunted and tortured her for about seven months before finally breaking and entering at her home. He attempted to attack her, but he picked the wrong one. Mattie has a black belt in Jujitsu. She took him down and, I mean, she *hurt* him."

I smiled at that. "Rough justice," I said. "It happens, but not often enough, in my opinion."

"Right," Anne said. "She detained him until the sheriff arrived. But here's the kicker… He's out on bail. His mother paid the bond. He's been living free to stalk more victims for the last three months. His trial is set for the beginning of September."

"Has he bothered Vilago since?" I asked.

Hawk shook his head. "No, not at all."

I mulled it over for a few moments. The MO wasn't quite

right, but then again, being overpowered by a woman could've done some damage to his ego and… on top of that, he'd lost his job and the right to practice law at all.

"I don't think…" I began. "No, I think we should look into it," I said. "The timing is about right, but… well, it can't hurt, and you never know."

"It is in the time frame," Anne agreed. "I don't know that it lines up, though, but at this point, I agree that we should look into it. You want us to bring him in?"

"Yes, bring him in," I said. But something about it made me feel uneasy. "And you need to find out why no one at Lewis, Scone and Petty thought to mention it. I don't like them withholding information."

"Maybe they didn't think it was relevant?" Anne suggested.

"Typical lawyer shiftiness, if you ask me," Hawk said. "I swear, they're always hellacious to work with. Tight-lipped and just want your money. They stick together like damn glue. What was it Shakespeare said, 'First kill all the lawyers?' When was that? Four hundred years ago. Even back then they were a pain in the ass."

I chuckled, the statement hitting me funny, especially coming from Hawk. And it was something I hadn't thought of all that much. I mean, granted, I knew there was a chance something nefarious was happening within LSP, but would they cover for something like this? *Absolutely, they would.*

"Okay, let's focus on Williams for now. Bring him in. Talk to him. See what breaks, if anything. Then go speak with the staff. Find out what they were covering up and why they didn't mention Williams. And be discreet. I don't want Williams to catch wind of it."

"Got it," Anne said. "We'll take care of it, and we'll let you know the progress."

"Sounds good. I have a lunch meeting with Paul Gerrick," I told them, just as Ramirez and Cooper joined the discussion.

"Paul Gerrick?" Cooper echoed, his brow furrowing. "He's another big-shot defense attorney, but I didn't think he had anything to do with the Lombardi and Mitchell killings. His name kept popping up in our search, but no one ever mentioned him as connected to the two."

"Apparently, he's worked with both of them," I said and folded my arms as Samson laid down under the desk.

"Seems promising," Ramirez said, making a face and nodding. "Maybe he has the dirt on them... or someone."

"He did sound nervous," I said. "Really nervous... when I think about it."

"You want me to tag along?" Corbin asked from behind me. "I don't mind crashing your lunch plans."

I shook my head. "Nah, I think it'll be okay. I'm going to the sandwich shop next door to his offices on Market Street. Shouldn't be a big deal. Besides, he might feel more comfortable if I'm alone."

"If he was already nervous, I'd agree with that," Anne said. "And the fact you've got a lawyer wanting to talk... I'd say that it's probably a solid lead."

"I hope so." I nodded. "But you two sort this Williams thing out, if only to eliminate him from the list."

"He comes from a privileged family," Hawk said. "All attorneys. My guess is that they've been pulling strings for him for years. That's usually how it goes, isn't it? My guess is they covered for him until they couldn't anymore, hence a forty-something Jujitsu champion takes him down."

"What?" Corbin laughed. "Someone is going to have to explain this one to me."

I turned to Anne and Hawk. "I'll let you fill him in. I'm going to do some digging into Paul Gerrick before I meet with him. I don't want to walk into it blind; that's never a good thing."

Little did I know!

22

Friday, July 1, 11:05 a.m.

I DIDN'T FIND MUCH ABOUT PAUL GERRICK, OTHER THAN HE WAS A damn good defense attorney. I spent more than an hour researching him and came up only with positive results. The man appeared to be squeaky clean, which, in and of itself, could be a red flag, but I let it go. At just after ten-thirty, I drove downtown and parked on the street outside the sandwich shop.

"Well, that worked out well," I told Samson. "Come on, let's go inside." I climbed out of the car and helped Samson down out of the back seat. I was about to go inside when I noticed a tall, blond man step out of the building next door. It was Paul Gerrick; I recognized him from the photos I'd seen while doing my search.

"Good morning, Captain Gazzara," he said as he joined me as Samson jumped down. "I see you have a canine partner. Is he friendly?" And he smiled at him.

Samson didn't return the smile, and that bothered me, a little.

"He has his moments," I said, giving Gerrick a smile. Samson wasn't always the friendliest of dogs, but that day he seemed a little... off.

"Shall we?" Paul said, holding out his arm toward the shop door.

"Of course," I replied and followed Paul into the sandwich shop, noting just how small the place was. However, the two women working behind the counter both waved at Paul.

"Hey, Paul," a heavyset woman called to him. "Good to see you." I could tell by the way she looked at him she was rather fond of the lawyer; the woman beside her, too, and there were several more people back there in the prep room behind the counter.

"This is my usual seat." Paul gestured to a booth at the far corner.

He took the seat facing the door, and as much as I would have preferred that spot, I let it go.

"I take it you know what's good here?" I said as I picked up the menu.

He smiled. "I prefer the BLT, but everything is good."

I nodded, scanning the menu as Samson settled in at my feet. "Well, it all looks pretty good," I said. "I'll have that, too."

He placed our orders with the heavyset woman.

"Thanks, Clara," he said, and she smiled at him, looking coy.

"As you might imagine, I eat here a lot," he said as he sat down again.

"I figured as much," I replied, and reached for my glass of water and took a sip. Then I looked at him and said, "So, why don't you tell me what this is about?"

He took a deep breath, sucked his bottom lip, then said, "Well, that's the thing. I don't know how much help this will be, but what you may not have heard is that Madison and David didn't have the best of reputations outside of the courtroom."

"What do you mean?" I asked.

"Well, in the courtroom and even beyond, they appeared to be… ethical… but they weren't, so I quit working with them. They both went about getting information in…" He paused, seemingly searching for the right words before continuing. "Let's just say they would use whatever means possible to win, even to the point of coercion, even..." He hesitated, then shook his head and said, "Blackmail."

"I see," I said carefully. "And...?"

"Well, you know," his voice lowered. "Tony Lombardi is a powerful man. He has connections all over the city, the nation, even. He knows some really *questionable* people. People who are willing to... cross the line."

He, too, was being careful in his choice of words.

"Hmm, well, okay," I said skeptically. "But we've cleared Tony of any wrongdoing."

"Of course, you have. He would never get his hands dirty, and he really backed off doing favors for Madison once he found out about the affair."

"We know all about that," I said frowning. "It ended years ago, so—"

"No, it didn't," he said, cutting me off. He glanced around as if he thought someone might be watching. "I know for a fact that they were still seeing each other. It made sense, too. They were both cut from the same cloth. They were power hungry, and they were both excellent attorneys."

I didn't like where this was going. We'd discarded the affair as a motive, and I wasn't happy thinking we'd have to reconsider that angle. "There's no evidence to suggest they were still seeing each other," I said.

"Of course not," he said, leaning forward. "D'you think they were stupid? They were lawyers, for heaven's sake; the best. D'you think they didn't cover their tracks? And you do know that affairs can be regarded as conflicts of interest, Captain Gazzara."

I nodded. "Yes. I'm aware."

"What they were doing bordered on collusion. And I heard..." He paused again.

"You heard what?"

"I heard some very powerful people weren't too happy with them."

I frowned and wrinkled my nose. "Like... who?" I asked.

He took a deep breath and leaned back against the booth. "The managing partners, Lewis, Scone and Petty, but I think pretty much everyone knew, though they won't talk about it. Between their underhanded tactics and the affair... well, you get the idea, I'm sure. Oh, and Colton Rhodes, another lawyer at their firm, was especially pissed," he added, almost as an afterthought.

Now that is news, I thought. "Did he talk to you about it?" I asked.

"Oh yeah," he said, nodding. "The morning Madison died, he called me. He was at home when it happened, running late, so he said. I was already at work—at Tooly and Watts. He told me about it, and then said he wasn't surprised, that he always knew something bad was coming for them. Like it was some kind of karma."

I nodded, trying to follow his train of thought. Where he was going, I still didn't know, and to that point, all I had from him was gossip and hearsay. But I wasn't about to give up.

"Okay. Are you saying that you think Rhodes had something to do with their deaths?"

"No," Paul said quickly. "Colton's clean. He rarely worked with either of them, and I know he has plans to leave the firm. He was planning to join me at Tooly and Watts. I'd already mentioned it to my managing partner, but Cindy Scone, one of the other named partners who he knows well, isn't a fan, and especially not a fan of Lombardi and Mitchell, and I don't think she was going to go for it."

"You say she wasn't a fan. Do you think she might have been involved..." I asked, trailing off, already knowing the answer.

"Not hardly." Paul shook his head, chuckled, then continued. "None of us have the kind of voodoo magic it takes to drop someone dead in the street like that. Hell, I don't even know how such a thing is possible. I was told they passed out and were gone within minutes. That's some pretty wild stuff."

Hmm. Clearly, he has no idea what killed them.

"All right, Paul," I said. "I'll have someone talk to Rhodes. Is there anyone else there that might have a grudge to settle? What about the interns? Clients?"

Paul nodded and leaned back in his chair as the heavyset woman, Clara, brought our sandwiches and set them down on the table in front of us.

Paul thanked her, and she sauntered away.

I stared at my sandwich. Samson began to whine, loudly, as if he was in pain.

"What's wrong, boy?" I asked, reaching down to stroke his head. But before I could, he was up on the seat and lunged at my plate, knocking it off the table and onto the floor.

"Samson!" I scolded him, shaking my head. "What's gotten into you?" But he jumped down and backed away, not even bothering to try and eat the food.

"I think your dog needs a little more training," Paul said, shaking his head. "I'll have Clara bring you another sandwich, but you might want to take the dog outside."

I shook my head, frustrated. "Forget the sandwich," I said angrily. "Let's just finish this conversation. I need to get back to the office."

But Samson wasn't done. He continued to whine, and then he lunged again, smashing my arm painfully against the edge of the table as he went for Paul's plate. But Paul saw him coming and swooped up his lunch just as Samson collided with the table.

"Hah!" he said. "You'll need to do better than that. I really think you should take him outside, Captain."

"Samson! Sit," I snapped. And he did. He banged his backside down on the floor, but he continued to stare at Paul.

"He'll be all right now," I said. "Though what's gotten into him... I don't know. Anyway, you were saying?"

Paul shook his head. "There was one client that *really* irked me. It was years ago, though. It was a case I was consulting with them on...." He paused, looked at Samson who was still staring at him, then he looked at me and said, "Look, Clara's giving us the evil eye. So let me eat this real quick and we can step outside before we get thrown out." He picked up his sandwich. Samson rose to his feet. Paul took a bite of his sandwich, chewed, swallowed and said, "The client was—"

"Paul?" I said as he froze mid-sentence. He stared at me wide-eyed, his mouth opened in what looked to me like a silent scream. The muscles in his face tightened, constricted. He dropped the sandwich, grabbed his throat with both hands and began to choke.

Samson began to back away as I slid out of the booth and went to Paul who was already convulsing wildly. I grabbed his arm. He looked up at me, choking, his eyes wide. And I knew then that there was nothing I could do for him.

I dug into my jacket pocket for my phone and dialed 911.

"What's your emergency?"

"This is Captain Gazzara, Chattanooga PD. I need an ambulance at Clancy's Sandwich Shop on Market Street—and be quick. I think a man is dying."

Paul's eyes rolled up. His hands fell away from his throat and he toppled sideways out of the booth. I tried again to grab him, but this time Samson turned on me and growled. I was stunned.

"Samson! What is it?" Then I got it. *He knows.*

Clara came rushing over, falling to her knees beside Paul. His body had gone limp. She put two fingers to his neck, feeling for a pulse, then heaved him over onto his back and began chest compressions. She pumped maybe six times then leaned over to apply mouth-to-mouth, but I grabbed her arm and stopped her.

"No, don't do that!" I said.

She gave me an incredulous look. "What? But—"

"He's been poisoned," I said.

I could hear sirens in the distance, but I knew they were too late. I could already see the rash appearing around his mouth. It was damn scary to see how quickly the cyanide worked. His face had already drained of color. His lips had turned blue. He was dead.

"How could he have been p-p-poisoned?" Clara leaned back, shocked. "*I* made the sandwich."

My stomach tightened. It was indeed a good question, and as the medics rushed in and scooted us out of the way, I knew I didn't have an answer.

But I sure as hell was going to find one.

I looked under the table at the plate and the sandwich. *My* sandwich, and then I looked at Samson. He cocked his head to one side, and I swear he showed me his teeth, smiling at me.

23

Friday, July 1, 12:40 p.m.

I WATCHED AS THE PARAMEDICS LOADED PAUL GERRICK INTO THE back of the ambulance, and then he was gone. His next destination? Erlanger Hospital and then, no doubt about it, Doc Sheddon's little shop of horrors.

Samson sat beside me as I watched Corbin pull up across the street. Uniformed officers had already sectioned off the restaurant and herded the few patrons and five staff members to the office building next door. Mike Willis was, so dispatch informed, on his way and would arrive within minutes.

Me? I remained stunned by the whole thing. In my mind, I played it over and over, the way Samson had gone for our plates.

"Don't let anyone touch that food or the plates," I said to a uniformed sergeant. "The sandwich on the table and the one under the table. They need to be collected for analysis."

He nodded. "You got it, ma'am. I'll stay close."

"You look like you've seen a ghost," Corbin greeted me, a sympathetic smile on his lips. "What the hell happened?"

I shook my head and put my hand to my forehead. "He was

poisoned. I'm sure of it. Cyanide. All the symptoms were there. He was obviously targeted, but how the hell they pulled it off, I have no idea."

"Could one of the staff have done it?" he asked.

"Possibly. They've all been moved, along with six or seven customers, to the law offices next door. We can interview there, I guess. Mike should be here soon." To tell the truth, I wasn't really thinking too clearly. I must have been in some degree of shock, I guess.

"How about you?" he asked. "Are you okay?"

"Yes, I'm fine," I said. "It was weird, though. It happened so quickly, and one of the staff members was about to attempt mouth to mouth… until I stopped her."

"Smart move," Corbin said.

I nodded, slowly, still thinking about Samson. I looked down at him. He was sitting quietly at my feet, panting slightly.

"He knew, Corbin," I said. "Samson knew. He knew there was something wrong with the food."

"You're kidding," Corbin replied skeptically. "How could he possibly have known?"

"I'm not sure," I said, "but he did. He knocked my plate off the table, and he tried to get to Paul's too, but Paul saw it coming and grabbed it before he could."

"Unbelievable," Corbin said, shaking his head. He looked at Samson, then at me. "You want to go next door and talk to these people?" he asked, changing the subject.

"I need to make sure nobody touches that food until Mike gets here," I said, just as Mike walked through the door.

I took a moment to fill him in, pointing out which was my food and which was Paul's, and then we left him and his team to it.

"Did you see anything, Kate?" Corbin asked as we walked the few yards to the office building next door. "Anything at all?"

I shook my head. "Not a damn thing," I replied. "Paul had the seat with his back to the window. I had my back to the room, something I almost never do. I couldn't even see who was coming and going."

"Hmm," Corbin said as I slipped past him into the lobby of the law offices, the door being held open by a uniformed officer. "I think we should start with the two women who were working the counter." He glanced down at his phone. "Lily Burns and Clara Dickens. We can get to the prep staff later. What d'you think?"

I shrugged. At that point, I wasn't thinking, and I really didn't care, but I complied. "Yeah, that's Clara." I pointed to the woman who had attempted CPR. She was sitting at one of the front tables, visibly distraught. Her face was muddy red, tears rolling down her cheeks.

"You talk to her, then," Corbin said, "and I'll take the other." He nodded toward the other woman, Lily Burns. She didn't look as upset as Clara, but I knew shock when I saw it, and the petite redhead was in shock. She was sitting, her back rigid, in an armchair, her eyes staring into space.

And I don't blame you, I thought as I took a seat across from Clara and forced a smile I didn't feel. "It's Clara, isn't it? I'm Captain Gazzara. Do you feel up to a chat about what happened?"

"Shouldn't you be getting interviewed, too?" she asked me hesitantly.

"Yes, of course. I'll be giving my statement later, but right now I need to get to the bottom of this... tragedy," I told her gently. "You said you made the sandwiches. Then what?"

"Well, I brought them out to you and Paul..."

"Yes, I know that," I said. "But you didn't bring them out straight away, did you?" I knew she couldn't have unless it was her who put the cyanide in the sandwiches, and I really didn't think she did. I could tell her shock and emotions were genuine.

She sucked on her bottom lip, then said, "I put them on the

counter and went out back." She frowned, looked me in the eye and continued, "But it was only for a minute... You don't think..."

"I'm just gathering the facts right now," I said. "Do you remember if anybody was standing at the counter?"

She slowly shook her head, obviously thinking hard. "I'm trying to remember," she said. "I don't think..." She looked at me, tears now streaming down her face. She took a tissue from her purse and wiped her eyes, saying, "I don't remember. There are always people at the counter. We weren't very busy. The rush hadn't started yet. I guess there could have been. How about you? Did you see anyone?"

Inwardly, I smiled. On any other occasion, I would have told her I was the one asking the questions, but I played along and said, "Unfortunately, I had my back to the counter, so no, I didn't." *Curses! I knew I should have grabbed that other seat.*

"How about your partner.... Lily, isn't it? Where was she?"

"She was out back, in the cooler."

"Why did you leave the counter, Clara?"

"Lily said there was a problem with the cooler and needed my help..." She trailed off and wiped her eyes again. "I was only gone a couple of minutes."

I reached forward and put a hand on her arm. "It's okay, Clara. Take a deep breath. Just a couple more questions, okay?"

She nodded, sniffed, and looked at me, so I said, "So you didn't see anything out front," I said. "How about the rest of the staff? Did anyone go to the counter while you were out back?"

Again, she thought for a minute, then said, "No, not that I can remember. But they wouldn't... They're all nice people."

I blew out my cheeks, my lips pursed. "Did you notice anything unusual this morning, anything at all?"

She shook her head. "No, everything was normal. Well, the fridge..." Her mouth dropped open and her hands flew up. "Oh my gosh, what if it was spoiled meat?" She started to sob, and I realized this woman was truly clueless about what happened—and she was blaming herself.

"What was wrong with the fridge?" I asked.

"We weren't sure. The lights… The lights were kicking off and on. Lily and I thought it might've been the bulb, you know, but it could have been the thermostat, and if it wasn't keeping everything as cool as it was supposed to… I've heard of spoiled meat doing that."

"Right, but we ordered BLTs. There was no deli meat on them."

"Yes, but the bacon is kept in the fridge, and then we heat it up."

"Okay." I let her think that I was taking the comment seriously. I knew that the bacon was already cooked before it was placed in the fridge. It was a reach at best, but I needed to move on. "Can you think of anything else?"

She mulled it over, her tears ceasing. "I… I don't think so? I got to the shop first this morning. I always do. I unlocked the door and started preparing everything as usual. We were slow today, and there were only four or five other customers in the restaurant when you came, and a couple more after that, I think. They were regulars. They work at several of the law offices around, you know?"

I nodded, the information leaving my throat feeling tight. "And no one came in while you were out back?"

She frowned, then said, "No, there was no one at the counter when I came back. Lily was working in the back. Like I said. She was in the fridge…"

"Right." I nodded and glanced over at the now-crying Lily. I sighed and nodded, sure now that neither of these two women had tampered with the sandwiches, and that only served to further unnerve me. Samson put his head on my knee, and I let him leave it there. "How well did you know Paul?"

"Not really that well. He comes into the sandwich shop, you know? Several times a week. He was a regular."

I leaned back in my chair and took a deep breath, trying to piece together how the hell something like this happened right under my nose. *What did I miss? Someone must have tampered with the sandwiches while I was sitting there. Someone? I don't think these two girls are lying.*

I took a wild stab. "Did you know Madison Lombardi or David Mitchell?"

She wrinkled her brow and shook her head. "No. Sorry."

I bit my lip. I had to be careful how much information I let loose. The last thing I wanted to do was start rumors. And I could see there was already one of the local news vans parked outside.

Clara burst into tears again. "It had to be the fridge."

I glanced over at Corbin. He looked at me and shook his head, and I had a feeling he was as frustrated as I was.

I turned my attention back to Clara and said, "Do you have security cameras, Clara?"

Clara shook her head. "No, we don't. There's never been a need for them... until now."

Oh, that's just great, I thought. "And you're positive that, other than the fridge, there was nothing out of the ordinary?" I was really fishing now.

She shook her head. "Oh, poor Paul," she said, sobbing.

I gave up, leaned forward, touched her arm again, excused myself, stood up and walked to the window, watching the camera crew setting up but not really seeing it. I was lost in thought, trying to play back my meeting with the now-dead Paul Gerrick, and getting nowhere. My mind was a swamp. The guy had died in front of me. That was a first—and not something I wanted to repeat.

I was joined a couple of minutes later by Corbin. He stood beside me, also staring out of the window. Samson was seated beside me. We must have made quite a picture, the three of us.

"That woman is absolutely clueless," Corbin said in a low voice. "C'mon, Kate. Let's leave them to it."

"Wait," I said. "Give me a minute."

I turned and walked across the room to where three uniformed officers were standing talking together.

"You interviewed the customers? I'm assuming you didn't get anything?"

"Nope," Officer Wagner said. "We were just talking about it. The interviews took less than a couple of minutes each. Nobody saw anything. So we got their contact information and let them go. Wild, really."

It's like a ghost had walked in and poisoned Gerrick, I thought as I rejoined Corbin and told him what Wagner had said.

"It's disturbing," Corbin said; an understatement if ever there was one.

I had to agree with him. And it happened right under my nose, and how had *no one* seen anything? It wasn't logical. If the two staff members were telling the truth, and I was sure they were, how would someone manage to poison two sandwiches and not be noticed?

"I'm going back to the shop," I said. "I need to talk to Mike."

"I'll hold Samson for you," Corbin replied, holding out a hand for the leash. I passed it to him and then headed back to the shop.

Mike Willis, our long-time head of CSI, met me just out front.

"Captain," he said and paused for a second. "This is one strange crime scene."

"That seems to be a word that's being used a lot," I replied. "What can you tell me?"

"I don't think you're going to like what I have to say," Mike said in a low voice, nodding toward a shady spot under one of the trees on the sidewalk.

"First," he continued, "the place is clean. Secondly, I got a call from Doc Sheddon. He suggested I bring my Quantofix Cyanide test strips. It was an odd request, but I'm glad I did."

"His sandwich tested positive for cyanide?" I said. "I'm not surprised. We know Madison Lombardi and David Mitchell died of cyanide poisoning."

He nodded, slowly. "But see, Kate, that's the thing. I wasn't surprised by the cyanide I found in Paul's sandwich either; it was *your* sandwich that's got me concerned."

I stared at him in silence, then said, "Continue..." It was all I could think of.

"Your sandwich also tested positive for cyanide. Now, I'm not saying that you were targeted specifically; you both ordered the same thing. Maybe the perp wanted to be sure he got Gerrick..."

I had a sick feeling in the pit of my stomach. "Right," I said, "that could be true, I suppose." I didn't know what to think.

"I heard Samson knocked your plate off the table? That's one hell of a dog you have. He saved your life."

"And not for the first time," I said. "He tried to get to Gerrick's, too."

I glanced back at Samson. *How the hell did he know? Geez, I wish he could talk.*

24

Friday, July 1, 2:50 p.m.

THE REST OF THE AFTERNOON PASSED IN A HAZE AS WE WENT through the motions of wrapping up the crime scene investigation. Nothing turned up, and the fact that it didn't, caused me no little concern.

I was in a state of stoic ambivalence as I buckled Samson in and slid into the driver's seat of my unmarked cruiser and started the engine.

"I don't understand it, Sammy," I said, meeting his gaze in the rearview mirror. "I don't know how no one could have seen anything, and yet, I believe them."

Samson leaned against the harness and placed a paw on the center console. I smiled, grasped it and squeezed. "Thanks for watching out for me, buddy. I didn't know you could sniff out cyanide."

He stared up at my reflection in the mirror, and I wished again, for the umpteenth time, that he could talk.

I turned on the radio, happy with the classic rock station, hoping it would take my mind off the fact that someone had just tried to kill me. I kept the volume down and stayed behind Corbin as we headed back to the office. I knew the rest of my team would be up in arms when we made it back. But me? I still wasn't convinced that I was specifically targeted. No, I would have been collateral damage. *Geez, I hate that term. It's so... impersonal.*

Why would someone target me, anyway? If that was the case, then that could mean that my team could be in danger, and that... was unacceptable. My stomach was growling, but I had no desire to eat, figuring I'd eat when I got home tonight.

I parked the car and climbed out. Samson and I joined Corbin, and we went inside.

"Geez, Corbin," I said. "That was some lunch meeting, huh?"

"You could say that," Corbin replied and chuckled wryly. "Did Paul say anything helpful before... Well, you know."

I hesitated, doing my best to recall the conversation. "Not really. He mentioned that Colton Rhodes had wanted to leave the LSP, and Lombardi and Mitchell were... borderline shysters—my words, not his—but you get the idea. What he actually said was that their methods were unethical. He also mentioned Tony Lombardi was doing them favors, until he found out about the affair, but never gave me specifics." I paused to think. "Oh, and he said the affair between Madison and Mitchell hadn't ended two years ago. They were still together, just being more careful about it."

Corbin raised his eyebrows. "I wonder if he had the answers."

"I don't think so." I paused as Corbin held the door open for me. "He was about to tell me about a client of theirs that wasn't too happy with them, but then he bit into his sandwich."

"They handled a lot of cases together," Corbin said. "That would have been good to know. It was an inopportune moment, him dying like that."

I stopped for a moment, put my hand on his arm and said,

"Inopportune for *us*, but not for the perp. For all we know, they just saved their own skin."

Corbin nodded. "You're not wrong. You think they might be targeting you? If they are—"

I cut him off, not wanting to think about such a scenario. "At this point, I don't know what the hell they're doing. I have no idea who it could be or why they're doing what they are. I'm at a loss, Corbin."

Corbin didn't answer, and I knew it was because he was on the same page as I was. The only hope I had was that someone on my team had made some progress, and without putting themselves in danger. This case had escalated to a new level of urgency, and I didn't like it; not one bit.

"Captain!" Anne called out as I made it to my office. "I'm glad you're okay. I can't believe what happened. I heard the call and—"

"I'm okay, Anne," I said, cutting her off. I couldn't handle that kind of sympathy, not then. I needed something to break. I wanted to solve the case. "Is everyone here?"

"Yeah, we've had one hell of a time trying to locate Victor Williams—"

"Have everyone come to my office." I cut her off again and immediately regretted it. "But give me fifteen minutes, Anne," I said, softening my tone.

But I wasn't ready to talk, not then. She nodded and turned away. It was my intention to brief them all together. Not to mention, I was still feeling the stress of the events of the afternoon and my head was pounding.

"We'll have to talk to Doc, you know?" I said to Corbin as he pushed open my office door.

"Yeah, he said he'd call," he replied.

"Good." I entered my office and went straight for the coffee maker. The last thing I probably needed was more caffeine on an empty stomach, but I was hoping it would help stave off the hunger.

"You haven't eaten, have you, Kate?" he said. "You want me to send out for something?"

"No, but thanks. I'll be fine." I looked at him wearily over my shoulder. "Not feeling up for takeout. I'll eat when I get home."

"Can't say I blame you."

"I wonder if anyone's heard from the chief," I said as I grabbed my mug from my desk. "I figured we'd have heard from him by now."

"Not that I've heard," he replied.

"You want coffee?" I asked him. "Help yourself."

He shook his head. "No, I'm good."

"You know..." My voice trailed off as I filled my cup, thinking. "What if Tony Lombardi *is* the one behind all this? Maybe he has an ax to grind we don't yet know about. Maybe someone in his family was pissed off about something his wife and Mitchell did."

Samson, sitting up in his bed, yawned and shook himself, then collapsed in a heap, his head on his paws, staring at me, as if to say, *Yeah, Kate, that's a bit of a reach.*

This entire case is a reach, Sammy, I thought as I turned back to Corbin. "I know it sounds farfetched, but..."

"But it's not impossible. I'll have someone go talk to him, see where he was and what he was up to at lunchtime this afternoon."

I shook my head. "Nah! Even if it were him, he'd have a rock-solid alibi. He knows how to cover his tracks."

"I guess," Corbin agreed, pulling out a chair at the table. He sat down and continued. "I'm thinking we're facing something bigger... Or someone who *really* knows their stuff. This thing stinks of mafia."

"Can we come in?" Ramirez said from the open doorway.

"Sure," I said, "come on in and sit down, all of you." And one after the other, they filed in and sat down.

"I heard what you said, Corbin," Ramirez said. "Whoever this perp is, they took a hit at us today. That's pretty frickin' audacious."

"We don't know if I was a target or just—"

"Of course you were a frickin' target," Hawk said. "From what I've heard, someone poisoned both sandwiches. That means the perp wanted to make sure one of you died. You're assuming Gerrick was the target. Why? He didn't work with them. But you, you're leading the investigation. It makes sense it was you they were after. Let's get frickin' real here."

He was obviously very angry, and, for the first time, I realized he could be right and felt a definite chill in the air. I pulled out a chair and sat down at the table, surrounded by my support team.

"We're all glad you're okay," Cooper said. "This is something… new, and it's about as unnerving as it gets. It's all over the department."

I shook my head. "I've been through worse," I said, thinking back to the time when Sergeant Dick Tracy saved me from what had been almost certain death. "But it was a long time ago… So… Let's get on with it, shall we?"

"From what I've heard, there's no witnesses," Anne said. "In a crowded restaurant? I would have thought that was impossible."

"It wasn't crowded," I said. "Just a half-dozen people, or so, and no, they saw nothing."

"Could it have been one of the staff?" Cooper asked.

"Not likely," Corbin said, then, "Kate, why don't you brief them?"

I nodded and then proceeded to share the events of the day, including the conversation I had with Paul, as best as I could remember it. I covered it all in thorough detail, trying to make sure I didn't leave anything out. My brain felt like concrete, and I was feeling exhausted. Some five minutes or so later, I was finished, and Corbin took over. When he finished, I looked around the table. Everyone was quiet.

This isn't good, I thought. Knowing them as I did, it meant they were stumped.

"So..." I cleared my throat. "Cat got your tongues? Okay, tell me about Victor Williams."

Anne shook her head. "We can't find him, but we'll keep looking."

"Someone snuck into that sandwich shop, poisoned the sandwiches, and then left without anyone seeing them," Hawk snarled. "That makes no sense. It has to be one of the staff."

"And none of the other customers were poisoned?" Ramirez added. "It's so specific."

"Well, we both ordered the same thing," I said, hesitantly returning to the conversation. "I guess they wanted to make sure they got the right person."

"That would rule out the waitress who brought the food," Cooper said. "She would've ensured which sandwich to give Gerrick. Unless she was after both of you..." He trailed off, then added, "That *could* be what happened."

"Okay, so we rule out the waitress," Hawk said. "Who made the sandwiches?"

"The waitress," I said.

"That only confirms it wasn't her, then, unless, as Cooper said, she wanted to kill both of you. But that's more than a stretch. I still think it was you they were after. So, who else could have done it? How does someone poison not one, but two sandwiches without anyone noticing? That's damn near an impossibility."

"But someone did, and you have to remember that they also poisoned two people in broad daylight," I reasoned. "And we have only *two* witnesses in the case so far, both of whom could give us only the vaguest description of someone in a trench coat with a hood."

"Whoever this is has stealth skills," Ramirez said as she

pinched the bridge of her nose. "It smacks of mafia to me, and Tony Lombardi has mafia connections."

"Or maybe they just blend in," Corbin said. "Maybe they're the kind of person who can walk into a room without being noticed. Someone... I dunno. Nondescript?"

I mulled the thought over. *Could that be possible? Could someone be so plain, so unremarkable, that they were able to fly under the radar without anyone noticing them?* It seemed like a stretch, but at the same time, I had to admit that maybe there was some validity to the idea.

At that point, I was ready to consider just about anything.

25

Friday, July 1, 5:15 p.m.

"Kate, a word," Chief Johnston said as he pushed past the members of my team as they shuffled out of the room.

"I'll finish my statement before I leave," I said, setting my empty mug on my desk as he shut the door behind him.

"Take your time," he said. "This is an off-the-record conversation. I heard what happened, and I'm here to tell you to be careful, Kate. You got lucky today. Thanks to him." He turned his head and looked at Samson. "You might not be so lucky next time."

"I'm not convinced that I was the intended target, Chief," I said lightly as I gathered up my things. I'd never been one to shoot out the door at five-thirty, but that day I was ready to get to my home. Home was my safe place.

"Regardless of whether or not you were the intended victim, the fact of the matter is that had Samson not knocked the sandwich off the table, my captain would be dead."

Well, geez, when you put it like that...

"I don't want you going anywhere alone, not even with

Samson. Not a single person saw anything out of the ordinary. Not even you. How does that happen?"

"Well, I had my back to the…" I wasn't one to make excuses, so I didn't. "I don't have an answer for you, Chief."

"Look," he said. "You don't have to continue with this investigation. Why don't you let Russell take the lead, if only for a while?"

I shook my head, then smiled wryly at him. "I don't think so. I'm fine… and more motivated than ever."

"I knew you'd say that," he said quietly. "But I was hoping you wouldn't. I think we need to dig deep into Paul Gerrick. If you weren't the target—and I'm still not convinced that you weren't—then he was, and that means he knew something that got him killed. I've sent officers back out to canvasss the area. I don't want you, or any of your team, going back out there right now."

"I can go talk to people at his firm—"

"*No!*" He cut me off, his voice sharp. "Absolutely not. I do *not* want you out there on the streets alone. You're too well known, Kate."

I couldn't argue with him. He'd made a decision, and I would have to respect it. "Okay. I'll do what I can from here unless I take Corbin with me, but Samson is the one to credit."

"I'm aware of that," he replied. "What do you think about the employees of the sandwich shop?"

"I don't think they know anything," I admitted and waited for him to respond. I was expecting him to argue and tell me not to ignore the obvious, that nine times out of ten, the obvious is the answer. But, to my surprise, he didn't.

"I agree. But I don't know how to advise you." He wearily rubbed his chin, then shook his head, and I knew what was coming next.

"The media have caught wind of it," he said. "You're high-profile, Kate, and there was nothing we could do to stop it from getting out. I have to give a statement."

"It might be the best thing," I said carefully. "There might be witnesses out there that haven't come forward because they don't know that what they saw was a murder."

"It's also going to scare the daylights out of the city. We're talking about the damn Grim Reaper here, slinking around the streets and killing people with a look and a handful of powder, and now... it's escalated to poisoning people in restaurants. It smacks back to the Tylenol poisonings back in eighty-two. If this thing goes national, and I have a feeling it will—" He cut himself off.

Yikes, I shuddered at the thought. "That doesn't bear thinking about."

"You can say that again," he muttered. "No one is going to take that well. And we can say we think it's isolated all day long, but it's not going to make anyone feel any better. Just be careful and remember what I said: you're not to go anywhere alone." And with that, he turned to leave.

"We'll just have to deal with it the best we can," I said, my mind running back to the stalker my team couldn't locate. It caused me pause, and before the chief could slip out of my office, I stopped him. "Can I get your opinion on something, Chief?"

He turned and looked at me, surprised. "Of course. What is it?"

I didn't ask his opinion often, but I couldn't get this one out of my head.

"Do you think it could simply be a stalker?"

"A stalker? You think the killings could be random acts of some crazy person? No, I don't think so. Stalkers don't kill people in restaurants."

"But couldn't it be a serial killer who's choosing their victims at random, without rhyme or reason?"

"There's always a reason, Kate. It might not make sense to us, but it does to them."

And I knew he was right.

"You're fishing, Kate, and that's not like you," he said.

"Maybe," I said, then, "Have you looked at Victor Williams in the case file? I had a copy sent to you."

He nodded. "I gave it a once over. I think you should bring him in. It wouldn't be a bad idea to interview him and talk to whoever was assigned his case. Do I think that he's capable of cyanide poisoning at this level? It seems like a stretch for someone who has a tendency to commit erratic crimes."

He opened my office door and stepped out, but not before calling back over his shoulder, "Stay safe, Kate."

"You, too," I replied, though the door had already closed by the time I said the words. I stood there for a few moments, staring at the door. I looked over at Samson, who looked more than a little forlorn. "I don't know who did it, Sammy. And I guess we won't be going for a run this evening. I guess I'll have to work it out on the treadmill in the garage. It's time to go home."

Samson rose to his feet and stretched. Me? I have to admit I felt a little leery about leaving the building, and I wasn't sure why. I've never been the type to back away from a threat, and my life had been threatened more than once in my career. Hell, I had faced more danger than most. But I still felt uneasy.

Maybe it was the idea, the image of the shadowy figure Shelly Seward had described. I didn't know. Neither was I one to contemplate how I might die someday—dying on the job... well, it's part of the job—but I did know one thing...

I did not want to go by cyanide poisoning.

As I clipped the leash on Samson's collar, my phone rang in my pocket. I sighed, fished it out and checked the screen. *Harry.* I tapped the button to answer. "Hey."

"I heard your pup saved you from an attempted assassination," he said, and while his voice had a touch of humor, I didn't miss the concern. "Amanda and I just want to say we're glad you're okay."

"Thanks," I muttered, pausing at the door. "Not everyone was so lucky."

"Yeah, I heard. I also heard that it was another shot of cyanide."

"You heard right. Willis confirmed it while I was still at the scene. He used some kind of test strip."

"I've heard of the method," Harry replied. "It has to be done within a couple hours or something. Not entirely sure of the parameters, but I get the gist. Cyanide isn't exactly something that I've bothered to study over the years. It's a rarity."

"Yes, well, I have to admit, it's damn scary, and not something I want to think about. Did you hear it was Samson who saved me?"

"I did. Good for him. You're lucky you have him. Any leads come out of it?"

"Nothing," I replied. "Not a damn thing."

"Well, I have to say, you've got my attention, Kate," he said. "It seems like it's going nowhere but also somewhere, and all at the same time."

"That's one very odd way to put it," I said, shaking my head. "But I suppose so."

"Your perp is getting bolder, you know that, right?" he asked. "Because if they have the gumption to go sneaking into a sandwich shop full of people, then they're damn sure starting to grow an ego. And that just might work in your favor."

"If it doesn't kill someone first," I said as I opened my office door and stepped out into the situation room, where I found Corbin lingering a few feet away. I guessed that he was waiting to walk me to the car, and as kind as that was, it was also annoying. But, with the phone still to my ear, I gestured toward the elevator, and he nodded, falling in step behind us.

"Now look, Kate," Harry said. "If you need any help, you know I'm always here for you."

"Yeah, I know, Harry, and I thank you for it. And I might have to take you up on that offer. From what the chief just told me, it's fixing to hit the news, big time."

"Ah," Harry said, and I could hear the humor in his voice. "I bet Johnston is tearing his hair out…" He paused for a second, then continued. "It might bring in some new leads, though. Whether they're helpful or not is another question entirely."

"I'd say," I said as I stepped out into the parking lot and huffed as a blast of warm air hit me in the face. I wondered if sucking in the thick, humid air felt anything like breathing in cyanide, and the thought unnerved me even further. I didn't want to know what it was like, but it was probably worse than ingesting it through a sandwich.

Another bullet dodged.

26

Friday, July 1, 5:55 p.m.

"Be safe," Corbin said to me as I helped Samson into the back seat. "If it wasn't for Samson, I'd be escorting you home."

I laughed. "You act like I've never been in a situation like this before."

He chuckled, but his expression remained tinged with concern. "You've been in plenty of tough situations over the years, but this cyanide poisoning situation has me on edge. It's hard to combat a perp you don't see coming, and from the looks of it, a ghost poisoned those sandwiches today."

"I don't believe in ghosts," I replied, "not ones that use cyanide, anyway," I added, shutting the rear door. "*Someone* saw who poisoned those sandwiches. They're either good liars, or we haven't found the witness yet. We still need to talk to the owner of the sandwich shop, too." I grimaced at that last statement. I wanted to go hunt the killer down right then and there.

"We'll get to it," Corbin said as if he knew exactly what I was thinking. "Ramirez tried to give him a call, but he didn't answer.

We'll pick it up first thing tomorrow. However, *you* don't need to worry about that right now."

"Yeah, right," I scoffed, sliding into the driver's seat. "We both know that's not how I operate. If someone was trying to stop me by poisoning me, it didn't work."

"Well, killing you would've definitely stopped you," Corbin said and rapped his knuckles on the top of the car. "And you're no use to the team if you're dead, so stay alive, Kate."

"Will do," I said, giving him a nod and shutting the door. I turned on the ignition and listened to the motor roar to life. My car was due for an oil change, but I wouldn't be dropping it off anytime soon, not until we'd found our killer. *Corbin was right when he said it's hard to fight someone you don't see coming... or at all.*

"I don't know who is doing this," I told Samson as I pulled out of the parking lot. "But I sure as hell hope we find them soon. I've never been so on edge."

Samson whined, and strangely, it made me feel better to think he might be a little worried, too. This was one ballbuster of a case, and I knew the answer had to be somewhere among the cluster of clues we already had, we just hadn't figured it out yet.

"You think our suspect might be the stalker?" I asked, looking at him in the rearview. I really wanted to get takeout, not having eaten all day, but I decided against it. I didn't trust food from anywhere but my own kitchen, and for all I knew someone was keeping a close eye on me. It had happened plenty of times before, though I'm not sure it had ever felt as ominous as it did that evening.

I pulled into the garage twenty minutes later, having navigated heavy traffic most of the way home. Chattanooga was still moving seamlessly, most of its citizens in complete oblivion to what was happening around them. That's how it had always been though, and that was one of the many burdens that we, as law enforcement, chose to carry. But I didn't feel like I was doing such a great job of keeping anyone safe right now.

"Home, sweet home," I said to Samson as I watched the garage door close behind us. I waited until it was all the way shut before I pushed open the driver's side door and got out. I took a deep breath of the stale garage air as if I might smell something... not really sure what I was expecting. But I didn't notice anything unusual. It was the same as it always was, musty, and it gave me little comfort.

"Come on, boy," I said as I opened the rear car door and unhooked Samson from his restraint. "I think we both need a good night's rest. I'm feeling more than a little frazzled."

He cocked his head at me as if to say, *Everything's going to be fine, Kate.*

I patted his head and then led the way into the house. Samson seemed at ease as he rushed for his food bowl, obviously hungry and ready for his dinner. I filled the bowl with his kibble, refreshed his water, and then went to the fridge and started digging. As I did so, however, I couldn't shake the one question hanging heavy in my mind...

How did someone poison those sandwiches?

It made no sense. If Gerrick and I were the only ones who received tainted sandwiches, it meant someone had been waiting... and watching. Had one of us been followed? Had they hidden somewhere in the shop? Was one of the workers lying? They were all questions to which I had no answers. I just didn't know how it was done... *yet.*

"We'll figure it out, won't we, Sammy?" I told him as I closed the fridge door. "We always do, don't we?" I'd found nothing in the fridge that turned me on. I was hungry, but nothing sounded good. I knew it was the events of the day that had caused my conundrum. "I have to eat something though, don't I?" I said, watching him snarf his food.

He paused, turned his head and looked up at me, his ears perked forward. He didn't look the slightest bit worried, and I chalked it up to our difference in species. Samson never missed a meal, no matter what he had gone through during the day.

I moved from the fridge to the cabinet, sweeping through the contents like I was on a mission. Five minutes and a thorough search later, I still hadn't come up with anything. *Ugh.* I pulled the tie out of my hair, raked my fingers through it and shook it loose.

Maybe I'll shower first, I thought. I eyed Samson, considering letting him out into the backyard to use the bathroom first, but he seemed content enough, so I slipped out of the kitchen and headed for my master bedroom.

I took a quick shower and then donned a pair of pajama pants and a T-shirt, my damp hair hanging loose. My stomach was still feeling a little queasy, but I felt refreshed. So, ironically, I made myself a sandwich and then walked outside with Samson into the backyard.

Without allowing myself to think about what had happened earlier, I devoured my simple dinner while watching Samson patrol in the yard.

I sat down in one of the patio chairs and set my empty plate on the table, watching the sun slowly begin to dip lower in the western sky. The days were longer, and so the heat of summer lingered. But it was going to be a pleasant evening.

I was certain my hair was a frizzy mess, but I decided I'd worry about taming it in the morning. I looked at the darkening sky, wondering at the colors... deep golds, pale purples, knowing that it would be but a blink and the summer would be over, and then we'd be in autumn and, hopefully, this case would be but a distant memory.

"Maybe," I thought aloud as Samson came bounding back to me, his pink tongue lolling as he panted. He sat down beside me and rested his head on my lap. I stroked his soft fur and scratched behind his ears, and he sighed, and I smiled. "You're a good boy, you know that?" I asked. "You saved my life today. How can I ever thank you?"

He closed his eyes and heaved another huge sigh. It was one of those moments. We couldn't have been closer, but then the moment was ruined when my cell phone rang in my pajama pocket. I shifted in the chair and fished it out, surprised to see Corbin's name on the screen.

"Corbin?" I said, dusting a strand of dog hair off my pajama pants.

"Hey, Kate," Corbin said, his voice heavy. I could tell he was still at work, probably hanging back late with the team. It made me wish I was there, too, but this time, they'd succeeded in running me out of there. "Brad Owens, the owner of the shop called."

"And?" I asked impatiently. "Don't just leave me hanging, Corbin."

"Well, he's coming in in the morning."

"And? Did he say anything else?"

"No, just that he'd be coming in around eight. He called in and spoke to one of the officers and left a message. That's all I know."

"Has it hit the news yet?" I asked. I hadn't bothered to turn on the TV.

Corbin sighed. "Not yet. Chief Johnston is trying to hold it off as long as he can, but he thinks it'll be on tomorrow morning, early."

I nodded. "Well, it could bring in some new leads... I suppose."

"And cause mass panic," Corbin said and laughed, though it sounded empty. He seemed stressed, which was unusual for him.

"Is everything okay at home, Corbin?" I asked.

"What?" He seemed caught off guard by the question.

"You sound stressed, and I don't think it's just because of the case," I said, not beating around the bush. That never did anyone any good.

"Oh, well..." He paused. "For the most part, I guess. The wife... Well, she's having some testing done for a couple of swollen lymph nodes. I don't think it's going to turn into anything, but you know how doom-and-gloom doctors can be."

My heart sank. "Oh, Corbin. I'm so sorry. If I need to come in—"

"No, no," he stopped me. "I'll be fine. We should have the results next Friday. You just worry about you, Captain. I'll be fine." With that, we said our goodnights, and Samson and I headed inside for the evening. I washed up the plate and put it on the rack to dry before zoning out on the TV for a while.

We went to bed early that night, but not before I had to ignore *another* phone call from Thomas Drews.

Will he never learn? I thought savagely.

27

Saturday, July 2, 6:45 a.m.

SLEEP DIDN'T COME EASY THAT NIGHT, THOUGH IT DID COME, eventually, so I suppose I shouldn't have complained.

Samson and I were up around our normal time, and despite it being Saturday and a holiday weekend, we were going to work as if it were just another weekday. And no matter how much the members of my team thought I should stay home, it wasn't going to happen. One, that's not me, and it never will be. And two, I wanted to hear what Brad Owens had to say, and I didn't want to hear it secondhand.

I dressed in a pair of dark-washed jeans and a white blouse, and tucked my hair up into a bun in order to smooth it out the best I could. Samson had his usual morning breakfast, and I opted for some toast and coffee at home, still not able to cope with the idea of grabbing something on the way in.

It was just after seven-thirty when I parked the car in the rear lot.

"You're here," Corbin greeted me as I walked to the interview room. "I told you—"

"Don't," I stopped him, holding a hand up. "You knew I was going to be here. I'm not going to sit around at home while my team puts in hard work. I'm not dead yet."

Corbin frowned but nodded. "Well, lucky for you, Brad Owens showed up early, too, and he looks nervous." He gestured through the open interview room door where a dark headed, middle-aged man was sitting at the table, a black plastic bag in his hand.

"What's that he's got?" I asked.

"It's a picture in a frame. They checked it before they brought him back here. No idea what it could mean, but there's no cyanide, if that's what you're wondering."

"I don't trust anyone at this point," I said.

"Join the club," Corbin muttered so low I barely heard him. "The rest of the team are working pretty hard, so I left them to it. They're digging into Paul's past... along with others. It's hard going, I think. They're trying to find connections other than the cases they worked together, and there are a bunch of those."

I sighed and stuffed my hands in my jeans pockets. Samson sat down at my feet. "I'm not surprised, and I'm sure they have their work cut out for them. Any update on Victor the stalker?"

Corbin shook his head. "Nope."

"All right. Well, then I guess we should sit down and have that chat with Mr. Owens," I said, inwardly deciding that Samson was going to join us in the interview room. I needed his expertise, especially now that I knew he could catch cyanide. That alone brought me comfort.

"You sure you're good for this?" Corbin asked. He sounded worried.

I nodded and chose not to give him a chance to protest. Instead, I walked quickly into the interview room and said, "Good morning, Mr. Owens. I'm Captain Gazzara."

He looked up, frowning, clutching his bag. "Morning."

"Thank you for coming in, Mr. Owens," Corbin said as he

took a seat at the opposite side of the table. I stood back against the wall facing the shop owner, Samson at my feet. He seemed to be oblivious to Owens, and I took that with some sense of relief.

"So, what do you have there?" Corbin asked, nodding at the bag.

"Well, it's something, that's for sure." Owens chuckled, setting the bag on the table. "But, before I go into what I found, I should probably explain myself."

"Okay," Corbin said, glancing round at me as Owens took the picture frame from the bag. It contained a photo of him standing outside the sandwich shop, a big smile on his face. He looked young, and there was a grand opening sign hanging above his head.

"I wasn't there yesterday when it happened," Owens said, crumpling up the bag and setting it on the table beside the wooden frame. "I'm working on opening a second location across town, and that's where I was."

I nodded, making a mental note of his alibi. "Okay, what does that have to do with your picture?" I tried not to sound impatient but had no patience for pleasantries that morning.

"Well." He let out a heavy, defeated sigh. "It all started a couple of months ago. Money started going missing from the register. I wasn't sure which employee was stealing from me, and I didn't want to install security cameras... that might make folks feel uncomfortable." He paused and looked up at me, then continued, "So, I got... this. It's a nanny cam, you know? They're used for watching the babysitter, or something along those lines. I don't have kids, so... well... you know! Anyway, I set the picture up on the wall opposite the counter and let it record."

I suddenly felt ten pounds lighter at the mention of a camera. "On the wall opposite the counter?" I repeated.

"Yes." He nodded. "I had it set up to catch whoever was at the cash register, but..." His voice trailed off as he fiddled with the digital photo frame. "You can see into the back room, too... when the door is open."

"Can we see the footage?" Corbin asked, eagerly leaning forward.

"Of course," Owens replied. "That's why I'm here, but I should warn you..." He paused, rubbed the back of his neck, looked up at me and squinted. "It's real strange. I don't know what to make of it, myself."

I didn't like the sound of that.

"Here." Brad pressed something on the back of the screen. The photo disappeared and it became a video screen. I knew such things existed, but it was the first time I'd seen one. I stepped forward, fascinated.

He tapped the screen and used his finger on the touch screen to navigate the footage. I leaned in closer as he chose the time stamp.

"This is where the weird stuff starts," he said, frowning. "I'm not real sure what to make of it—but someone knew everything about the sandwich shop."

It was quiet as the footage scrolled across the screen. I watched the two women as they chatted. The smaller one, Lily, disappeared into the back room, while the other started making the sandwiches.

"Seems routine, doesn't it?" Owens commented. "But wait."

Lily stuck her head back in, gesturing to something behind her. And I continued to watch as the two women engaged in some kind of conversation.

"Does it have sound?" I asked.

"Unfortunately, no," Owens said. "I have no idea what they're saying. Just watch."

I nodded as Lily continued to talk, animatedly. Clearly, she was frustrated about something. And then... they both disappeared into the back room, leaving the sandwiches unattended on the counter. And I leaned in even closer in anticipation of what I was sure was going to happen next.

Someone wearing a black hoodie slipped into the frame from screen right, walked right up to the sandwiches, paused for just a few seconds, took something we couldn't see from their pocket and, less than two seconds later, slipped out of the frame again, in the same direction from which they'd come; never once showing their face to the camera.

"Where is... whoever it is, going?" I demanded, looking at Owens.

"That's what I meant when I said they knew all about the shop. There's a supply closet at the far end of the counter with an exit on the west side of the shop. It leads to the dumpsters. We use it to take out the trash. They had to have come in, waited, and then you know... well... waited."

"What happened in the back?" Corbin asked. I knew what he was thinking. Something must have caused a diversion.

"Well, they said the fridge was going out, but turns out the settings had been messed with, and it had been turned off and was beeping. That's what it does when the power goes out."

"Or someone turned it off," I said, shaking my head. "Is there an entrance to the back?"

"Yeah, the shop has three entrances." Brad sighed. "Front, dumpster, and then the back room. I was planning on sealing that one up."

"Complex plan," I said. "Whoever that was knew exactly what they were doing. Either that or... they had an accomplice. I don't know if I buy it."

"Could've been an opportunist," Corbin reasoned. "I mean, if they'd been watching Gerrick, it would make sense that they saw their chance and took it."

"Risky though," I said thoughtfully.

"Not really," Owens chimed in. "That's the problem. Customers can't really see what's going on behind the bar.

Everyone is angled away from it, which wasn't intentional. It's just the way it was set up."

Corbin folded his arms. "But the two girls working could've seen them."

"Could've," Brad agreed. "But they were fighting that damn fridge. I looked at it, it's fine now."

"Hmm, wonder if that's just a coincidence. Have you managed to catch who's taking the cash out of the register?"

"Not yet," Brad grunted. "But I sure hope I do soon. They've taken a lot, and it's adding up quick."

"Why haven't you reported it?" I asked, studying his changing expression.

"Well, to be honest with you, I don't like to jump to conclusions. I don't want to upset my employees. If I can handle the manner internally, it makes things a hell of a lot easier. Plus, sometimes people just go through a rough time. They need a little pick me up, so they swipe from the drawer. It's not the first time it's happened." He seemed frustrated by my question, and it had me thinking…

Did he know more than he was letting on?

"What was your relationship like with Paul Gerrick?" Corbin asked, clearly on the same page as me. "Any tension between you two?"

"You gotta be kidding me." Owens threw his hands in the air. "I came here to help you people, and now you're trying to pin it on me, and just because I care about my employees? Come on. Paul was a good guy, a good customer. He was never a problem." He paused, meeting my gaze with an icy stare. "And I damn sure wouldn't try to poison a cop. That's just asking for trouble. I'm just trying to help, okay?"

"Okay," I said. "Good enough, Mr. Owens… I'll need a list of your employees, current and previous." I decided not to press him further. We knew he wasn't around the shop at the time it happened, but the sticky fingers mixed with what we'd just watched... I wasn't convinced there wasn't a connection.

"Yeah, and you can have this, too." Brad handed over the photo frame camera. "I think you need it more than I do right now. I don't know anyone who would want to hurt Paul, but you know, he was a lawyer. They seem to get on the wrong side of people all the time. Oh yeah, and there's a thirty-two gig SD card in the back of that thing."

It was at that moment the door opened and Chief Johnston stuck his head into the room.

"As soon as you wrap this up, Captain, I need you... everyone in the conference room. *Pronto.*"

Corbin and I exchanged glances. That couldn't be good.

Saturday, July 2, 9:30 a.m.

WE WRAPPED UP THE INTERVIEW WITH BRAD OWENS shortly after Chief Johnston's visit. I wasn't sure what to make of it, but he never corralled everyone in the conference room unless it was a dire situation.

Brad Owens' camera needed to be scrutinized and the image picked apart. That was a job for Jack, not me.

"I wonder what it's all about," Corbin muttered as he reached for the door.

"I guess we'll soon find out," I said, eyeing Samson as he trotted out into the hallway at my side. He'd been a little quiet this morning, and I wondered if maybe he wasn't happy about having to spend the weekend in the office. Though, on thinking about it, it was just another day to him.

My team was already sitting around the table, and Chief Johnston was standing in the corner with his arms folded across his chest. No one looked happy. There was what looked like a sheet of white paper and an envelope inside an evidence bag lying on the table.

"What's that?" I asked, breaking the silence in the room.

"Our perp is getting bolder," Anne Robar said as I sat down. She slid it across the table to me. "Maybe you can decipher what it means. It showed up in the mail this morning, no return address."

"Has it been checked for prints?" I asked as I picked it up.

"No. Not yet," Anne replied.

I looked at the paper through the glassine front. It was a type-written letter. It was short, and it didn't make a lot of sense.

You might think my behavior displays willful and wanton conduct, Captain, but you don't understand. Now you're standing in my way as one of them.

I dropped it back down on the table. "Interesting," I said thoughtfully.

"It's a threat," Ramirez said, shaking her head.

"And what's *wanton* mean?" Cooper asked, glancing around the table.

Jack's chair squeaked as he leaned back. "It means immoral behavior according to Google. It's a word that's used a lot in law."

"What's the exact definition?" I asked, still thinking the wording strange. I'd had plenty of threats on my life during my career, so I wasn't that surprised by it. But this perp's confidence was increasing, and that really was a problem.

Jack coughed, cleared his throat, and began typing on his laptop before answering. "*Deliberate and conscious indifference to the safety of others.*"

"You're going to have to lay low, Captain," Johnston finally spoke up. "This story hit the Saturday morning news, and we've already started getting phone calls and even a few leads. You need to disappear for a while."

"What leads?" I ignored the mention of me laying low. I could lay low and still work on the case. I'd done it before and, knowing how things typically go for me, it probably wouldn't be the last time I had to do it, either.

"Mostly sightings," Hawk answered. "And then of course, there's always the people who think a family member might be involved. We'll follow them up today."

"Any word on Victor?" I asked.

"No," Anne said, shaking her head. "He seems to have disappeared into thin air, which is suspicious in and of itself."

"I agree," Johnston said. "What'd you get from the sandwich shop owner?" He nodded to the picture frame camera, still in my hand.

"Video footage from yesterday," I answered and then handed it to Jack. "The picture's grainy, and it's difficult to make out any details. But someone walked right into the store, poisoned the sandwiches, and then walked back out again. It was done in less than thirty seconds and, so it seems to me, they somehow managed to turn off the fridge and create a diversion."

"I don't like the sound of that," Cooper muttered. "Whoever's doing this is getting bolder."

"And that can be helpful in catching them," Corbin said. "They'll mess up eventually."

"Hopefully before anyone else gets hurt," Johnston added, looking right at me. "It's only going to continue to escalate."

"Maybe with some analyzing, we can figure something out," Jack said, already tinkering with the camera. He removed the SD card and stuck it into his laptop. "These nanny cams have terrible quality video, but we should still be able to get an approximate height, weight, and maybe more."

"Anything will help." I glanced down at Samson, who had laid down at my feet, his eyes closed.

"I think from the verbiage of the note, we need to look harder into the two law firms," I said. "We haven't spoken in depth with Paul Gerrick's intern or his secretary. We need to do that ASAP."

"I say we bring them in," Corbin said. "It's a controlled environment."

"And secure," Anne added.

I took a deep breath, knowing what they were saying. "That's fine, but let's get them here sooner rather than later."

"You and I can handle that," Corbin told me. "And the rest of the team can work on following leads. I think it would be best if you stayed here at the station."

I wanted to argue with him, but at that moment, and with the chief watching, I didn't feel like putting up much of a fight. So I decided I could work out of the station, at least for the moment.

"Well, then. It appears we have a plan," Chief Johnston said. "Any information... I need it as soon as you have it. Now that the story's out, they're going to be hounding us."

"Great," Cooper muttered.

At least Thomas Drews will have someone else to bombard, I thought, feeling a little relief. We all rose to our feet, and I couldn't help but look down at the note on the table. The tone was borderline egotistical, but then, most killers had an air of superiority. Hah! I've yet to meet a humble killer.

Corbin and I spent the next hour tracking down Tanner Westling, Paul Gerrick's intern, and Nancy Bridges, his secretary. I was able to reach Nancy through her husband, who readily agreed to bring her in.

"Well, that's one of two," I told Samson as I poured myself a cup of coffee. "I just hope that someone can point us in the right direction."

Samson wrinkled his brow and lowered his head to rest between his paws. And, once again, I had the feeling he was totally bored by the whole affair. Either that, or maybe he somehow knew we were barking up the wrong tree. Barking? No pun intended. But was that even possible? Did he know something I didn't? I shook my head at myself and took a sip of the burning hot, bitter liquid.

Then I sat down again at my desk to think. *Judging by the note, it seems clear the perp has some sort of connection to, or interest in, the law.*

But that doesn't necessarily mean they're working at either of the two law firms... does it? I frowned. *But it seems like a solid theory...*

"But what would the motive be?" I asked Samson, turning in my chair to face him. He picked up his head and cocked it sideways. "Doesn't make a lot of sense unless there was bad blood, now does it? But wouldn't we have found that out? And what about the affair? The relationship between David Mitchell and Madison Lombardi wasn't null and void just because Paul Gerrick's been targeted."

Do I even count? Am I just a roadblock, in their way?

Samson laid his head down between his paws again and stared up at me, his brow wrinkled, his eyebrows twitching this way and that.

"What?" I said. "Is there something you want to say to me?" I laughed, patting a hand on my knee for him to come. He happily came, resting a paw on top of my hand. "You're a strange dog, Sammy. I wish I knew where you came from."

He rested his head on my thigh, and I sat my coffee down and used my free hand to scratch behind his ears.

I was still scratching behind his ears, lost in thought, when there was a knock on my office door and Corbin stepped inside.

"Tanner Westling is on his way. He sounded really shaken up."

"I don't blame him in the slightest. It would be unnerving to be any criminal defense lawyer at either of those firms right now. I'd probably be thinking about taking a vacation."

"No kidding." Corbin chuckled. "Glad to see you're in good spirits, given the circumstances and what with that letter. I don't like where this case seems to be heading."

"It's like a ticking time bomb, you mean?" I said lightly.

Samson picked his head up off my thigh, and I glanced down at him. He turned and ambled back to his bed.

"I hope we can get some kind of break," Corbin said, looking aimlessly around. "I mean, I really don't know what to think of it, Kate. We're trying to find a solid connection between the three dead lawyers, but no one's coming up with anything."

"Maybe that's because they don't *want* us to find a connection," I said thoughtfully.

"These people tend to stick together."

Saturday, July 2, 10:50 a.m.

Tanner Westling arrived first, and Corbin got him settled in the interview room while Samson and I watched from the control room.

"I think you should let Corbin handle this," Chief Johnston said from behind me.

I turned to face him, shaking my head in disagreement. "No one is going to get in here with cyanide. I'll take my chances. I'm not backing down just because someone thinks I'm in the way."

Before Johnston could protest, Corbin stuck his head in, nodded at me and said, "You ready?"

I didn't waste a second. "Yep." And I followed him with Samson at my side.

I took a moment to size up Tanner Westling. He was seated at the table, his hands clasped together on the tabletop. His blond hair was perfectly styled, swooped to the side. He *looked* the part: an eager law intern, dressed in slacks and a nice crisp white dress shirt. However, the dark circles under his icy almond eyes were telling.

This kid hasn't been sleeping, I thought.

"This is Captain Gazzara, my partner." Corbin gestured toward me as he took a seat facing him. Once again, I chose to stand a few feet back facing Westling.

"Why the dog?" Tanner asked wearily, his voice strained and airy. "Is he a drug dog or something?"

"Would that be a problem?" I asked.

"N… no. Of course not. I don't do drugs. I don't—"

"Relax," Corbin cut him off, his voice calm. "You're here because we need information; nothing more."

"Right… right." Westling's stubby nose crinkled as he spoke. I watched him closely. From his obvious discomfort, it was my guess that he knew more than most. Then again, it could have been the grief from losing his mentor.

"Why don't you start by telling us where you were yesterday lunchtime between eleven and noon," Corbin began. "You weren't in the office when I got there, and you've not been interviewed before."

"That's correct." Tanner swallowed hard, his pronounced Adam's apple bobbing. "I was in court that morning. Nate invited me. Paul wanted me to get courtroom experience, so he let me go."

"What time did you finish up there?" I asked as Samson sat down on my foot.

"It was late," he replied. "I didn't go back to the office, actually. I didn't find out what happened to Paul until I saw the email from Nancy, Paul's secretary. Nate and I went out for drinks. I didn't leave the courtroom until five, I think."

"And Nate is…" Corbin's voice trailed off.

"Nate Shaw," Westling said. "He's an intern with Lewis, Scone and Petty. We were at school together. He's like, a friend."

"So he worked with David Mitchell and Madison Lombardi, correct?"

"Yeah, he did. Him and uh… Oh… I can't remember the other

one's name. I didn't go to school with her. She's from out of state... Uh... Barbra something? I don't know." His cheeks reddened. "Sorry, I thought I came prepared, but I should've written more of this down."

"Take a few deep breaths," I said. "You're fine. Was Barbra at the trial?"

"No, no. No one from that office was there except Nate. We just wanted to sit in on the case. It's a civil trial, actually."

"How long have you been an intern for Paul?" Corbin asked.

"Oh, not long. I started on January ninth, so... Uh, seven months? Something like that."

"Did you ever see Paul with David Mitchell or Madison Lombardi?" I asked.

Westling didn't answer immediately. He looked down at the table. It was telling. "Tanner?" I said.

He shifted in his seat before raking his fingers through his hair, disheveling it. "Yeah... Well... No, not exactly. I don't know."

"It sounds to me like you *do* know something," I said. "Why don't you just tell us what you know?"

Tanner let out a long, ragged breath. "Can I have some water or something?"

Corbin nodded. "I'll go grab some water for you." He pushed back from the table, slipping past me and giving me a knowing look. The kid had something to say—something on his mind— and it was important.

Or, at least, *Tanner* thought it was.

As Corbin left the room, I stood there, watching the young man breathing slowly, taking controlled breaths. He was obviously nervous, and his face had lost some of its color.

"Are you okay?" I asked.

He nodded. "I just need some water."

I didn't get another word in before Corbin reappeared, a paper cup in his hand. He handed it to Tanner, who swooped it up and downed it like he'd just spent a month in the desert.

Corbin's expression remained unchanged as Tanner wiped his mouth with his sleeve.

"Okay," Tanner said, looking up at me. "Here's the thing. I don't *know* a lot, but I know that something was off. I knew that Paul was planning to meet with the police to discuss a case that he worked on with Lombardi and Mitchell."

Now we're getting somewhere...

"He was really secretive about it though, and when I asked him, he told me it was better if I didn't know the details. After he... well... you know." Tanner paused, grief flashing across his face. "After that, I went to the office, and... I snooped."

"You snooped?" Corbin echoed, his tone urging him to continue.

Tanner nodded. "I had this gut feeling, you know, that the case must've been important. But that's the weird part... Paul has a really efficient filing system, and it's easy to locate anything you're looking for..."

He trailed off, and I had a sinking feeling I knew where it was going.

"I dug through all of his files, and there was *nothing* there that included the three of them. It was like they'd never worked together at all. I even went as far as to go through his desk, his bag, all of it. I *know* he worked on a case with them, and I think maybe it's connected. I was planning on coming in on Monday after I put in my resignation."

"Resignation?" I said out of surprise. "Why are you resigning?"

He glared at me. "Would you want to work with a bunch of people that keep getting murdered? I don't want to die before I even reach thirty."

Fair enough, I thought.

"So the files are missing?" Corbin said.

"Yeah, they're missing." Tanner's tone eased a little. "But I didn't do any more looking after that. I decided it might be best to cut my losses and get out of there. And I didn't want anyone to catch me searching the files, either. I thought it could make me a target, too."

"Do you recall anything strange happening to Paul prior to yesterday?" I asked. "Did he mention being followed? Things being out of place?"

"No," Westling answered. "He was kind of antsy and worried, but tight-lipped. He wasn't the kind of person who would run his mouth, you know? I really liked working for him..." His voice dropped off and his expression fell. "Sorry." He wiped his eyes.

"It's okay." Corbin reached out and patted his shoulder. "You're doing fine."

Westling sniffed hard and then looked up at us, his eyes wide. "I haven't worked for Paul long enough to know much about the cases, but Nancy, his secretary, has been working for him for *years*. She'd know about the cases, I think. Well, maybe."

I nodded and said, "We'll need to speak with her, too."

"I hope that you find who did this." Tanner crumpled up the paper cup. "Paul didn't deserve to die like that. He was a good man, and... Why would someone want to kill him? I mean, he got threats *all* the time from all kinds of people."

"Really?" I wrinkled my brow. "Any that you can recall, particularly?"

He shook his head. "No, he just ignored them. Par for the course, so he said. Most were just generic, you know? Like... *'I'm going to sue you.'* You know, that kind of thing."

I looked at Corbin and said, "Do we have a copy of the letter handy?"

"I think so," Corbin said, already rising to his feet. "I'll go get it."

He was gone but a few minutes. "Here, take a look at this," he said, and handed the copy to Westling. "Does this look familiar?"

Westling took the note from him and studied it for a second or two, then said, "I... No... This is... This is weird." He looked up at us. "I get that it's a threat, but I've never seen someone write something like this. It almost doesn't make sense."

"Why not?"

"It's like the 'wanton and willful conduct' is stuck in there forcefully. It's not natural. It's like they wanted to sound smart. Those are terms a lawyer would use."

"So, in your opinion, it doesn't fit?" I questioned.

"Uh, I mean, it does, but who uses that kind of wording in a threat? It's silly. If they're trying to sound smart, they're not doing a great job of it. To a lawyer, it sounds ridiculous."

"Thank you, Tanner," Corbin said, glancing at me. "Anything else?"

Tanner hesitated but shook his head. "I can't think of anything… But for the record, I'm going home to Nashville for a while. I can't… I just… I want to get away from here for a while."

"Noted," Corbin said, handing him his card. "And thank you, Tanner. You've been very helpful. If you think of anything else, please give us a call."

I watched as the young man rose to his feet. He appeared a little more at ease, having lifted the burden he'd been carrying. While the information he'd provided was helpful, it didn't move the case forward, but it at least gave me the feeling we were heading in the right direction… maybe.

30

Saturday, July 2, 12:20 p.m.

I WAS STARVING WHEN NANCY BRIDGES TOOK HER SEAT IN THE interview room. I thought about postponing the interview for thirty minutes while I sent someone across the road to get me something to eat, but I didn't. I wanted to get the interview checked off the list. Time was ticking by, and I was sure the answers we needed were at our fingertips. They had to be—well, at least something that would point us in the right direction.

We took up the same positions as we had for the previous interview, and Samson, again disinterested in the person sitting at the table, parked his rear on my foot.

Nancy Bridges, tissue in hand, eyes on Corbin, seemed just as ill at ease as was Tanner Westling.

"You were Paul Gerrick's secretary?" Corbin said, pretending to look through his notes. Then he looked up at her.

"Yes, that's right," she answered with a sniff.

"And you worked for him for a long time," Corbin said. It was more a statement than a question.

"Nearly fifteen years," the short, stubby woman replied. Her gray hair was cut pixie-style, and her makeup was nearly as bright as the turquoise blouse she was wearing. "I've known him for most of his professional career."

"And where were you between eleven and twelve yesterday morning?" Corbin asked.

"In the office, of course," she answered. "I always bring my own lunch. The sandwiches at Brad's shop are just too expensive. We've been saving money to visit our grandchildren in New Mexico."

Corbin nodded and again consulted his notes. "How was Paul that morning? Did he say anything that indicated he was worried about… anything?"

"I already talked to one of you detectives about the day," she said, squinting at him. "I didn't see or hear anything out of the ordinary. I did think he seemed a little nervous, a little… distant, I suppose, but that's the way he was, sometimes."

"Such as?" I asked.

"When he had a big case coming up, hiring new interns, you know, just the normal kinds of things lawyers have to deal with. He handled stress well, though. He never took it out on his staff. Though sometimes he'd go for a walk or call his wife."

"Had he done anything like that lately?" Corbin asked.

"No, he hadn't. Though I do know he had something important he wanted to discuss with you, Captain." She looked up at me, her face hardening. "And maybe had you come to the office instead of meeting him at Brad's, he'd still be alive."

I didn't think there was any truth to that statement. I was by then pretty certain that Paul Gerrick was a target and would have been killed no matter what, though I also believed I, as lead investigator, was also a target.

So I ignored the statement and said, "Who knew he was planning to meet me, and when and where?"

"Just me, I think," she replied, without having to think about it. "Well, and maybe Tanner. He knew Paul's schedule, but that boy is as harmless as a fly. He doesn't have the gumption it takes to be a good lawyer, either. I think he's just trying to live up to his daddy's reputation. He's a judge, you know."

"I see," Corbin said. "And can you think of anyone that might have had a grudge against Paul? Someone who might have wanted to harm him?"

"Plenty of folks," she scoffed. "Let's be honest here, shall we? Most people hate attorneys. Paul received a lot of threats over the years; all of them empty."

I nodded but couldn't shake the fact that I hadn't heard similar for Lombardi and Mitchell. Neither of them had seemed to have a history of threats... Or was it that maybe we just hadn't been told of any? Everyone at Lewis, Scone and Petty was much tighter-lipped than the people at Tooly and Watts. I'd thought it was because they were, well, lawyers, but now, I was beginning to wonder if there was more to it.

"No recent threats, though," Nancy continued. "At least I can't think of any. But you should know that Paul was an honest attorney. He never crossed the line. He wasn't like those other two." Her body stiffened. "There was something badly off about those two. I know they were romantically involved, but that's only the tip of the iceberg, as they say. I think they were corrupt, both of them."

"What makes you say that?" I asked. No one else had made that kind of an accusation.

"Well, for starters, Madison was married to a mob boss. I think that says something in and of itself. I heard he'd killed nearly twenty men in New York City."

I frowned. I was starting to question this woman's veracity. Even Samson tipped his head sideways at that one.

"And I'm telling you, Mitchell was no better. He would do whatever it took to break a witness. It was... disturbing. Paul was never more stressed than when he worked a case with those two."

"When was the last time they worked together?" Corbin beat me to the question.

"Oh, let's see…" Nancy sighed. "It's been years. He wasn't a fan of those two, as I told you, especially because of their affair. He said it made him look bad. Paul didn't want to look bad. I didn't want that for him, either. He was an upstanding man and lawyer."

And Lombardi killed twenty men in New York.

If she's stretching that truth about Lombardi, I thought, *maybe she's stretching the truth about Paul Gerrick, too.* It was never a good thing when a witness was this hostile. It was hard to tell when they were telling the truth and when they weren't.

"Do you remember any of their cases… any in particular?"

"No," she said flatly. "It's not like they talk to me about them, either. I'm just the woman who answers the phone and coordinates the Christmas party. Paul kept me out of the loop. And I think it's better that way, too."

"I see," Corbin said, sounding a little defeated. "You were his secretary, so would you happen to know where we could obtain his records? I'm… We'd like to see the ones he worked with Lombardi and Mitchell."

She pressed her lips tightly together, then relaxed a little and said, "In his office. That's where he kept everything. He was very careful about his files. They stayed locked away, and once the case was over, he never removed them. He was a stickler. He never wanted to lose anything of importance. And, I might tell you, you'd need a warrant; lawyer-client privilege."

Corbin nodded. "We've heard that the case files the three of them worked together are missing. Would you know anything about that?"

But Nancy shook her head. "No, I wouldn't, and I doubt very much that they are missing. He would never have removed them from his office. Even if he intended to share them with you, he would've made a copy. He was like that. I don't think you understand how meticulous he was. He wouldn't have moved those files."

Then we need to go look for them ourselves, I thought, *and she's right—we'll need a warrant.*

"I'm sorry I'm not being more help," Nancy said with a sniff. "I just want whoever did this to him to be caught, and soon. Those other two might've had this coming, but not Paul; he never did a damn thing wrong."

"Thank you for your time," Corbin said, sliding the card across the table. "We appreciate your time. If you think of anything, let us know."

"Very well," she muttered, pushing back from the table. "As I said, I wish I could have been more help."

She rose to her feet with an effort and a huff, giving both of us a hardened stare as she turned and walked toward the door. Corbin jumped to his feet to escort her out, and I let them go. I needed a minute to mull over everything we had learned that morning.

I led Samson to my office and dropped down in my seat behind my desk.

I stared up at the clock. It was almost one-fifteen. I shook my head and blew air out through my lips, making a noise like a horse.

Samson looked at me, his mouth open, tongue lolling out.

"I don't even know what to think about that last interview, Sammy." I sighed. "And my stomach thinks my throat's been cut."

I looked at him. He looked at me. "It seems like Nancy had a lot of opinions, most of them negative, even hostile and, based on what we know, I think she has Tony Lombardi pinned all wrong."

Samson tilted his head and then shook himself violently, his feet skittering around on the floor. Then he headed for his water bowl.

"You're not a great listener today," I joked, swiveling my chair back to the computer. I swept my mouse across the pad and checked my email; *nothing!* I thought.

I rocked my chair back and forth, my hands linked together behind my neck, while staring up at what looked like a small spider.

That lasted for just a couple of minutes until Corbin walked in and sat down.

"What did you think about Nancy?" he asked.

"I think she's a typical old gossip," I said, letting my chair fall forward and clasping my hands together on my desk. "In fact, I'm not sure we can trust anything she said."

"She didn't really give us much, did she?" Corbin said.

"Nope," I replied. "However, I do think we should carry out a search of Paul's office. We need to find those files."

"I agree," Corbin said. "Anne's ordered lunch for all of us, by the way. I think we need to have a meeting this afternoon and see where everyone's at. Maybe then we can—"

"I think we need to do Paul's office first," I said, cutting him off. "Or at least see if we can get a warrant... I'd better call Henry."

Corbin frowned. "I don't think you should go with us, Kate. I think you should let me take the rest of the team and go through the place."

I sighed, not surprised by his words. "Samson will be there."

"But these attacks—with the exception of the one on you and Gerrick—they came out of nowhere. You'd have no warning. I don't think it's a good idea."

"You all could be putting yourself in jeopardy," I reasoned.

"The letter was directed at you."

I pursed my lips. "I was the one meeting with Gerrick. I'm sure that's the only reason I was targeted."

He nodded but didn't change his stance. "The chief will never go for it, and I'd support him. Sorry, Kate. I think you should go home and lay low for a while."

"It's safer to be here," I snapped back at him. "I'm not running out right when we're on the brink of solving this."

"I know how you feel," he said grudgingly. "You're one of the best detectives here. And if anyone's going to solve this thing, it'll be you."

"No, not just me," I corrected him. "We're a team. I can't do what I do without you and…" I smiled, glancing over at Samson. "…him, too."

Saturday, July 2, 5:15 p.m.

IT WAS ALMOST TWO WHEN I CALLED JUDGE HENRY STRANGE AND explained the situation. He wasn't happy about issuing a warrant to search an attorney's office but, considering the dire situation, he issued a limited warrant for Gerrick's office only and files pertaining to the three lawyers working in concert, and only under the supervision of one of the partners. The judge's chambers were in the Federal building conveniently only minutes away from the offices of Tooly and Watts.

The search went quickly—too quickly, in my opinion—and at just after five that afternoon we all gathered together in the conference room.

"Well…" Corbin said, looking around the table, "we searched Paul Gerrick's office and came up with nothing. The files are indeed missing."

Chief Johnston, sitting at the head of the conference table, didn't look happy.

"And Victor, the stalker," Anne said, "was located this morning. He's in Tucson, Arizona, and has been for more than a month. He has alibis for all three killings, so we can cross him off the list."

"You sure about those alibis?" Ramirez asked. "You know how easy they are to fabricate."

"For now," Anne said with a shrug, "we have to take them at face value. The Tucson PD has promised to check them out..." Again, she shrugged.

"Okay, and do we have the list of the sandwich shop employees yet?" I asked.

"He sent it over this morning," Ramirez said, "and we're working on it, but so far there doesn't appear to be any connections to anyone at either of the two law firms. We're still digging, but it doesn't look promising."

"But the missing files." Cooper leaned back against his chair. "That *is* a lead. It's the best one we've got. All the other leads we followed up on today were fruitless. A lot pointed to Tony Lombardi, but his alibi for the sandwich shop has already been confirmed. He was at a meeting with a client."

"He wouldn't necessarily have to get his own hands dirty," Corbin pointed out. "I think it's been said many times, but he could have had all three killings arranged and be entirely hands-off."

Cooper shook his head. "We've gone through him two times over, searched his house and office. There's nothing there. If there was, I think we would've found it by now. I don't think he's involved. Maybe he's not the cleanest guy in the neighborhood, and I certainly wouldn't trust him myself, but he just doesn't fit this crime."

"Why not?" Corbin snapped.

I was surprised at his sharp tone. It wasn't like him, and, given that Tony Lombardi had been a total bust—my opinion—I thought Cooper was right.

"Cooper's right," I said. "I don't think it's worth digging any further into Lombardi. He had no connections to Paul Gerrick that we know of. I think any further action on that front would be a waste of our time and resources."

"Agreed," Chief Johnston said. "Leave Lombardi alone. I don't think he'd talk to us, anyway. And, quite frankly, I don't blame him."

"Well, I'm not writing him off yet," Corbin muttered, though mostly under his breath.

"I think whoever the killer is took the files," Ramirez said, neatly changing the subject. "But I don't know how they got into the office. The security seems pretty solid."

"Cameras?" Hawk asked.

"No, of course not," Ramirez answered. "There are no cameras in attorney's offices. You should know that, Hawk."

He grinned at her and said, with a tilt of his head, "Just asking, Tracy. No need to get in a tizzy."

"I'm not—" Ramirez cut herself off. Hawk continued to grin at her.

"Jack," I said. "Were you able to pull any details from the camera footage from the sandwich shop?"

"The footage isn't great, but we already knew that. I was able to figure the height, to within an inch either way. Whoever it is stands around five-seven, slim build, weight around one-sixty."

"So, we're looking for a *small* man…" Anne said thoughtfully, "or an average-size woman?"

"Couldn't tell, so my guess would be… yes, the perp could be male or female," Jack said. "And they know how to cover up their appearance."

"You think they knew the camera was there?" Hawk asked.

Jack answered with a shrug. "It would be a stretch… I think. They never looked at the camera. They kept their head down, and they would, wouldn't they?"

"You would have thought someone in that shop would have noticed something," Ramirez said, "them being covered up and stooped low like that. *I*… It would have caught my attention."

"Not the way the seating is arranged," I said. "I was there, remember? And I didn't notice them…" I shook my head as I trailed off.

"You can't beat yourself up for that," Anne said. "It's not like you knew they were coming, and no one in the restaurant spotted them, not even the staff."

"Okay," Chief Johnston said. "I don't want to sit around all evening and shoot theories back and forth. We have one solid lead: the missing files. I have no update for the media, and I'm not going to give them one. Tomorrow is Sunday, so go home and rest up. We'll reconvene Monday afternoon." He turned to me. "I'm scheduling security for your house. I don't think we have a grip on this thing yet and I don't want anything happening to anyone, including you. You keep your weapon handy; you hear?"

I blew air out through my lips and shook my head. I wasn't happy, but I looked at him and nodded.

"I'll keep working on the video," Jack said. "There are still a few tricks I can try to nail the build of this… person a little bit better. I want to get it as precise as possible." Jack scratched his chin. "That's all I know to do right now. They don't keep the case files online."

"I'm still working through the employee list that Brad Owens sent over," Anne said. "I'll continue to make my way through it. It's longer than I expected, but then again, turnover rates are high for part-time restaurant employees. I haven't found any connections or anything that stands out thus far, but I still have a way to go."

"It seems to me it all rides on the case files," Cooper said, "so I think we should all do some digging into what we can find online about the three of them working together. For all we know, there could've been something high profile enough for the media to cover it."

"It's worth a shot," Chief Johnston said. "I'll see you all on

Monday. And, Kate, you lay low. Don't go out. I'll have a cruiser outside your house twenty-four-seven."

I nodded, though I would have to see where the weekend took me. While I was leery of who might be out there, I had no intention of living in fear. Besides, I had Samson, and his senses were better than any uniformed officer. I glanced down at my canine partner, quietly sitting beside me. *You'll keep me safe, won't you, Sammy?*

He looked up at me, expectantly. I smiled at him.

"That it then?" I asked. "Nothing to say, anyone? Very well then..."

"Good night, everyone," Johnston said, then turned to me. "Go home, Kate, and stay there. Understood?"

I nodded, not meeting his eyes, and everyone stood and began to file out of the room.

I stopped by my office to gather the rest of my things. I was hungry again, having skipped over the food Anne had ordered in. I took one last look around my office, double-checked my email one last time and grabbed Samson's leash.

And wouldn't you know it? Just as I was about to leave, my phone began to ring. I took it from my pocket, looked at the screen and was relieved and a little intrigued to see Harry Starke's name. I tapped the answer button and put it to my ear.

"Calling me on the weekend, huh?"

"Well, I saw the piece about the cyanide poisonings on the news, and I was surprised they didn't name you specifically. I might've had to record it then."

"Ha ha," I said, shaking my head as I led Samson out into the parking lot. "It generated a lot of calls but no credible leads."

"Well, I'm sure they'll run it again tonight," he said.

I eyed the blue and white patrol unit, parked behind my car. "Johnston's tagged me with round-the-clock security, and I'm confined to quarters." I waved at the officer; he waved back.

"Geez, he must feel strongly about the situation then."

"I think it's gotten everyone off-kilter," I replied. "I suppose it's difficult to fight what you can't see... Though Samson *did* sniff it out."

"That's one incredible dog," Harry remarked. "Why don't we chat this over? I'll provide security for you tonight. I could use something to do. We're a little slow, and Amanda took Jade to her parents for the weekend. You know, bonding with her grandparents and all that. She's been curious about this case, too. So, maybe I ought to have something to tell her when she gets back."

"Fair enough," I said. "But I'll let you call Johnston."

Harry laughed. "As usual, you're trying to push the heat off onto me, Kate."

"Always," I joked as I opened the rear door. I let Samson jump in and then buckled him up, noticing just how humid the car was inside. Hurriedly, I closed the door, climbed in myself, and started the engine. "I'll see you later then, Harry."

I hung up as the blast of air from the vents hit my face. It was humid, hot, and miserable, as if you were breathing in a gulp of warm water. I've never been a fan of mid-summer, but then again, I guess it's better than snow-covered roads and waiting for the heater to get warm.

"How do you feel about all this?" I asked Samson, meeting his gaze in the rearview mirror.

He tilted his head, his ears perked forward, his tongue lolling out.

"I take it you're just as frustrated as I am then," I said and laughed as I navigated toward home, ready to chill out and eat something. I was feeling a little lightheaded and I knew it was because I hadn't eaten since breakfast. I would have to get over what happened at the restaurant, and I knew I would, sooner or later.

The traffic was light, and I made the drive home in near record time. The patrol car was on my tail all the way. But, as I turned into my subdivision, I noticed that he continued onward.

Harry must've made the call, then. I smiled, wondering what Johnston must have thought about that. He and Harry didn't get along, but I knew he trusted Harry with his life. In fact, Harry was the one he turned to when his daughter went missing, and he had, on occasion, allowed me to bring him in on a case as a consultant, unpaid, of course.

I pulled into the garage, sucking in a long, tired breath as the door closed behind me.

"I'm sure Harry will be here soon," I said to Samson as I turned the car off and helped him out. I dabbed the sweat from my brow. "I don't know about you, but ten minutes out in this heat, and I might as well have taken a shower in my own sweat."

Samson seemed to make a face at that, and I laughed, leading him into the house. I knew that Harry would want to talk about the case, but I was sure hoping for a break from it.

32

Saturday, July 2, 6:45 p.m.

I HAD JUST GOTTEN SAMSON SETTLED AND FED WHEN MY DOORBELL chimed. Samson jumped up and headed straight for the door, his tail wagging. I followed him to the front door and opened it to see my old friend standing on the doorstep.

"It's a scorcher," he grumbled, shaking his head. "I can't blame Amanda one bit for taking off to someplace cooler."

"Me neither." I chuckled, stepping to one side to let him in. "I'm thinking maybe when this case is done, I'll take a vacation. I'm way overdue."

"Good idea," Harry said as he stood in the entryway as I closed and locked the door behind us. "TJ is posted in the car, in case you were wondering. I'm not the only one who wants to keep you safe. I'm not here just for the juicy details. Hey, Sammy," he said as he bent down and scratched Samson behind his ears.

"Right." I laughed, leading the way to the kitchen. "Have you eaten?"

"No, I haven't." He held up a paper bag. "But I brought some food, and don't worry. It's Maria's homemade enchiladas. No cyanide. Guaranteed!"

"Oh… m'God, thank you," I said. "I'm so hungry I'm starting to get hangry, and we don't want that."

I got out a couple of plates, split the food in two, and then heated it up in the microwave. I opted for water, and Harry grabbed a beer before we made our way to the kitchen table.

"So," Harry began as he slid onto his seat. "Give me the rundown on what you have so far."

"Well," I said, taking a bite of the food. The warm meat, cheese, and tortilla melted in my mouth causing me pause. "Let me enjoy this for a few minutes and then I'll tell you."

Harry laughed. "Sounds reasonable, I guess."

"I haven't eaten anything since breakfast this morning. I dunno, Harry. Something about takeout… I can't seem to face it right now."

"Can't imagine why," he quipped. That had always been one of the best things about Harry. He never overreacted or stressed when he knew my life was in danger, and he knew how to make light of it. As someone who had experienced it even more times than I had, he knew we had to cope… somehow. He taught me a long time ago not to worry about the things we can't change. And he's right; worrying never does anyone any good.

After I finished my food, leaving some scraps for Samson, I briefed him on what we had so far, which as I recall, didn't seem like much. He listened while I talked about the missing files and Nancy Bridges.

"I wouldn't take anything she said too seriously," he remarked as I finished. "The woman seems unreliable—or maybe she just really believes it. Who knows."

"Maybe," I replied, "but you know how the gossips are. Most of what little information they have is bad."

"But the files are missing," he said.

"And I'm certain the answer is in them," I muttered, more to myself than to him.

"I agree," he said. "You said they worked on more than one case, right?" Harry took a sip of his beer.

I nodded. "I'm guessing they took them all because they don't want to pinpoint *which* case is missing."

"Or maybe," Harry paused. "Maybe they took them all because they weren't sure which one they were supposed to grab."

"Could go either way," I admitted, leaning back against the kitchen chair. Samson was lying quietly on the couch in the living room, and as I watched the sun set, I couldn't help but feel the draw to the great outside. "How about you?" I asked. "How have your investigations been going?"

"Oh, you know." He laughed. "They're going. Always going. We're a little slow right now, but I'm enjoying it. I almost went with Amanda and Jade. Can you believe how big she is now?"

I nodded, recalling the pictures Amanda had sent me. "She's really growing. Looks just like her mother."

"No kidding. She's a smart kid, too. She's already started reading. Can you believe that? She hasn't even started school yet."

"Some kids pick it up quickly," I said.

"She's one of them, I suppose." Harry stabbed his fork into the last bite on his plate and stuck it in his mouth. I looked out the front window, my mind swirling around in circles. While Harry had family and personal matters to consume him when he wasn't at work, I didn't have much of anything. Just Samson. I frowned.

"I'd really like to go for a run this evening," I said bleakly.

"Well, give me an hour to digest dinner and we can go on one," he replied. "I could use the exercise myself. I haven't pounded the pavement in a while."

"That's surprising," I said. "Not at all like you."

"Amanda got us *gym* memberships." Harry grimaced but then smiled. "And the funny thing is, we're actually putting them to good use. There's even childcare. Jade has a blast in the play area."

I smiled. "It's a family affair."

"Just like that." Harry winked at me, smiling.

I pushed back from the table, gathered up my plate and Harry's, took them to the sink, rinsed them off, and then stuck them in the dishwasher.

We still had some time to kill before going for a run, though I doubted Harry would be up to my pace given the fact he'd just downed a beer. Back in the day, when we were twenty years younger, downing a beer and then going for a run didn't seem like much at all; these days, though... I'll pass.

"You know," Harry began as he followed me into the living room. "I did a little research on that fella you mentioned; you know, Thomas Drews."

"Oh yeah?" I raised a brow as I dropped down beside Samson. "He was a cop, a good one, got a lot of accolades, so I saw. Then he threw it all away for journalism."

"Tell me how you feel without telling me how you feel," Harry said with a chuckle.

I shook my head and leaned back on the couch, my arms stretched out along the back. "People like him can be helpful, but they can also be a real pain in the ass."

"Yeah, maybe so," Harry said, "but have you listened to the man's podcast?"

I rolled my eyes. "No. Not interested in amateur work. I've heard enough from those online sleuths. They think they know everything, theorizing and pointing the finger at people who've done nothing wrong. It's all just garbage."

"Once again, another strong opinion." Harry leaned back in his chair and steepled his fingers. "But I'm going to go out on a limb here. I usually would agree with you—and I do for most of those podcasts—but his is good, Kate. It really is. He seems to know what he's doing. He works on cases that haven't been solved. And he's helped solve several of them."

I pressed my lips together, still unimpressed. "The media

helps solve cases all the time, but I still don't find myself enamored with them, any of them, and neither were you when you were a cop, as I recall; one in particular."

He laughed. "Amanda, you mean. To quote a cliché, 'but she's different.' No, I do agree with you. Most of them are like ravening wolves. I'm just saying that the guy isn't a lunatic. I think maybe you should hear him out. I'm not saying go on the show with him or anything like that, but who knows? Maybe he has some pertinent information."

"Or maybe he's just sticking his nose into the case to gain followers, or whatever the hell these people do. If he had pertinent information, he could come to the station and sit down with anyone on the team; not just me. And, bearing in mind his history, he knows how things work."

"You're not wrong," Harry mused. "But I still think you're letting your prejudice prevent you from potentially exploring a lead. It could be what you need to—"

"Again, Harry?" I cut him off. "If he had something to say, he could've come down to the station."

"Yeah, yeah," Harry waved me off. "I get it. You're not changing on that."

"But those missing case files…" I thought about them again, Thomas Drews fading away into the dark in the corners of my mind. "You think maybe you could lend a hand? There's got to be some way to find the cases they worked on without the actual files."

"I'm sure there is," Harry said. "And I've already accepted the offer to help out. You know Chief Johnston is always happy to have me on board."

I narrowed my eyes at him. "When did you talk to him about helping?"

"Oh, earlier today. As it turns out, he's worried about your safety, and in that, he's worried that you'll just keep working yourself to death, literally. He wants someone to keep an eye on you."

"Are you serious?" I scoffed. "Of course, he does. I'm just a little put out he didn't bother to mention you'd be joining us sooner. You could've come in early today when we were discussing the case. Eh, whatever. Welcome aboard, Harry."

"Thanks, Kate. I didn't join you earlier because I had some things I had to get done in order to clear my schedule for you, but I'll be with you from here on out. We're going to get to the bottom of it. I'd really like to take a look at that footage you have of the perp."

"Jack is in the middle of analyzing and enhancing it," I said. "Apparently, the quality is pretty crappy."

"I find the sandwich shop to be of particular interest," he said. "And the notion about the fridge. My guess is someone tampered with it."

"I agree. It's too much of a coincidence, that the thing turned itself off at just the opportune moment." I paused, breathed deeply, then looked at him and said, "I need to change into my running gear... I guess. I could run in jeans, but I don't like that."

"I hear you." He laughed. "I'll go grab my change of clothes from the car. Hopefully, by then, we'll be up to a quick run."

I nodded and then turned to Samson. "You want to go for a run, Sammy?"

Apparently, he did, because he jumped to his feet and ran to the door.

33

Saturday, July 2, 7:55 p.m.

I GOT CHANGED, GRABBED SAMSON'S LEASH, AND HARRY AND I
took off along the street at a steady clip. It was still humid,
though it was easing up a little. I gave TJ a wave as we passed by,
and he returned it.

"How's he doing?" I asked Harry as we trotted along.

"Terrific. The whole team is. Life is good, Kate. Really good."

I laughed. "Well, I'd say the same for myself, but I have to
admit, things right now could be a lot better."

He chuckled and, after a moment, said, "How far are we
going? I'm thinking the beer wasn't a good idea."

"If we make it to the light pole at the end of the road, then it'll
be a little over a mile-and-a-half back to the house."

"Ah, that's not so bad. I can handle that."

I nodded, though I felt I could go twice as far.

I focused on the rhythm and sound of our shoes slapping the
pavement, and our steady breathing. It was... relaxing, soothing,
even, which was exactly what I needed.

The modest suburban homes were already lit up. Our pace

quickened as we got closer to the light pole, and before I knew it, we were almost there. It was, by then, getting on for nine o'clock and the sky was already darkening.

We were maybe twenty yards from the turn when Samson suddenly put on his brakes.

"Whoa!" I called out and jerked so hard that I nearly went down to my knees. "What the heck, Samson?"

Harry stopped a few feet ahead and as he turned to us, Samson's hackles rose, and he let out a low growl. The hair on the back of my neck stood on end as I looked around, not seeing anything.

"What's wrong, boy?" Harry asked, wiping the sweat from his brow.

Samson was laser-focused on the woods just beyond the light pole, and suddenly, he surged forward, dragging me with him. The growl morphed into angry barking that resounded throughout the entire neighborhood. I was now hanging onto the leash with both hands, trying to hold him back as he continued to slowly drag me toward the pole. It was almost more than I could do to hang onto the raging, one-sixteen-pound tractor of a dog.

"Samson, *stop!*" I yelled, digging my heels in and finally bringing him to a stop. "What is it, boy?" I said as I glanced down at him. My attention was diverted to him for no more than a couple of seconds.

"Kate!" Harry yelled, now some ten yards or so behind me. "Look out!"

I looked up and saw a hooded figure wearing a ski mask running toward me with what looked like a small, open glass jar in hand.

Oh no. No, no!

I stumbled backward, dragging Samson with me. He was still fighting to get loose, now six or seven feet in front of me, growling and barking and struggling on the end of the leash.

Chapter 33

The figure came to a stop some ten feet in front of Samson, staring at him, then at me, then at Samson again, then at...

Harry stepped forward, his CZ75 in his hands pointed at the masked figure.

"Get your hands up," he snapped. "You're under arrest."

The figure slowly shook their hooded head, holding out the container, and I wondered what would happen if they threw it.

"Set it down on the pavement," Harry shouted. "Do it slowly. Try to throw it, and I'll shoot you dead."

The figure stood there for a moment. It was impossible to even guess what might be going on in their head; all I could see were the eyes, glittering in the light of a street lamp. The person was dressed from head to toe in black, shorter than me, and slim, almost... *petite.*

And then, the person spun around and took off running into the woods beyond the pole.

Samson lunged forward. I dug my heels in and held him back. Whoever it was still had that open container in hand, and I didn't want anything to happen to him.

Harry charged past me into the woods. Samson and I after him. Sammy pulling so hard I had a job staying on my feet.

Whoever it was, they were quick and had an escape route already planned out. Wanting a little peace and quiet, I'd left my cell phone at home and was mentally kicking myself for it.

Harry continued to shout, but it fell on deaf ears. They were moving *fast.* In fact, impressively quick. They rounded a large pine tree and made it out into the next street. Not more than ten seconds later, Harry burst out onto the sidewalk; me, a few seconds later.

"What the hell?" Harry said as we looked up and down the street. "Where'd he go?"

I tried to suck in a deep breath as I spun, searching the line of parked cars and moving traffic. "He?" I said, breathing hard. "You think? I don't know, but I hope you brought your phone."

"I'm guessing you didn't?" he replied.

"Nope," I huffed, glancing down at Samson. He was alert, though no longer growling or barking.

They couldn't have gone far... I thought, my hand on my knees, trying to get my breath. *Unless they had a car.*

I didn't pay attention to what Harry said as he placed the call, my eyes focused on the line of parked cars. My heart was still racing and my lungs burning as I began to walk the line.

"Be careful, Kate," Harry called after me. "They could be hunkered down somewhere."

I paused but then continued on, watching Samson carefully as we walked. I could hear sirens in the distance. By the time I made it to the fourth car, two patrol units screeched to a stop.

"Where the hell did they go?" I thought aloud, shaking my head in disbelief. They must have had a car. It made no other sense.

"Kate," Harry called. "Come on."

I turned Samson around and jogged back to where Harry was talking to the two officers.

"They dropped whatever it was back there among the trees," Harry said.

I'd missed that in the chaos of the chase.

"We need to find it and bag it," he added.

"Agreed." I nodded, giving Samson a pat.

"We've got a BOLO out on the perp," the officer named Lopez said, "but there's not much to go on when all you can tell us is that they were dressed like the Grim Reaper."

I shuddered involuntarily. *That's exactly the description I would've used. But how did they know Harry and I would go for a run? Had they followed us? Or had they been watching me and knew my routine and the route I'd take to the light pole?*

"I don't like this," Harry said, his words pulling me from my thoughts. "I don't like it one bit. They're watching us, and they're bold."

"We'll keep searching," the officer named Paulson said. "But my guess is they got away in a vehicle."

"I agree," Harry said. "And they were quick. I didn't see anything."

Two more officers showed up, along with Anne Robar and Cooper, and we began the search.

"You're sure they dropped it?" I asked Harry as we headed back into the woods.

"Oh, I'm positive. They tossed it away to the right."

"Damn, they got away," I muttered, more for something to say than to be helpful. My head was spinning, so I shut up, and Samson and I walked slowly through the trees together.

It was Harry who found the container. White powder had spilled out onto the ground.

I paused. There was quite a lot of it, and yet, from a distance, it didn't seem so threatening. But I knew that same substance had already taken the lives of three people.

"I can't believe they're watching you like this," Harry said.

I thought about it and then said, "Maybe they're just trying to up their ante? Maybe they feel threatened... by me. They *could* have thrown it, you know. I think they were close enough."

"Maybe," he replied. "Who knows? But there is one thing..."

"And what's that?" I glanced at him.

"Why cyanide?" he said. "I think maybe it's because... Well, not because it's the most efficient way to accomplish their goal, but because it's what they know. And it wasn't a big fella."

"Right," I said. "He, or she, is quite petite."

"Could be a small man," he said. "I guess this one is clever, clever enough to fight smarter, not harder."

"Hah!" I said. "I wouldn't give them the compliment, Harry," I snapped, shaking my head. "They're wreaking havoc. And maybe that's just what they want."

"You're right," he said, placing his hand on my shoulder. "But it's still the truth. When can we get a look at that video footage? I think we should let these people take care of the search and get you back to safety."

"Yes. Anne and Cooper can handle it. As I said, Jack is still working on the footage, but we can go back to the house and look at it. I need to change first, though... Maybe Jack can send me a link to it."

He nodded and called TJ, who came and picked us up at the light pole. While we were waiting, I couldn't help but wonder how they knew where to wait for me. I had no answer, and, as we rode back to the house, I had the thought:

Sunday's not going to be a day of rest after all.

34

HARRY AND I MADE IT BACK TO THE HOUSE, AND AFTER A thorough check, locked down for the night. Neither Chief Johnston nor Harry wanted me to participate in the search for the culprit, and while I wanted to object, I didn't. I was exhausted. I made a quick call to Jack and then took a shower.

Since Harry was staying over, I dressed in a black sweat suit, thanking my foresight to buy a three-bedroom house with two bathrooms.

Harry was already seated at the table when I entered the kitchen and sat down. He, too, was wearing sweats.

The smell of brewing coffee gave me little peace as I opened my laptop and clicked on the link Jack had sent me. "I don't know what good this is going to do," I said, trying not to grumble.

"I just want to see it," Harry muttered. "To make sure it's the same person we just encountered."

"You think there might be more than one perp?" That thought hadn't crossed my mind.

"Possibly," he said thoughtfully. "They got away pretty damn quick, like they dove headfirst into the back seat of a car."

"Two people could have worked the sandwich shop, too," I said. "Think about it. It would've been easier with two." I paused, then continued, "They came out of nowhere tonight." I looked over at Harry as he took a seat beside me. "And they must have been lying in wait... or following us."

"You could be right," Harry said. "I don't have any answers... yet, but..." He gestured at the screen. "Let's see what we have, because then I'm sending you to bed, Kate. You need to get some rest."

I wanted to argue, but I didn't. He was right. I hit the play button and, once again, I watched the video play out just as it had before. Harry leaned over, controlling the mouse. He watched it over and over, rewinding and moving forward, changing speeds. I nearly laughed at how erratic his search was.

"I don't know how the women didn't notice," Harry suddenly spoke, gesturing to the screen. "If this person was in the supply closet, they would be able to watch them from the small window in the door, right?"

"Right." I rubbed my eyes. "But they didn't so..."

"I dunno." Harry hummed thoughtfully as he watched the video. "This is the same person though. I do know that. You can tell by the way they move."

I rested my chin in my hand, my elbow on the table. "Yeah," I said. At that moment I didn't really care. My eyes were drooping. "Looks like he has a bit of a limp."

"Yeah," Harry drawled, checking out the parts of the video that showed the perp walking. "You could be right, Kate."

I pushed up off my elbow and stood up. "I think I'll have some coffee."

"No, no, no," Harry said. "The coffee is for me, Kate. You need to go to bed. There's nothing more you need to do tonight."

"Well, you can tell me that all you want, but this is my home, and if I want coffee, I'll have some. I'm not going to bed until I'm certain that you've gotten all you can from that video."

"Hah!" he said. "You still have that dry sense of humor, then."

Harry chuckled as he rose to his feet, stepped past me and grabbed a couple of mugs from the cupboard.

"Well, if you insist on caffeine before bed, I won't stop you."

I nodded, my eyes drifting to Samson. He met my gaze, and then spun around and bounded to the back door, then turned around and stared at me.

"He needs to go out," I said. "I usually go with him and sit outside, but…"

"Ah! No worries," he said. "Let me pour the coffee, and I'll go with you. I know Samson's a smart dog, but you never know… You went on that run unarmed. That's not like you, Kate."

I sighed, not surprised he picked up on that.

"I figured since I was running with you, it'd be okay," I said.

"Here." Harry handed me a mug of fresh-brewed coffee.

Samson whined anxiously at the door.

"Hold on, Sammy," I said opening the door and turning on the porch light.

"You have a nice place," Harry said as we stepped out onto the deck.

"Thanks," I said, as I watched Samson run almost crabwise across the backyard, his nose to the ground, snapping at lightning bugs. "I sometimes catch myself these days though."

He scrunched his eyebrows at me. "What do you mean?"

"Well… Oh… I don't know. I guess it has kind of been on my mind lately that I spend a lot of time alone. I have Samson, and he's a great companion, but I'm not getting any younger. When I'm not working, I don't have much else to do."

"Ah, so you've been thinking about what I said?" he asked.

"I've been thinking about it for some time now. You just brought it to my attention. Maybe it is time for me to think about… I don't know… taking a vacation." I couldn't even bring myself to mention the prospect of dating. Hell, I just almost lost my life again to some madman.

That wasn't exactly the kind of conversation you shared over dinner.

"A vacation for the two of you would do you good," Harry said, sipping his coffee. "But you deserve someone—someone who's human—to spend time with, too. I think it would be good for you."

"I don't know if I could share my space, Harry." I laughed, shaking my head.

"Ah, yeah. I know that feeling. I dealt with it a lot before Amanda. But you know... I can't imagine it being any other way now. When you meet the right person, it works out."

"Even if your job puts them in danger?" I approached the subject carefully, not sure if it was still a sore spot for Harry or not. He had never intended to put Amanda in danger, but she'd almost died at the hands of one of Shady Tree's henchmen. It seemed to be a byproduct of the work we did.

"She knew what she was getting into," Harry said wryly. "She might not be like us, but she's similar in the fact that she craves the thrill of the job. If we're not putting ourselves in harm's way, we get bored. Restless."

"Hmm," I said as Samson came jogging up to me, his tail wagging as he smiled up at me. I gave him a good rub all over, catching that sensitive spot that all dogs seem to have that sends them into an ecstasy of scratching.

We went back inside. I sipped a little coffee and then dumped the rest out into the sink. In truth, Harry was right. I *did* need to get some rest.

"Calling it a night, then?" Harry asked as I washed my cup.

"Yeah, I think so. You should, too. I don't think there's anything more to be learned there." I nodded at my still-open laptop.

"True." Harry took a seat at the table again. "I'll get my team started on it first thing Monday. I don't think anything will surface tomorrow. And, while tonight feels like it was a big event, it was really nothing more than a sighting."

"DNA or fingerprints on the container," I reasoned, setting the cup on the dish rack. "That could break it wide open."

"We won't get that information overnight." Harry shook his head. "But I wouldn't get your hopes up about that. They were wearing gloves, and I don't think they'd have dropped it if there was evidence there."

I took a deep breath. "You're right. I noticed the gloves, too. I also think they know what they're doing... But, Harry, they are taking some pretty big risks."

"That, they are. Go on to bed. I'll see you in the morning. I'll be right here. I'm going to watch the footage a little more... You never know!"

"Yeah, right," I said dryly. "There's nothing there, Harry. You should give it a rest and go to bed, too."

He looked at me and grinned, and I knew I was wasting my time. Well, if he wanted to waste his, too, who was I to argue?

"Good night, Harry."

"Night, Kate."

Samson followed me up the stairs, the fatigue hanging heavy on my shoulders. I was glad Harry was staying the night. I'd spent many a night alone, sleeping with the burden of knowing someone was out there, watching me. With Harry and TJ on hand, I was able to relax and breathe easier.

For a while, anyway.

35

Tuesday, July 5, 6:30 a.m.

NOTHING BECAME OF THE HOLIDAY WEEKEND—OR THE MONDAY after. Samson and I could see the fireworks show from the back-yard, and Harry, TJ, and Jacque joined us. It wasn't much of a celebration, but it was one. The investigation had stalled, and not a single new lead had been brought in. It seemed as though the world had gone quiet...

The quiet before the storm, I thought to myself as I slipped into a lightweight denim jacket that Tuesday morning. TJ was outside my house, and I caught sight of his car through the window as I tightened my ponytail.

Fifteen minutes and a slice of toast later, I was in my car and backing out of the garage.

"Do you think today will be the day?" I asked Samson as I clicked the garage door opener and watched it close.

As I backed out onto the street, I waved at TJ, and he returned the gesture.

"Good thing I packed my lunch," I told Samson as I eyed my

black lunch bag. I hadn't used the thing in I don't know how long, but I'd dusted it off that morning and it would be in use until we found the cyanide killer.

It was almost seven that morning when I pulled into the parking lot at the rear of the PD, TJ just a couple of car lengths behind me. I sucked my bottom lip, frustrated and more than a little embarrassed that I was being forced to accept the fact that I needed such an escort; not that I didn't like TJ. I did. I loved the old man, though that does not fairly describe him. The Vietnam hero was in better shape than most men half his age. But I wasn't going to argue, and the slight feeling of annoyance quickly dissipated when I saw Harry Starke standing outside the door.

"What's he doing here already?" I wondered aloud as I climbed out and Samson hopped out after me.

"Ah, Kate!" Harry gave me a wave. He was wearing a crisp white shirt—cuffs rolled back—and a pair of dark blue jeans, his CZ in its holster on his right hip.

"The two ladies who were working in the sandwich shop that day are on their way here. I know you interviewed them, but I'd like to hear what they have to say for myself. Okay?"

I shrugged. "Of course. But you watched the video... for *hours*, and you didn't see anything," I said, shaking my head. "I don't think they're going to have anything else for us, Harry. We need to focus on those missing case files, and the cases Mitchell, Lombardi and Gerrick worked together."

"Yes, that," he replied. "I understand your IT man—Jack North, right?—he found a couple files. He's a good one. I thought about having Tim come over and get a couple of lessons."

I stopped walking, turned to him and said, "That's a ridiculous thing to say, Harry. Tim has no peers. He's the best." I laughed.

"I was joking, Kate," he replied dryly.

"Ah, yes, of course you were," I said as I stepped through the door Harry was holding open for me.

We took the elevator to the second floor and then crossed the situation room to my office where most of my team—Jack, Ramirez, Cooper, Hawk and Anne Robar, were already sitting at the table.

"Hey, everyone," I said. "Good morning. I hope we all had a wonderful Fourth," I continued dryly, having spent most of it locked down with either TJ Bron or Heather Stillwell parked outside my front door.

There were mumbled replies from around the table.

"Good," I said. "I see someone made coffee. Even better." I poured myself a cup, sent Samson to his bed under the window and sat down at my desk, leaving the empty seat at the table for Harry.

"Good morning," Harry said as he sat down. "It's been a while. Good to see you all again. Great job finding the cases, Jack."

I swear Jack blushed at the compliment.

Having said that, Harry continued, "Why don't we discuss them? Is there anything there?"

"Yes, let's do that," I said, "but let's make it quick. Clara Dickens and Lily Burns will be here soon."

"Well, okay," Ramirez said. "I looked through them yesterday—"

"You worked on the Fourth?" I said.

"Yes, some," she replied. "I figured if Jack was willing to work, I could do no less. Anyway, both cases are pretty cut-and-dried. In fact, they aren't even all that interesting. The defendants got off with a lighter sentence than they deserved. Everyone seemed happy with the results."

"Still, I'd like to hear about them," I said. "So?" I leaned back in my chair and folded my arms.

"The first took place nearly six years ago," Anne began, picking up her notebook. "It was an armed robbery. Took place in a convenience store. The defendant was an eighteen-year-old kid, but he was seventeen at the time of the robbery. The second person—who they didn't represent—was twenty-nine. They were able to get the defendant, Marshall Avery, off with just eighteen months, the defense being that he was forced to partake in the robbery."

"Okay," I said. "So how about the co-defendant? Maybe he's pissed off they tried to pin it all on him? And now he's reacting?"

"Not possible," Cooper said. "He got three years. He was killed in a motorcycle accident a couple of months after he was released."

"And where is Marshall Avery now?"

"He did only twelve months," Anne said. "Got out on good behavior, got married, and moved to St. Louis."

"That one is a bust," I said, leaning forward to grab my coffee. "How about the other one?"

"It's a little more complicated," Hawk said.

"I don't think it's pertinent to the case," Anne said, leaning back in her chair, coffee in both hands. "It was a homicide, but the method and motive…" She shook her head. "I don't think so."

"Okay, well, why don't you just humor me?" I said. "I'd like to hear it." I took a sip of my coffee, stood up, and walked around to the front of my desk and sat on the edge.

"So, Lombardi and Mitchell were working as Nelson Villa's defense attorneys—"

"Wait," I said, cutting Anne off. "Nelson Villa? That was what? Two years ago? Didn't he kill his wife? He pleaded self-defense and got off, as I recall."

"Correct," Anne said. "Which is why I don't think it makes a lot of sense for the guy to be suddenly throwing cyanide around. He's been quiet ever since."

"Yeah, but wasn't there someone else involved?" I asked, trying to put the pieces together in my head. "And when did Paul Gerrick get brought in?" I remembered the case, but I hadn't been involved. That case had been handled by Lt. Garvey out of

Chapter 35

Homicide. The self-defense plea and Villa's release had been controversial, to say the least.

"That's what isn't so cut-and-dry," Hawk said. "We're not sure at what point Paul Gerrick joined the case, but we do know he was only involved for a short time before he pulled out. My guess is that he wasn't a fan of how they were... *handling* things."

"Okay, so Nelson Villa, where is he now?" I asked. "He still around?"

"Yep. He still lives here in the city; well, just outside the city limits—south side," Hawk said. "Though from what I hear, he's become something of a recluse. Can't blame him for that, though. He gunned down his wife, didn't he? Kinda reminds me of that famous football player who went to trial for supposedly killing his ex-wife, only Villa's defense was that his wife attacked him with a knife."

"She did have schizophrenia," Ramirez interjected. "And a knife was found at the scene. But, to answer your question, the other person who was brought in was his cousin, Ricardo Villa. The prosecutor said he played a role in the planning of the crime."

"And did he?"

"Well, Nelson Villa got off with just self-defense," Ramirez said, "so the short answer is, he didn't. But if it was homicide... Well, maybe he did. There was a life insurance policy on the wife, though it wasn't much. However, she was seeing someone outside of the marriage."

"Who?"

"Ricardo Villa," Cooper said, laughing and shaking his head.

"Oh, *geez*," I muttered, shaking my head. "It's one of *those* cases."

"Uh-huh." Hawk chuckled. "And Paul Gerrick came in when charges were potentially going to be filed against Ricardo Villa, but from what I understand, they were able to prove he didn't

231

have anything to do with it. He took a big hit from the mess though."

"How so?" I asked and sipped my coffee.

"Lost his job, and his place on the school board," Hawk said. "He no longer lives in Chattanooga. He moved just up the road to McDonald, close to his daughter."

"Maybe he's upset with how things turned out?" I said. "Suppose he's upset enough to—"

"I don't think so," Anne said, cutting me off and sighing.

"Why not?" I asked.

"Well, for a start, the guy is six-feet-three."

"*Crap!*" I muttered.

"And Nelson Villa?" I asked. "Is he tall, too?"

"Yep," Hawk said, "and so are his kids. They're all six-feet-plus, including the daughter. Look, I think we're on the wrong track here."

"You're probably right," I replied, "but I'd still like to dig into it some more... and... Tanner Westling," I continued, as I had a thought. "He said he was at a hearing with a couple of the other interns from Lewis, Scone and Petty when Paul was killed. Let's figure out what case that was, and if it could somehow be significant."

"Ramirez and I are planning to head down to the DA's office this morning," Cooper said, pushing back from the table. "Maybe we can find some more cases there."

"They also handle cases outside of Chattanooga," Harry said as everyone rose to their feet. "And that's another avenue we're going to have to explore."

Before I could say anything to that, Chief Johnston stuck his head in. "There are two ladies here to see you, Kate."

"I'm on it, Chief," I replied. "Harry?"

He nodded and said, "Let's go see what they have to say. It's hard to believe they *really* missed someone slinking in and poisoning those sandwiches."

I gestured to Samson, and he jumped to his feet.

Me? I had my tongue in my cheek. I was skeptical. Harry might've been hell-bent that they didn't miss seeing the sneaky SOB, but I was the one who interviewed them and, while I wasn't one hundred percent, I was pretty damn certain we were wasting our time.

Tuesday, July 5, 9:45 a.m.

"LILY BURNS AND CLARA DICKENS," HARRY SAID TO ME AS WE stood outside of the interview rooms. "Separate or together?"

"Separate for starters, though like I told you, Harry, we've already done this. Corbin and I interviewed them right after it happened."

"Sure, but people forget details in the middle of the chaos. Let's give it a shot and see where this goes. We both know what happened in the shop, so we know that *someone* was in there right under their noses. I think we should dig deeper. Maybe we can jar their memories."

"Okay. I'll take Lily. I've already talked to the Dickens woman."

He nodded, and we stepped into the rooms. Samson perked his ears forward when he saw Lily. She was sitting at the table, and obviously nervous.

"I don't know why I have to be here again," she said, her hands clasped together on the table. "I know I didn't see nothing. I swear."

"Well, thanks for coming anyway," I said pleasantly. "But we do have video footage of what happened that day."

"We don't have cameras." Lily's brow furrowed. "I kept telling Brad that he needed to get one, because I was tired of the money going missing, but he kept telling me he couldn't afford it, what with the new location and—"

"I know," I stopped her, pulling back the chair and taking a seat opposite her. "As it turns out, your boss did put a camera inside the shop. He just didn't tell anyone."

"Oh," she said with a frown. "That was real nice."

I nodded, taking a second look at her. She was young—maybe twenty-one or two—and she was one of those petite women who could probably pass as still being in high school. Her voluminous curly red hair was pulled up in a messy bun on the top of her head.

"Has anything out of the ordinary happened since that day?"

She shook her head. "No, but I'm trying to find somewhere else to work. I don't want to be there anymore."

"Really? Why's that?" I asked, then realized what a stupid question it was.

She gave me an incredulous look. "Duh! Someone *died.* You were there."

I smiled at her and said, "You're right, of course. Sorry. That was stupid of me. But there *has* been a lot going on there lately."

"Yeah, because someone is taking money," she snapped, "but I don't know who it is."

"I'm sure you don't," I said, opening my laptop. "But for now, I'd like to focus on the days up to and including the day of the murder. I need you to think hard about it. Did you see anything? Anything at all. Anything you can tell me might be helpful."

She sat there for a few moments, wringing her hands on the table in front of her. She shook her head but then stopped mid-shake. "Actually, when I think about it... There has been quite a lot of strange things going on."

Now that was not what I expected, I thought. "Really," I said, leaning forward. "Why don't you tell me about it?"

"Well, for starters," she said and then cleared her throat. "The freezer was just fine until the day of the… you know. Like, I know Clara says that the fridge was going out—but it wasn't. She don't have a lick of sense about her, really! The fridge was just fine, and the thing is, when I went in and checked the freezer, there was a big ole mess. A gallon of milk had been busted open and it was ruining all the meats."

"And when did this happen?"

"Not sure," Lily said, shaking her head. "We hadn't been open very long when it all happened. The other thing is… the back door wasn't closed all the way. I figured it was 'cause Clara came in that way, but it was shut all the way after the milk spill."

"Maybe Clara shut it?"

"No. Clara was in the front. I went and got her, and then we both worked to clean up the mess because, like I said, it was gonna ruin the meat."

"Okay, but was it the freezer or the fridge?" I asked.

"It's a huge, double-door fridge/freezer with the fridge at the top and the freezer underneath. But the milk was spillin' from the fridge. It was gettin' everywhere. It was like it had exploded. And like I told you, it was getting all over the deli meat. We had to get it cleaned up real quick."

"What'd the milk container look like?"

"Like milk?"

"Was the plastic container damaged?" I asked, fighting frustration.

"I don't remember. We threw it away. Took the damn thing right out to the dumpster."

"From the back door?"

"Yeah. I didn't want to go through the front with it. It would've dripped all over the floor." She gave me a look as if she thought I was stupid.

I reached for my computer and flipped it open, navigating to the video. I was on the fence about letting her watch it, but she was already telling me more than either of them had the day of the murder. I turned it around to face her.

"Is this... Is this a camera? In the shop?" She once again looked perplexed at the mention of it. "I just... Wow. This was smart of him."

"Mm-hmm," I muttered, as I pressed the space bar, starting the video.

"That's when I realized the milk was everywhere," Lily said, pointing to the screen when she whipped the door open and started talking to Clara. "She tried to tell me to just clean it up while she finished Paul's sandwich, but I was real worried about the meat getting spoiled—and the trouble we might get into."

Humm, the killer was taking a risk by setting this up... It could've easily turned into nothing for the killer, leaving no window of opportunity. That wasn't much different than my run that night, either. It had all been a game of chance. *Do they get off on that?*

"Oh my gosh..." Lily's eyes widened, and I glanced down at the screen to see the black figure walk quickly to the sandwiches. No matter how many times I watched it, it never got any easier.

"They came outta the dumpster door!" She looked up at me. "If we would've just... Paul..."

"It's okay, Lily," I reassured her. "Whoever it is would have gotten to him sooner or later. It's not your fault."

"I guess..." she said, her eyes glistening. "I should've cleaned it up on my own and left Clara to do the sandwiches."

She continued to stare wide-eyed at the screen, seemingly hypnotized by what she was seeing. But then, "You know..." Lily's voice trailed off as she dabbed her eyes. "I think... I think I might've seen that person somewhere before."

"You what?" I snapped, making her jump and Samson sit up.

"Well... I can't be for sure... But she looks a lot like the girl that I saw outside of Paul's firm a few weeks ago. She walked just like that."

I stopped, blinking a couple of times. "*She?*"

Lily nodded. "Yeah, it was a girl. Not real old, either. I don't know, maybe around my age... maybe a little older, say twenty-five... or so? She was outside of Paul's firm, dressed in the same kinda black outfit. Only it wasn't raining and there wasn't anything hiding her face or nothing. She's a pretty girl."

"Okay," I said, trying to remain calm. "When was this?"

"Uh... It had to have been..." She hesitated, wrinkled her forehead. "It was the last time I worked... before Paul... So, it would've been Tuesday of that week. It was the middle of the afternoon. I was fixing to head to my biology class after my shift. She was standing outside, just staring in."

"Did you speak to her?"

Lily shook her head. "Oh, no. She was crying. I was gonna check on her, but she glared at me when she saw me... And then she left. It was real weird. I can't believe I didn't think of it earlier. But I just didn't, I guess 'cause I didn't realize that it was a girl doing all this stuff."

I nodded. "Had you seen her before?" I asked.

Lily paused, thought for a moment, then said, "Nooo, not really. She looked kind of like the girl who worked at the shop before me, but she had blond hair. This one had dark hair."

"When did she work at the shop?" I asked.

"Well, I don't know if it was her, but if it was, she woulda worked there last year. I didn't really know her, but from what everyone said, she was real weird."

"How so?"

"I can't say exactly. I didn't know her. That's just what I was told." She glanced down at her watch. "But look, I got my shift I have to get to."

"Okay," I said with a sigh, pulling my card out. "If you think of *anything* else, call me." I gave Samson a pat as Lily Burns rose to her feet.

After I saw her out, I went to find that list of employees that Brad Owens had given us.

I was almost certain the answer lay somewhere in that list, and that something was about to break.

Tuesday, July 5, 11:30 a.m.

"We'll find the tie," Anne said to me after a short chat in my office. "Ramirez and Cooper are at the DA's office right now... but how could someone who worked in the sandwich shop have anything to do with this?"

"That isn't clear yet," I answered. "This is from my interview with Lily Burns. I'm not sure if she's totally reliable, but it's a lead, and we need to follow it up."

"Is Harry still speaking with Clara Dickens?"

I nodded. "He'll wrap it up when he's ready."

"I guess," Anne said with a chuckle. "Here's the list of employees." She took a small sheaf of papers from the file and handed them to me. There were five sheets stapled together, and they looked as if they'd been worked hard. I flipped through them. There were at least seventy names.

"The sandwich shop had a lot of turnover over the last eighteen months. I looked into all of them, and I couldn't find anyone that piqued my interest." She shrugged.

"Let's narrow it down a bit to say the last twelve months."

Anne took the papers from me and flipped through them, tearing through the staple. "This takes us back to last July," she said, handing me three sheets.

That's still a lot, I thought.

"You said female?" Anne took the three sheets of paper from me, grabbed a highlighter and marked the names of the female employees. "That narrows it down a bit," she said, looking up at me.

"No one older than twenty-six," I said.

"Got it." She grabbed a pencil and began crossing out anyone who didn't fit the age requirements. It wasn't many, but it did narrow it down to nine.

"We can work with this," she said. "I've done some preliminary fishing on most of these, but I was checking for criminal backgrounds."

"Any of them have a record?"

"Two, actually," she replied. "Gabby Collins has a trespassing charge, and Carly Matherson has a DUI."

"Look into the trespassing case first. I don't think a DUI is a fit... but you never know."

"Got it. I'll let you know if I find anything."

I gave her shoulder a squeeze and then headed back toward the interview room. I wanted to know if Harry had found anything.

"Then we can eat some lunch," I told Samson as we made it to the observation room and looked in through the window.

Clara was talking animatedly, her hands waving all over the place. She looked fired up, and I couldn't help but wonder what it was about.

I turned the handle, pushed the door open, and slipped inside. "Don't mind me," I said. "How's it going?"

The look on Harry's face told me the answer, while his voice said something else entirely. "Great."

"I told you, I know that place is haunted," Clara said loudly.

The look on her face was one of passion. She believed what she was saying.

"I'll let you finish this up," I told Harry, giving him a nod before heading back out of the room.

"You sure you don't want to sit in, Kate?" Harry called after me.

"Nope," I said with a hidden smile as I exited the room. I led Samson back to my office, settled in at my desk and grabbed my lunch box, opened it and took out my sandwich, chips, and water bottle.

"Why would someone working in the sandwich shop want to murder three lawyers?" I asked Samson as I unwrapped my turkey and cheese on wheat bread. "It doesn't make any sense." Samson licked his lips, and I glanced down at my sandwich. "Really? All you care about is your stomach getting filled."

I tossed him some of the crust, trying to ignore that weird feeling in the pit of my stomach. My gut was telling me that today was the day.

I ate my lunch slowly, tossing Samson the crust and a couple of Doritos now and then.

I finished eating, wiped my hands on the napkin and then downed the rest of my water. I looked out the window. The sun was high in the middle of the clear sky. It was another scorcher, and without the cloud coverage, there was no relief.

"Lucky for us, we have the air conditioner," I said to Samson as he snuffled the floor at my feet, looking for crumbs. I tossed the empty sandwich wrapper and water bottle into the trash and zipped up the lunch bag. "How much longer do you think Harry will take, Sammy?"

Before Samson could even react, the office door swung open and Harry walked in. He looked taxed and frustrated and was shaking his head.

"That was the biggest waste of time. The woman is convinced the place is *haunted* and a ghost killed Paul," Harry said, obviously frustrated as he dropped down in one of the chairs. "Who the hell thinks like that?"

"Clara Dickens, apparently," I said, laughing. "But it wasn't all a waste. I've been waiting for you to finish up. Lily Burns has provided us with a new lead."

"Really? Does she believe in ghosts too?"

"Well, I don't know about that," I said with a laugh. "But from what I can gather, she believes she's seen the person in the video before, and that she possibly worked at the sandwich shop last year. She also says she saw her outside Paul Gerrick's office the day before the attack, and she was crying. She said she didn't think about it at the time; not until she saw the video, in fact."

"Tell me everything," Harry said, leaning forward, his elbows resting on his knees.

I quickly filled him in on what Lily had said—from the busted milk container to the girl standing outside Paul's office, crying. Harry listened carefully, nodding along. As I finished, he blew out a heavy breath.

"It could be nothing..." he said thoughtfully. "Or it could be everything."

"I agree," I said, "but what makes me think there might be something to it is what Lily said about the way the woman walked. We picked up on the gait as well."

"Yeah, but it could be all in her mind," he said.

"Always the skeptic," I said.

"Have to be," Harry said. "So, what motive would this... person have, and can we tie any of the employees on the list to Paul or the other two attorneys?"

"Anne is working on that right now."

"So, what if..." Harry began, frowning. "What if... Maybe the three lawyers were in the sandwich shop and someone saw or overheard something they shouldn't."

"That's farfetched, even for you, Harry," I said, smiling. "And it would've been over a year ago. It's too much of a stretch."

He shrugged.

"We're close, Harry," I said. "I know it. I can feel it. We're just missing a piece of the puzzle."

"That's always the way it is before we solve it," Harry said and sat up straight. "We'll figure it out, Kate. It might not be today, but I think we're moving in the right direction."

I nodded. "We are, I think. I just hope no one else gets hurt before we find the answer."

Harry went silent. "If the only lawyers on the case were Lombardi, Mitchell, and Gerrick, then the only person left is…"

I pursed my lips, not liking the answer. "Me."

"Yeah," he said thoughtfully.

"That could potentially put my team in danger, Harry. I don't like that."

"True, but that's something you can't change," he replied.

"So, if she—and I'm assuming our perp is a she—has achieved her goal—to kill all three lawyers—why wouldn't she simply disappear?"

"She could," he said, "but now she's killed three times. One is scary. Two is easier. Three is a thrill. I think by now she's addicted."

"Lombardi and Mitchell were killed right outside their offices… so she is a risk taker," I said, thinking aloud.

"And then she steps it up," Harry said, "and goes for Gerrick—and you—in the sandwich shop. That's an escalation."

I shook my head. "Maybe not so much. If she worked there, she would have known the layout and the procedures, which would have made the plan less risky. And now that the task is done, it's not enough. She wants me, too."

Harry nodded. "It's possible."

Just then, there was a knock on my office door. It opened and—

Thomas Drews?

38

Tuesday, July 5, 1:30 p.m.

MY FIRST INSTINCT WAS TO TELL HIM TO GET THE HELL OUT OF MY office, but then I spotted the file he was holding.

Drews stepped into my office with an aggravated expression on his face, and I noted Harry's look of amusement at the situation.

"Captain Gazzara," Drews said, "with all due respect, I don't appreciate the way you've been avoiding me. It's clear your stance on journalists is negative, but I do more than just report on cold cases. I was twenty years in law enforcement, and I do have my P.I. license. Just give me a damn moment and take a look at this."

He dropped the file on my desk in front of me.

"How did you get in here?" I asked, glancing down at the file.

"Chief Johnston pointed me in the right direction," he answered. "Now will you give me a few minutes?"

I took a deep breath and glanced at Harry, who raised his eyebrows and tilted his head, smiling.

"What is this?" I asked quietly, looking again at the file.

"Well, in the beginning, I was hired by Tony Lombardi to

research the death of his wife. I was skeptical. Tony isn't the easiest fella to get along with, but, after you searched his home and offices and came up with nothing, I decided to take it on."

"And what have you found?" I asked, narrowing my eyes.

"Why don't you open the file and take a look, Captain?" The smirk on his face was beyond irritating, and his handsome features only furthered my frustration.

I flipped open the file, both Harry and Thomas hovering over the desk. Inside, on the top of a stack, was a baggy with a note in it. It didn't take but a glance to see that it was a near copy of the one I'd received.

Ms. Lombardi. You failed him. Miserably. You will pay.

"Where did you get this?" I demanded, holding up the baggy with the note. "And why didn't you bring it in immediately?"

Drews stood back, folded his arms and said, "No need to get fired up, Captain. Tony found it when he was cleaning out Madison's office over the holiday weekend. He dropped it off to me this morning and I brought it in."

What could I say to that? Nothing! So I changed tack. "So what's... all this?" I said as I set the note off to the side, staring down at the stack of papers in the file.

"Those are the cases that Mitchell, Lombardi, and Gerrick worked on together. The most important, high-profile case they worked together was one in Charleston, South Carolina. Originally, Brandon Nickson—"

"Brandon Nickson?" Harry asked, cutting him off. "The serial killer? He was never in Tennessee. It wouldn't have made much sense for LSP to take it on."

"You're right," he said, holding out his hand to Harry. "I'm Thomas Drews, by the way, and you, I assume, are Harry Starke. It's nice to meet you, sir. And yes, you *are* right. It wouldn't have made sense, except that Nickson's mother lived here in Chattanooga. She also has extended family here, and they knew of Lombardi and Mitchell's success rate."

"So, you're telling me these three attorneys took a case in South Carolina? The Brandon Nickson case was indeed high profile, but as far as I know the fact that he was represented by a team of Chattanooga attorneys was never mentioned."

"That's true," Drews said. "It wasn't mentioned, except on a few odd occasions. Tony Lombardi could have told you." He looked at me, then continued. "Gerrick pulled out after two weeks." He leaned forward, turned the file and riffled through the papers, then continued on, "Gerrick said that Nickson was a liar and he couldn't work with him. Lombardi and Mitchell, however..."

"I see," I said coldly as I turned the file back again. "How did *you* get this? It appears to be Gerrick's personal file."

"It is," he said. "I was following the case for my podcast, and when Gerrick pulled off the defense team, I talked to him. He was very candid about it. He gave me the file and asked that I not release the information until after the trial. I agreed. Lombardi and Mitchell were working behind the scenes with a local attorney, Jeremy Hulser. Hulser died in a car crash about a year after the trial. His brakes had been tampered with, but nothing ever became of it."

That's four, I thought and looked at Harry. His face was a mask.

"And Nickson?" I frowned. "I don't understand. He's in prison. He was charged on multiple counts of murder."

"He was," Drews replied, "four, actually, and they think he's responsible for at least three more." He stopped talking and looked quizzically at me. And I could tell there was still more he had to say.

"What about the cyanide?" I asked. "His mother? She doesn't fit the description."

Drews laughed. "No, Nickson died five months ago, which might have been the trigger for someone close to her, don't you think?"

"I'm following," I said.

"Barbra Nickson is Brandon Nickson's daughter. He had sole custody of her. Her mother passed away when she was four under... odd circumstances. She stayed with him until he was booked for murdering Cathleen Dobson, which was the case that broke the serial killer investigation wide open. Barbra went to her grandmother in Tennessee."

"Does Barbra, by any chance, have a limp?"

Drews grinned. "She does. She was in a car accident with her father when she was seven."

Barbra. Barbra. Barbra. I'd heard that name. I stood up and went to the door.

"Kate, where are you going?" Harry called after me.

"Incident room! I'll be right back."

"Hey, Kate." Corbin looked up at me. "What's up? I just heard from Coop that the DA pointed him in the direction of a big case out in South Carolina."

"Brandon Nickson, I know," I said.

"Anne," I said as I stepped up to her desk. "Does the name Barbra Nickson mean anything to you?"

"Uh..." Anne shuffled through some papers. "No Nickson, but there's an intern at Lewis, Scone and Petty. Her name is..." She took a sheet of paper from the pile, looked at it and said, "Barbra Edmonds. Why?"

"How about the sandwich shop? Anyone named Barbra Nickson on that list?"

"No," she said slowly as she looked at the list from the sandwich shop. "There's an Edmonds, though. Louise Edmonds."

"Barbra Louise Nickson," a voice behind me said. I turned to see Drews and Harry. "Edmonds is her mother's maiden name."

"Geez," I said, slowly shaking my head. "That's it. Has to be. Do we have a picture of her?"

"I can get one, I think," Anne said and turned to her computer.

We waited impatiently for what seemed an age while she searched.

"There," she said triumphantly. "This is her DMV photo." She turned the monitor a little so we could all see it. I leaned forward, my hands on Anne's desk.

"She has blond hair," I said, staring at the face on the screen. She was young. "I wonder if she's dark-headed now."

"Let me see what I can dig up," Anne said slowly, already searching for a particular file. "I know she was interviewed after Madison died." She started to sift through the pile of reports and interviews. "I think she had an alibi."

"I bet it won't hold up," I said.

"Ah, here it is," Anne said, taking an interview form from the pile. "She said she was in her car when Madison was killed, waiting for the rain to stop... But no one questioned it; probably because she's a dainty little thing."

"It's her," I said. "It has to be."

I looked at Drews. His face was blank, but I knew what he was thinking. And yes, maybe we would've gotten there faster had I listened to him, but it wasn't a guarantee. We still hadn't found her. So I ignored him.

But wait...

"The person we chased through the woods was fast." I turned to Harry. "How could this girl—with a limp—manage to run that fast?"

Again, it was Drews who answered. "She was the star of the track team her senior year. Her injury didn't affect her ability, just her gait. She could run faster than most."

I shook my head. "But cyanide? Why cyanide?"

"Easy," Harry said. "It was easy. It was deadly. It was silent."

"While also allowing her to get up close and personal," I said. "The perfect weapon for someone with a hefty grudge."

"I think she's too much like her father to stop killing," Drews said. "She's getting bolder, and she's taking risks. She's escalated. It's only a matter of time before she kills again."

"Then let's go get her," I said and turned to face them. "Now."

"She'll be at work," Anne said.

"Then let's go," I said, spinning on my heel. "Have backup meet us there, Corbin."

"Whoa, Kate," Harry called after me as I took off across the incident room.

Tuesday, July 5, 2:45 p.m.

I HESITATED AS I PASSED BY MY OFFICE DOOR, PEEKING IN AT Samson. He was sleeping peacefully in the corner. I was about to call him but thought better of it. Something in my gut told me to leave him where he was. I didn't know if it was my fear of him getting injured again or something else... Whatever it was, I listened to it and closed the door softly so as not to wake him.

"We need to think this through," Harry said as I slid into the driver's seat. "We don't want to panic her and have her do something stupid."

"If she's at work," I said as I started the engine, "we'll grab her before she can do anything stupid." I pulled out onto Amnicola, blue lights flashing, and headed west toward downtown. I looked at the clock on the dash. It was almost two forty-five; we'd be there by three. Not soon enough for me.

"What a hell of a case." Harry chuckled. "Maybe you should've listened to Drews earlier, though he did say he didn't make the connection until he got the note."

"Yeah," I said as I turned left onto East Fourth and hit the gas. "I guess he's a lot smarter than I gave him credit for."

"Maybe so. Handsome, too."

"What?" I glanced at him.

"Oh, come on," Harry said, laughing. "I saw your cheeks getting red, Kate. Is that why you were avoiding him? That is your dating MO."

I rolled my eyes. "Hah! No thanks."

"He's on your level."

"Shut up," I said, shaking my head. "I'm not interested. Right now, I want Barbra Edmonds in our interview room in cuffs. We need a confession."

"Her dad was a tough nut to crack," Harry said.

"He had years of experience. She doesn't."

Five minutes later, I pulled up outside the front entrance of the LSP building. I was about to open my door, but hesitated and looked into the empty back seat, wishing that I had brought Samson with me.

"Why'd you leave him?" Harry asked. "You never go anywhere without him."

I nodded. "Something told me to leave him." I turned to Harry. "I almost wish I hadn't listened, but I still feel like it was the right choice."

Harry's expression was serious. "Intuition can be a lifesaver, Kate," he said. "And we don't know what we're walking into, here."

"Well, I guess we're about to find out, aren't we?" I unhooked the strap over my Glock and slid out of the car. Still thinking about Samson.

I shook my head. *It's just the apprehension talking,* I thought. I've always been levelheaded, but I was definitely feeling a little off that day. Maybe it was because I'd left Samson behind. But I also felt better knowing he'd be safe back in the office. *I'll be back to get you when we're done, Sammy.*

However, something about that thought was tugging at me, but I didn't have time to process it as we stepped through the front doors and into the lobby.

"Stay cool," Harry said in a low voice as we stepped inside. I saw Anne drive by in her SUV with Drews in the front seat.

"Good afternoon," the woman at the front desk greeted us. "Colton Rhodes is out for the day. Can I help you with something?"

"Is Barbra Edmonds available?" Harry said, beating me to it.

"Down the hall; last office on the left," she said with a smile. "Nathan and Barbra are both here this morning."

"Thank you." I gave her a smile, and together, Harry and I walked past the desk and down the hallway.

The door was closed. I tapped lightly, two times, and a couple of seconds later, "Come in," a male voice shouted.

And we did.

It was a small office with two desks.

"Oh, hello," Nathan Shaw said, frowning.

He was seated at one desk, and the woman I took to be Barbra Edmonds was seated at the other. She was no longer blond—her hair was dark brown—but it was easy to tell that she was the same woman as in the DMV photograph.

"I'm Captain Gazzara, Chattanooga police. This is my colleague, Harry Starke. We're here to talk to Barbra about the deaths of Madison Lombardi, David Mitchell, and Paul Gerrick."

"Oh." Nathan frowned. "Well. Okay. I guess you don't need me then."

I nodded, glancing over to Barbra. She remained still, and silent, staring at me as I stepped to the side to let Harry enter. I stared right back at her, then stepped up to her desk, maybe six or seven feet in front of her.

She continued to stare at me, ignoring Harry.

"What questions do you have, *Captain?*" Barbra's tone was borderline taunting.

"You're Brandon Nickson's daughter, aren't you?" I said quietly.

"What?" Nathan gasped, and I wondered why he hadn't left the room.

I ignored him. "Are you?" I asked again.

She almost leaped to her feet.

I drew my weapon and trained it on her.

She smiled. "*Nervous,* Captain?"

"Kate..." Harry's voice sounded distant as Nathan backed himself into a corner of the office.

"Nathan, you should leave," I said, but he appeared frozen in place.

"Barbra Edmonds, you're under arrest for the murders of Madison Lombardi, David Mitchell, and Paul Gerrick," I told her. And I suddenly realized I couldn't see her hands.

"Put your hands up, where I can see them," I said.

She didn't move.

"I said, put your hands up where I can see them," I repeated. Did she have a firearm? Cyanide? With her actions escalating, I couldn't rule it out.

Barbra laughed. "Are you really going to shoot me here?"

"Hands in the air," I barked at her, knowing I couldn't shoot unless she drew a weapon or made a move. She must have known it too. I didn't like that Nathan and Harry were both in danger. I could hear footsteps running down the hall, and voices shouting for us.

So could Barbra.

Her eyes went wide and then... I swear they visibly darkened. "Oh captain, my captain."

"Nathan, go. Now!" I commanded, looking at him out of the corner of my eye.

"Kate!" Harry shouted, but it was too late. She flipped her right hand up and something flew across her desk. I reacted instantly. I tried to cover my face, but I was too late.

I felt the powder hit my nostrils. Then the burning started. I panicked. I began to choke. I gasped for air and grabbed my throat. I couldn't breathe. I couldn't see. I could *hear* the chaos around me, but I couldn't see it.

I couldn't feel anything but pain searing through my lungs. I even heard the thud as I hit the floor. I could hear shrill laughter, seemingly somewhere off in the distance.

"Get out of the way," I heard someone shout. It sounded like the annoying Thomas Drews, but I was too far gone to be sure. It was, however, the last thing I heard before everything went black.

I'm sorry, Sammy.

40

Saturday, July 9, 2:30 p.m.

"IT'S A MIRACLE THAT SHE SURVIVED," DOC SHEDDON SAID. HIS voice sounded muffled. The blackness began to lift. I saw bright lights overhead through my eyelids. "Amazing the things that fella knows."

"Yes, the man's a frickin' prodigy," I heard Harry Starke say.

"She was refining that stuff in her basement," I heard Doc say. "Did you hear about that?"

"I did," Harry said. "The girl was obsessed. Never got over her father being locked up for life. I heard from Anne Robar that they're trying to connect her to Jeremy Hulser's death, too."

I took a long, deep breath. The lights grew brighter. They hurt my eyes. Was I dreaming? Was I dead? Doc? Was I lying on the medical examiner's table?

This is not what I imagined it would be like after I died...

I wriggled my toes. My head was pounding, and I squeezed my eyes tight shut. I heard a beeping sound. *A heart monitor? I'm not dead?* I could feel my heart beating. I slowly opened my eyes.

Bright lights? Hospital? And then the memories of what had happened came flooding back. They hit me like a ton of bricks.

Wait... But I should be dead.

I heard a whine. I turned my head. Samson was standing with his front paws on the bed, smiling at me.

"Hey, Sammy," I mumbled, reaching out to him and noticing an IV in the back of my hand. He whined again, snapped his jaws and licked my hand. I was never so happy to see him. I let my hand flop back down on the bed. I felt... so weak. But the fact that I was feeling anything at all was, as Doc Sheddon said, a miracle.

"Ah, you're awake at last," Harry said. I looked up at them, Harry and Doc Sheddon.

"I thought I was dead and on one of your examination tables," I joked, eyeing Doc. "I promise, it's the worst thing that can happen, to hear your voice while semi-conscious. I thought for sure I was a goner and you were about to carve me up."

"Ha! Good to see you still have your sense of humor," Doc said. "I'm here to check on your progress. Looks like you'll survive, I'm happy to say. And you can thank our friend Drews for that."

"How? What happened? I—" I stopped talking. I didn't feel too good.

"Oh boy," Harry said, taking a seat. "Well, you got a face full of cyanide. That kid had it in her hand. I didn't see it, and I know you didn't. It was the damnedest thing. She was so quick."

"And you survived," Doc said. "It was one of the most amazing things I've ever seen. That fella Drews, the uh, podcaster? He had a kit in his bag. He knew to intravenously administer thiopentone sodium. That brought your blood oxygen levels up. Then he called for an ambulance and told them to bring hydroxocobalamin. He saved your life. Your ECGs came back a little wacky for a while, but they've leveled out now. It's nothing short of a miracle."

I was unable to process most of what he said, but I got the gist of it. What he meant was that I was damn lucky to be alive. I glanced over to Samson.

"I knew there was a reason not to have you there," I whispered.

"I agree," Harry said. "Even if Samson had detected the cyanide, I think Barbra still would've thrown it, and it would've killed him much quicker than it got you. He wouldn't have survived. Good on you for listening to your intuition, Kate."

I nodded, full of emotion. "I'll be sure to listen to it from now on."

"Your heart is doing well now," Doc Sheddon said. "Granted, I'm more of a doctor for the dead, but that's what they said fifteen minutes ago."

I laughed, then said, "Great! So when do I get to go home?"

"Tomorrow, I should think," Doc said as Harry's phone buzzed, and he answered it.

"You have a visitor," he said. "You up for more company?"

"Well, you two are here," I muttered. "So I guess you might as well let them in."

"Good, he's been hanging around a lot," Harry said with a wink.

"I have to go," Doc said. "It's good to see you looking better, Kate. We'll talk soon." And with that, he left, leaving me alone with Harry... until Thomas Drews walked in, a vase of flowers in hand.

"Ah, so you're awake, Captain Gazzara. I'm really glad you pulled through." He gave me a smile and set the flowers on one of the bedside tables. I looked around. The room was full of them.

"Thanks," I managed to say, which struck me as a little funny as I took in the sight of the man in his black polo and light blue jeans. Maybe it was the medication I was on, but I couldn't help but think how stunningly attractive he was.

"This guy's the reason you're alive," Harry said, standing up and patting him on the shoulder. "He's a sharp one."

Drews' face flushed. He appeared to be embarrassed.

"I... You... Look, I did some research into cyanide as things were heating up. You never know what you might encounter and I... well, the girl is unhinged. It just made sense to be prepared."

"What happened to her?" I asked as Drews and Harry sat down.

"The only cyanide she had on her," Drews said, "she threw at you. And then she tried to run, but Harry here grabbed her, and that was that. Kind of hard to dispute an attempted murder in that situation."

"Where is she now?" I asked.

"In the county lockup," Harry said, "awaiting her court hearing. The DA is working on multiple indictments."

"Did she admit to the murders?" I asked.

"Sure did," Harry said, nodding. "That kid has an ego bigger than a house. She was out for blood on behalf of her father. She was after revenge, and killing the lawyers that she said failed him was her way of going after it. Having done what she set out to do, she went after you, knowing you were out to get her."

"The truth is, though," Drews said, "even if she'd succeeded in killing you, she would've gone after someone else. She's developed a taste for it. She was an embryonic serial killer. She had to be stopped, just like her father."

"Female serial killers are rare," I said, "but that's how they work. She must be deranged."

"Yes, and lied her way into the internship," Harry said. "She didn't have a college degree and has never seen the inside of a law school. That's why her use of her law verbiage was... ineloquent."

I grinned at him. "That your word of the day?" I asked, but then continued before he could answer. "Makes sense, I suppose."

I glanced down at Samson. He whined again, and I sighed.

"Come on." I patted the bed, and he jumped up and snuggled down beside me and rested his head on my shoulder.

"You're going to get me into trouble with the nurses," I said, but he took no notice.

"That dog hasn't left this room," Drews said and laughed. "I had to fight him like hell just to get him to use the bathroom outside."

"Sorry," I said, but I couldn't help but smile. "He's a good dog."

"I know," Drews said.

"Thanks for saving my life," I said.

"Oh." Thomas blushed slightly. "Yeah, no problem. You're welcome."

"And... I apologize for blowing you off the way I did. We might have saved Gerrick if I hadn't been so pigheaded."

"I didn't have it put together then, so no. It would have made no difference. But..." He paused, looked at me, took a deep breath and continued, "I'd like to discuss it further with you. When you... If you'd... like to."

"Oh?" I glanced at Harry. He was grinning widely. "Is there more to the case?"

"No, I was just thinking it might be nice to chat with you, is all," Drews said. "Maybe over dinner?"

I slowly shook my head. "I really don't want to be on your podcast, Thomas."

He laughed. "Who said anything about a podcast? That's not what I want, Captain Gazzara. But I would like to get to know you better. So, how about it? Dinner?"

"Oh," I said, this time it was *me* who blushed. "Well, yes... I suppose. I guess I could go for that." Samson nudged my shoulder. "As long as he can come, too."

"Why not?" Drews said and smiled at me.

MADISON

Thank you for reading **Madison: Case 19 in The Lt. Kate Gazzara Murder Files.**

I hope you enjoyed this story, and if you did please help others find Blair Howards Books by leaving a few words about it in the form of a review.

From Blair Howard

The Harry Starke Genesis Series

The Harry Starke Series

The Lt. Kate Gazzara Murder Files

Randall & Carver Mysteries

The Peacemaker Series

The Civil War Series

From Blair C. Howard

The Sovereign Star Series

ABOUT THE AUTHOR

Blair Howard is a retired journalist turned novelist. He's the author of more than 50 novels including the international best-selling Harry Starke series of crime stories, the Lt. Kate Gazzara series, and the Harry Starke Genesis series. He's also the author of the Peacemaker series of international spy thrillers and five Civil War/Western novels.

If you enjoy reading Science Fiction thrillers, Mr. Howard has made his debut into the genre with, The Sovereign Stars Series under the name, Blair C. Howard.

Visit www.blairhowardbooks.com.

You can also find Blair Howard on Social Media